The

Mapmaker's

Apprentice

GLASS AND STEELE
#2

C.J. ARCHER

Series by C.J. Archer:

Glass and Steele

The Emily Chambers Spirit Medium Trilogy

The 1st Freak House Trilogy

The 2nd Freak House Trilogy

The 3rd Freak House Trilogy

The Ministry of Curiosities

Lord Hawkesbury's Players

The Assassins Guild

The Witchblade Chronicles

Stand-alone books by C.J. Archer:

Redemption

Surrender

Courting His Countess

The Mercenary's Price

DEDICATION

To Joe, Samantha and Declan. Thanks for the love and laughter.

CHAPTER 1

London, Spring 1890

"How are your acting skills, India?" my employer Matthew Glass asked me. We sat at diagonal opposites in the brougham, our knees bumping when the coachman took the corners too fast, something he did at regular intervals. Matt had hired the fellow after winning the brougham in a poker match only a week before. We'd ridden in it every day since, visiting watchmakers throughout the city, but today we were on our way to the Bank of England in Threadneedle Street.

"That's an odd question," I said. "They're adequate, I suppose, as long as I'm not asked to remember entire Shakespearean soliloquys. I never was very good at memorizing the classics. Why do you ask?"

"Can you play the part of a concerned granddaughter?"

"Ah. I see, now. What a clever idea. I'll try my best, but I can't promise I won't be tripped up by a clever clerk."

We were heading to the Bank of England in an attempt to find out if a watchmaker named Mirth continued to collect the guild allowance that was paid regularly into his account. He could be the watchmaker called Chronos, whom Matt needed to fix his life-giving watch—a watch that he required more frequently every day to restore his health. Although Abercrombie, the master of the Watchmakers' Guild, had assured me that Mirth wasn't the right fellow, I didn't trust him. The horrid man had tried to have me arrested on false charges of theft, and refused to allow me into the guild. It wouldn't surprise me if he had lied about Mirth to detract us from our search. Aside from Mirth, we'd not learned of any other watchmakers who were the right age and had been overseas five years ago, when the mysterious Chronos had teamed up with a magical doctor to save Matt's life in America. We couldn't rule him out yet. Not until we'd seen him.

"I'm sure you'll be up to the challenge," Matt said with a small smile that didn't quite reach his tired eyes.

Despite the tiredness, he looked particularly handsome in a new charcoal gray suit, delivered yesterday by his tailor. He cut a fine figure with his long legs, broad shoulders, and dark hair framing a face made up of strong angles and smooth skin. I often found myself studying his intriguing features and wondering how much more handsome he would be if tiredness didn't plague him.

"Just remember Mirth's personal details, and you should be believed," he assured me.

"Oliver Warwick Mirth," I recited from memory. "Date of birth, April ninth, eighteen-twenty. Recently residing at the Aged Christian Society on Sackville

Street, however he went missing and we, his family, are very concerned."

"And your name?"

I frowned at him. We hadn't been given names of his family members by the Society. A staff member there had provided Mirth's personal information, after Matt passed him some money, but he'd not mentioned family. No one had visited Mirth at the residence. We knew from Abercrombie that Mirth had a daughter, however. I could be that daughter's daughter.

"Jane," I announced. "Jane Bland. Will that suffice?"

He studied me with a wry twist of his mouth. He had an easy countenance and an expressive face, one that made his thoughts clear. Usually. There were times when he schooled his features to keep his thoughts to himself. He was as good at that as he was at making people feel comfortable in his presence, when he chose.

"You don't look like a Jane Bland."

"Oh? What does a Jane Bland look like?"

"Small."

"You do realize that women like to be considered small and that you have just insulted me." I added a smile so that he'd know I wasn't hurt by his observation. Truly, I wasn't. I may not have the tiny waist of many females, because I didn't lace my corset to painful extremes, but I had a generous bosom and was tall enough that I could reach the top shelf in the pantry, yet short enough that a man like Matt towered over me. At twenty-seven, I'd become used to my proportions and accepted them as being as much a part of me as my straight brown hair and greenish eyes.

"Let me rephrase that," he said, a pink tint blooming on his cheeks. "Jane Bland sounds like someone who blends into the background. *You* do not. Let's call you Jane Markham."

"And who are you? My brother?"

3

"Lawyer."

"You? A lawyer?" I laughed.

He bristled. "What's wrong with being a lawyer?"

"Nothing, but you don't look like one."

"What do I look like?"

Handsome. Intriguing. Charming. "A gentleman of means who has lived an interesting life. Your accent makes you sound like a man who has never settled in one place long enough to consider any particular country his home."

His smile faltered before returning. "You're very observant."

"Those are facts you told me yourself, Matt."

"Only the part about moving a lot. I never mentioned that I consider myself a foreigner wherever I am."

"Oh."

The coach suddenly swerved, sending me sliding across the leather seat to the other side. Matt reached for me with both hands, but wasn't quick enough to stop our knees smacking together. He did manage to stop me slamming into the side of the cabin.

"Are you all right?" he asked, helping me to sit up straight. His hands relaxed on my arms but didn't let go. For one brief yet fierce moment, our gazes connected, propelling my heart into my ribs. His fingers gently squeezed before releasing me.

"Thank you." I righted my hat, taking my time so as to hide my hot face. "Your new coachman seems to always be in a hurry."

He pulled down the window and shouted at Bryce to slow down. The brougham dutifully slowed to a walking pace. "So," Matt said, settling on the seat once more, "if I don't look like a lawyer, who should I be?"

"We should say we are both Mr. Mirth's grandchildren since no one knows otherwise."

"We hope."

We'd not found any records of Mirth's descendants beyond his only daughter. According to Abercrombie, that daughter had fled to Prussia, beneath a somewhat scandalous cloud, but we didn't know for certain if she'd subsequently returned to England or if she had children of her own. Hopefully the bank wouldn't know either.

The coach pulled to a stop and we alighted in front of the colossal Bank of England building. It dwarfed its surrounds and the men coming and going like busy ants. There wasn't a woman in sight, except for me.

"Come, Sister," Matt said, extending his arm to me. "Let's find out if our dear grandfather is still with us."

Inside, earnest young men stood behind the long polished counter, their fingers working swiftly to dole out bank notes to their customers. The *swish swish* of paper underlaid the hushed voices, punctured occasionally by the decisive *thunk* of stamps.

We approached a clerk and Matt stated our names and business, but when the clerk said he couldn't help us, I decided a more feminine approach might be in order.

"Please, sir," I said, clasping my gloved hands on the counter top. "We've just returned from Prussia, where our mother recently passed, and wish to know if our grandfather is still alive." I injected a measured dose of desperation into my voice. Hopefully that would be enough. If not, I would increase the dose to hysteria levels. Causing a scene in public tended to move even the most conservative man into action. "The staff at the Aged Christian Society were not helpful. Apparently he just walked out, but no one knows where he went. Please, are you able to help my brother and I? We're quite at a loss as to where to go next."

"The police," the clerk said, sounding bored.

"We've made inquiries there," Matt said. "They claim they can't help."

The clerk spread out his hands and shrugged.

"We only wish to know if he's still drawing from his account." I pulled a handkerchief from my reticule and dabbed the corner of my eye with it. "If not..." I pressed the handkerchief to my nose and sniffed. "If not, then I'm afraid we'll need to notify the police that he's not missing, he's...he's dead."

Matt put his arm around my shoulders. "There, there, Jane. We'll get to the bottom of this, one way or another." He cast a forlorn look at the clerk. "If you can't help us, perhaps your superior can."

The clerk sighed. "Prove to me that you are who you say you are and I'll see what I can do."

We gave him our false names again, as well as Mirth's personal details. He wrote them down and handed them to a spotty-faced youth who disappeared through a door behind them. Three minutes later he returned and gave the clerk a file.

"According to our records," the clerk said without looking up from the file, "your grandfather is still drawing on his account. He comes in every Wednesday afternoon, in fact."

My heart lifted. Mirth was alive!

"Is there a current address for him?" Matt asked, trying to peer at the documents.

The clerk snapped the file closed. "According to this, he still resides at The Aged Christian Society."

Matt gave the clerk a sad smile. "Thank you for your time."

We climbed back into the waiting carriage, and Matt thumped the ceiling once we'd settled. The coach lurched forward and drove off at speed. It would seem Bryce had already forgotten his instructions for a more sedate journey.

Matt stared out the window, his gaze distant. He must be terribly disappointed. We were little better off than we had been before we entered the bank.

"I'm sorry we didn't learn anything more useful," I said quietly.

"It wasn't a complete waste of time." He gave me an encouraging smile. I admired his optimism. He rarely showed frustration for our lack of progress in the search for Chronos. Few people in his predicament would be able to maintain such unwavering optimism. "We know he'll be in the bank next Wednesday afternoon."

Today was Thursday. Only six more days to go. It felt interminable. "You plan to wait for him at the bank?"

"I do. I'll know Chornos when I see him. If Mirth is Chronos, I'll recognize him."

I smiled, hoping to prove that I too could be optimistic. "It's progress."

"It is."

Neither of us sounded particularly convincing, but our smiles didn't waver.

Bryce let us out at the front of number sixteen Park Street, Mayfair, then drove off to the mews behind the row of townhouses. Duke and Cyclops met us at the door.

"Well?" Duke asked before we'd even removed our coats. "Is he alive?"

"He is," Matt said, assisting me out of my coat. "But we don't have a current address."

Duke swore under his breath.

"Another dead end," Cyclops muttered with a shake of his head.

"Not quite." Matt told his friends about Mirth's regular Wednesday afternoon visits to the bank. "I'll watch for him next week."

The lack of response was an overwhelming indication of what both men thought of that.

"In the mean time, India and I will continue visiting the watchmakers in the city," Matt said.

We'd already been to many, perhaps most, and there were only a few remaining Clerkenwell factories to search now. "We'll continue after lunch, shall we?" I suggested cheerfully.

He merely grunted. Although I used the excuse of lunch, he must have noticed that I avoided mentioning his need to rest and use his watch. If there was one thing Matt disliked intensely, it was being reminded of his weakened state.

"Duke," Cyclops said with a jerk of his head toward the back of the house. "What've we got to eat?"

"Why is the cooking always left to me?" Duke whined.

"Because no one else likes cooking."

"Because you're good at it," Matt said with a glare at Cyclops.

Cyclops's good eye beaded with humor. It was at odds with the ugly, ragged scar extending from beneath the patch over his other eye. He was a frightening looking man with his gigantic height, solid girth and scar, but I'd quickly learned that he was quite the gentle soul. Like Duke and Willie, he was also fiercely loyal to Matt.

"Hopefully we'll have a new cook, soon," Matt added. "You won't have to continue with kitchen work. Any of you."

"I don't mind the work," Duke grumbled. "As long as everyone pulls their weight."

"Things are done differently here. This is Mayfair, after all. We need staff."

"We don't. We'll be going home soon."

Matt lowered his gaze. Duke's audible swallow filled the silence. No one knew how long they'd be in London searching for Chronos. And if they didn't find him here...their next step was unclear.

Cyclops shoved Duke's shoulder. "I'll help you."

"You? You couldn't cook toast."

Cyclops's rumbling chuckle lingered after they'd both disappeared to the service area downstairs. Matt and I had hardly finished removing our hats and gloves when the door to the drawing room burst open and a slender woman strode out, her steps purposeful. Her severe black brows crashed together over a beaky nose.

"I refuse to work in such an immodest and ill disciplined household!" she declared as she stalked past us to the front door. "Americans," she added in a mutter without so much as a glance at Matt or myself as she threw open the front door and left.

Matt shut it behind her, just as Willie, Matt's American cousin, emerged from the drawing room. "Interviews not going so well?" he asked in a lazy drawl.

"That woman!" Willie stabbed a finger at the door and uttered a sound pitched somewhere between a growl and a scream. "Englishwomen!"

"Yes?" I inquired with a lift of my brows.

"You're all..." She threw her hands in the air, as if that explained everything. "Missish prudes!"

"Is that all?" I said as I swept past her into the dining room. "You had me worried there for a moment, Willie. I thought you were going to say something cruel about my countrywomen."

I had the great satisfaction of hearing Willie emit that odd noise again as she stomped after me.

Miss Glass, Matt's elderly aunt, touched her ears and winced. "Do cease that infernal racket, Willemina," she pleaded. "My ears are too old to be subjected to it."

"Interviews definitely aren't going well, then," Matt said to his cousin and aunt.

"They would be more successful if I were allowed to interview potential housekeepers on my own," Miss Glass intoned in her haughtiest manner. She was upper class to her bones and managed to convey as much with a mere tightening of her lip, something she generally only reserved for Willie.

The two of them clashed terribly. Miss Glass considered Willie crass, unladylike, and working class at best, while Willie considered Miss Glass snobbish, stiff, and self-important. They were both right, yet they both had marvelous qualities too. It would take some time before either of them recognized those good qualities in the other, however. Certainly longer than this morning. They'd rarely been left alone together, but both had wanted to interview potential staff. Matt had hoped it would bring them closer. It would seem he'd misplayed them.

Willie folded her arms over her worn leather waistcoat and narrowed her gaze at Miss Glass. "*She* wants a housekeeper with airs and graces. I won't be looked down on by the damned help. I won't be looked down on by anyone!"

Miss Glass's back stiffened. "I am trying to employ someone of upstanding moral character. Unfortunately, your foul language discourages such women."

"Ain't nothing to do with my language." She waved a hand at the door. "That one called me unnatural. Unnatural!"

"She was referring to your masculine attire. No *normal* woman dresses as you do."

Willie hitched up one leg of her trousers and rested her booted foot on the low table. "The one before that said I was immoral. I may dress like a man, but that don't make me no loose woman."

Miss Glass merely sniffed.

Willie gave her a hard smile. "Got nothing to say on that score, Letty?" Willie had taken to calling Miss Glass the informal version of her Christian name to annoy her. It worked. Miss Glass presented Willie with her shoulder.

"Ladies," Matt groaned. "Can you please stop squabbling? Were there *any* applicants you both liked?"

Willie and Miss Glass looked at one another. "No," they said in unison.

Matt sighed. "Perhaps India can sit in on future interviews."

"Why?" Miss Glass asked.

"Yes, why?" Willie added, lowering her foot.

"She can act as intermediary," he said. "She's got a calming, no-nonsense nature that will sort the good from bad with minimum fuss."

He thought that of me? That I was calm and no-nonsense? Had he already forgotten our first meeting where I'd railed at my former fiancé, Eddie Hardacre? I'd created quite a scene. So much so that Matt had needed to forcibly remove me from the shop and Cyclops then restrained me. Granted, that wasn't how I usually behaved, but I'd found the experience so cathartic that I'd not fully returned to my quiet, acquiescent manner. I quite liked speaking my mind now, when the occasion deemed it necessary.

"I am calm," Miss Glass said, smoothing her hands over her black skirt.

"And I ain't got no truck for nonsense," Willie cut in with a glare at me, as if I'd been the one to make the

11

suggestion that I sit in on the interviews. "We don't need her."

"I quite agree." Miss Glass gave me a friendly nod. "No offence intended, India."

"None taken," I said. "I have no wish to be involved anyway. It's not my place."

My answer seemed to please both Miss Glass and Willie, but not Matt. "Prove to me that you can come to an agreement on a housekeeper without a third party's interference," he told them. "Otherwise, I'll hire the next woman who walks in off the street. Is that clear?"

"Quite," his aunt said.

Willie merely grunted, which was as good as an agreement in her language.

Matt excused himself, only to have Willie run after him as he departed. She probably wanted to ask him how our inquiries at the bank fared. We'd decided to keep Matt's health problems from his aunt. Her mind could be somewhat fickle, occasionally slipping into madness, and we didn't wish to alarm her. Nor did we want to try to explain how a watch could rejuvenate him, albeit temporarily. But that meant we couldn't openly discuss our search for Chronos around her. As far as she was aware, I was employed partly as her companion, and partly to assist Matt in running his business affairs while he visited London—a visit she was convinced would never end. We'd given up trying to tell her that he would return to America one day. She refused to believe it.

In truth, I didn't like thinking about that day either. What would become of me then, and Miss Glass, too? Not to mention I'd grown rather fond of my new American friends.

Matt rested in his rooms for the rest of the morning then we all ate lunch together in the dining room. Miss Glass no longer commented on the presence of Duke and Cyclops at meal times. She'd given up calling them staff, too, and seemed to accept them as members of the household, equal in status to myself and Willie although not to herself and Matt. In her mind, she and her nephew were placed in an elevated position through their birth and God's will. Poor Willie butted up against the English class system every day, calling it unfair and archaic, sometimes in Miss Glass's presence. She would learn, eventually, that it was a centuries-old system too ingrained to change over the course of a few weeks.

The arrival of a visitor after lunch surprised us all. It was our first since capturing the American outlaw known as the Dark Rider a week ago. Not even Miss Glass's brother or sister-in-law had called. Miss Glass had refused to have any friends over for tea until we installed proper staff befitting a townhouse belonging to Mr. Matthew Glass. Police Commissioner Munro's arrival saw her fretting over how and where to receive him, until Matthew suggested they retreat to his study. Going by Munro's quick agreement and stiff chin, it wasn't a social call.

"After you, India," Matt said to me.

I gave him a blank look. "You want me to join you?"

He flicked an apologetic gaze at Munro, standing at the foot of the staircase, and stepped closer to whisper to me. "You are my assistant."

"I thought I was more Miss Glass's companion than your assistant."

"I would like your presence."

I led the way up the stairs, Willie's glare stabbing me in the back. No doubt she wanted to know why I received special privileges. So did I.

"I have a task for you, Mr. Glass," the commissioner said as he sat.

Matt sat behind his desk while I pulled up a chair beside it and waited for him to pass me a piece of paper and pencil. He did not. He merely rocked back in his chair and waited for Munro to go on.

Munro stroked his white moustache with his thumb and finger and looked lost for words. In my brief encounter with him, after my run-in with the Dark Rider outside Scotland Yard, he'd shown himself to be direct and never short of an opinion. Something must be amiss.

"What's the task you have for me?" Matt prompted him.

"My...friend's son has gone missing."

Matt sat forward. "I see."

Munro's face sagged. The moustache drooped over his downturned mouth, and his eyes became moist. He must be very close to the boy and his parents to be so concerned. "He's a brilliant cartographer. He produces exquisitely fine maps and globes, with pinpoint accuracy. Here." He pulled out a rolled leaf of thick parchment from his inside breast pocket and handed it to Matt.

Matt spread it out on the desk. It was a map of central London, drawn in exquisite colored detail. Even the smallest lane was rendered and named in writing so tiny as to need a magnifier to read it. Ships crowded the docks, their ropes blackened with tar so glossy it shone, their cargo piled on the jetties in perfect miniature. The water of the Thames and the occasional window appeared to reflect the sunlight, and I could distinguish between brick, stone and wooden buildings. It was a work of art.

"It's lovely." I skimmed my fingers over the lines and was surprised to note that some felt raised. How had he achieved such an effect?

"It's all accurate," Munro said again with a hint of pride.

"You want me to find him? Isn't that a task for one of your detective inspectors?"

"They've tried. I've tried. He just...disappeared. That's why I need you." His face no longer looked long or his eyes sad. He was once again the formidable, proud police commissioner. "You told me that your specialty is infiltrating criminal gangs, pretending to be one of them as you moved within their ring. I telegraphed my counterpart in California and confirmed this with him. He told me you have brought down several dangerous gangs from within, often single handedly. He called you fearless, determined, and without equal. You, sir, are precisely the man I need. My inspectors are good men, but I need someone better than good. I need a competent and intelligent man, someone who can think quickly and act accordingly. I believe you're the only man who can help me find my...find Daniel."

I turned to Matt, aware that my eyes were huge and my mouth ajar. I couldn't help but stare at him. I knew he'd brought down outlaw gangs in America, including that of his own grandfather, but the praise from his employer was excessive. He didn't so much as blush.

"Clearly you have some notion of who is responsible for your friend's son's disappearance," Matt said. "What group is it you'd like me to infiltrate?"

"The Mapmakers' Guild. There's something odd going on there, and I'd like you to get to the bottom of it." He leaned forward, and once again his countenance changed from commanding to concerned. "Find my boy, Mr. Glass. Find Daniel."

CHAPTER 2

"*Your* boy?" Matt asked.

The commissioner stretched his neck out of his crisp white collar and a flush infused his cheeks above his whiskers. He pulled out a small photograph of a youth from his pocket. The young man's intelligent, direct eyes peered at the camera from beneath a mop of fair hair. He was slender, unlike his robust father, but the firmness of his mouth mirrored Munro's.

"His full name is Daniel Munro Gibbons," the commissioner said.

The boy must have been born out of wedlock, taking his father's name as his middle name but not his last. I wondered if Mrs. Munro knew.

"He's nineteen years of age, blond hair, blue eyes." The commissioner spoke matter-of-factly, as if he were briefing his men on a stranger's disappearance. It would seem he didn't know how to react, oscillating between indifference and concern, spanning the range of emotions in between. "He's clever but naive. He lives with his mother and maternal grandfather, and he went

16

to a good school. His grandfather was a mapmaker, and the boy showed an aptitude for cartography from a young age. He began his apprenticeship with the Mapmakers' Guild's master a little over a month ago. Three days ago, he left his master's shop at the end of the day and set off for home. He didn't arrive." The hand that held the photograph shook.

"May I keep this?" Matt asked, reaching for the picture. "And the map, too?"

Munro hesitated, then gave a curt nod. "There's more. That night, as the entire family was out searching for him, making inquiries of his friends, there was a burglary at the house. The only things stolen were Daniel's maps. He'd made them over the years and kept them in a box under his bed."

"Nothing else?"

"Nothing. The following day, there was another break-in, again while the family was out searching. They took nothing but left the house in a mess."

"They were looking for a particular map, perhaps. One that wasn't in the box under the bed. " Matt studied Daniel's map in front of him. "This one?"

"I don't know. Daniel asked me to take care of it a week ago. He didn't tell me why or who'd commissioned it, and I wasn't interested enough to ask." He cleared his throat. "I wish I had. It might be important information."

I picked up the map again and traced the line of the river's bank with my fingertips. It felt slightly raised, yet a closer inspection showed that it was simply a flat drawing.

"His mother is beside herself with worry." The commissioner swallowed heavily. "Find him, Glass. Even if you learn the worst, just find Daniel."

"I'll do my best." Matt reached into his top drawer and pulled out a notepad and pencil, which he slid across the desk to me. He turned Daniel's map to face Munro. "Is the route he usually took between work and home on here?"

"The shop is here, at Burlington Arcade." Munro pointed to the arcade at the edge of the map. "Daniel walked to Victoria Station and got off the train at Hammersmith." Neither were on the map.

"Did he have friends?" Matt asked.

Munro gave me two names, which I wrote down. "My men have already spoken to them. They didn't see Daniel that day. The last time they saw him, he mentioned being troubled by something at work but wouldn't tell them what. I spoke to his employer myself, but he claimed Daniel was his usual self and nothing was amiss."

"Did you believe him?"

"I think he's lying. I think he knows what happened to Daniel but won't tell me. That's why I need you, Glass. I need inside information on the guild and on Jeremiah Duffield."

"I'll see what I can do. I have other commitments—"

"No!" The commissioner slammed his palm down on the desk, causing me to jump. Matt didn't so much as flinch. "Set aside everything else, and give all your time to finding Daniel."

Matt nodded. He was agreeing?

"That won't be possible," I cut in. "Mr. Glass's other commitments are of vital importance."

"As important as finding my son?"

I leveled my gaze with his. "Yes."

Matt put up his hands. "I have six days before I can do anything on the other matter," he said to me. "I can spend that time searching for Daniel."

"Good." Munro stood.

"There are other things you can be doing in those six days," I said. There were several watchmakers' factories still to visit, and inquiries to make. We wouldn't be idle.

"He's nineteen, India," Matt said quietly. "I have to help if I can."

"Quite," Munro said with gruff finality. "Thank you, Glass. You'll be rewarded handsomely, of course."

Matt simply lifted a hand in dismissal. "If you learn anything that might be important, send word to me here."

"How do you plan to go about becoming part of the guild?" he asked as Matt walked him to the door.

"Yes," I chimed in. "How, when you have no mapmaking skills?"

"I'm yet to plan all the details."

I followed them down the stairs and saw Munro out to his waiting coach. We'd hardly closed the front door when the entire household descended upon us, including Matt's aunt. She wasn't interested in Munro, however, but in Willie.

"You talk to her, Matthew," she said crisply. "I'm at the end of my tether."

"I offered India's assistance," he began, only to be interrupted by Miss Glass.

"Not that. *That!*" She waved a hand at the pipe drooping from the corner of Willie's mouth. "It's filthy."

Willie managed to grin while clenching her teeth around the pipe. "It ain't so bad. Good for the lungs." She breathed deeply, only to end up coughing.

Duke snorted. "I agree with Miss Glass."

"Nobody asked your opinion," Willie said, choking out the words along with a cloud of smoke. "Besides, you smoke one sometimes."

"But I ain't a woman."

She rolled her eyes.

"I wouldn't want a man blowing filthy smoke in my drawing room either," Miss Glass said. "If you insist on continuing with the disgusting habit, take it outside."

"Or into the smoking room," Matt added before Willie pointed out that the drawing room, or any other part of the house, didn't belong to his aunt.

Miss Glass looked horrified. "The smoking room is for men!"

"I hardly think it makes a difference where Willie's concerned."

"What will our staff think?"

"We don't have any staff. When we do get some, they'll have to put up with it, just like we do." Matt glared at Willie.

"I'm going," she muttered. "After you tell us what Munro wanted."

"Gladly." Matt sounded tired, and I couldn't blame him. I grew tired listening to his aunt and cousin bickering too. "His son has gone missing. He wants me to find him."

"Missing?" Miss Glass echoed. "Poor Agatha. Poor dear, Agatha. Her husband missing again."

We all looked at her. Miss Glass's madness hadn't appeared for a week, and I'd begun to suspect we'd imagined the previous episodes. This new rambling proved we had not.

"I'll take her to her rooms," Willie said, handing the pipe to Cyclops. "Duke, fetch her maid." With surprising gentleness, she steered Miss Glass toward the stairs while Duke headed to the door leading to the service rooms below the house.

Matt watched them leave with a small dent between his brows.

"Polly will see that she's comfortable," I assured him.

He nodded and rubbed his forehead.

"Didn't you get enough rest earlier?" Cyclops asked.

"I'm fine," Matt said. "We need to discuss a plan for finding the lad."

"And a plan for finding Chronos," I added. "We're not giving up on that in favor of this new assignment."

"Aye." Cyclops managed to instill more menace with his one good eye than most people did with two. Matt, however, seemed unaffected by it.

Willie returned and we convened in the library to discuss Munro's visit.

"So how're you supposed to go about finding the missing boy, then?" Willie asked.

"He's not a boy," I said. "He's nineteen and was—is—apprenticed to Jeremiah Duffield, the master of the Mapmakers' Guild."

"Must be good, then," Duke said, sprawled in the deep armchair with his feet angled toward the fireplace.

"He is." Matt produced Daniel's map and spread it on the table. "He made this."

Willie swore softly. Duke's eyes widened as he pored over it, while Cyclops pointed out places of note.

"Touch it," I said. "Some of it feels raised."

They each touched roads, buildings, the river, tracing the outlines with their fingertips as I had done.

"He's an artist," Cyclops said. "A genius."

"How'd he do that?" Duke asked, wonder in his voice.

"He turned it over and pressed hard from the back," Willie said. "The back would be the same map, but reversed."

"Except he hasn't." Matt picked up the map and held it flat at eye level then flipped it over. It was unmarked.

Nobody had an answer. The map's creation was a mystery.

Matt rolled it up and set it aside.

"My question still stands," Willie said, stretching her legs in front of her and crossing them at the ankles. "How're you going to find him if the police couldn't?"

"Munro wants me to infiltrate the guild and see what I can learn from the inside," Matt said.

"How? You can't draw maps."

"He could try," Duke said. "He ain't a bad doodler."

"Trying ain't going to get him into the guild," Cyclops said with a roll of his eye.

"I'll need another way in," Matt said. "Guilds require servants, the members have customers, friends, wives."

"You wouldn't make a good wife," Duke said, fighting back a grin. "You ain't obedient enough."

"Obedient?" Willie snorted. "No wonder you ain't married."

Duke crossed his arms and gave her a smug smile.

"I'll get a job as a servant," Matt said.

"What if they're not hiring?" I asked.

"They'll be hiring after I pay one of the servants to disappear."

Cyclops shook his head. "I'll be the servant. You look and sound like a gentleman."

"I can act like a servant if necessary."

"Why don't you be the customer," I said. "Cyclops can be a servant, and I'll befriend Mr. Duffield's wife, if he's married."

Matt nodded. "A three-pronged attack. I like it."

"What about Willie and me?" Duke asked.

"You're both needed here. Too many of us will set alarm bells ringing."

Duke sat back with a grumble, but Willie seemed unconcerned. "What if the guild has nothing to do with his disappearance?" she asked. "What if it were a simple robbery as he walked home, but something went wrong and he got killed? Maybe he had enemies. His father definitely would, a man in his position."

"Munro is convinced that it's linked to the guild. He also seems to think Daniel's still alive."

"That could simply be a matter of hope." I shuddered as an icy shiver trickled down my spine. "I do hope he's right and Daniel hasn't met a terrible fate."

"The question is," Cyclops said, "why would someone kidnap him?"

That was a good question, and one that had so many potential answers that it was impossible to speculate without knowing more. I picked up Daniel's map and studied it again. It truly was beautiful, yet also functional. Whatever technique he'd used to raise some of the lines hadn't left a mark. As I ran my fingers over them again, I felt a faint sensation, a slight warming, so light as to be hardly discernable. I closed my eyes and focused all my attention on the map. My fingertips warmed again, but barely. If I moved my fingers off the raised lines, the sensation stopped.

"What is it?" Matt's voice sounded close behind me. I hadn't heard him approach.

I opened my eyes to see him leaning over my shoulder, his face a little above me. I handed the map to him. "Touch the lines." He did as asked, even closing his eyes as I had done. "Do you feel anything?"

"Such as?"

I touched his hand and his eyes sprang open. His gaze locked with mine in a brief, fierce moment before I broke the connection. "Close your eyes again," I said. I guided his finger to the raised lines. "Do you feel anything?"

He drew in a deep breath and let it out slowly. He shook his head.

"No warmth?"

That dent appeared in between his brows again. "No." He opened his eyes. "Did you?"

"I...I think so." I touched the lines once more, but my focus had slipped away with his presence. I felt nothing but the rough parchment. "It was a little warm."

He dragged a chair closer and sat, his knees brushing the cotton of my skirt. "Did it warm in the same way the watches do when you touch them?"

"Not as much. They're made of metal so it's understandable."

"Or you simply respond to them at a deeper, stronger level because your magic is watch magic, not map magic."

My fingers curled on the tabletop. My heart slowed to a sluggish beat and my mouth went dry. "I...I'm not convinced that I have any kind of magic."

"I am." He rested his hand over mine. It was warm, gentle, solid. "India, there's no other explanation for clocks and watches to move of their own accord. Clocks and watches that *you* have tinkered with."

"But...how do I do it? And why me? Why am I capable of such a thing?" Why couldn't I fix his watch?

"I don't know. But we'll find someone with answers. Someone who can help you understand your gift."

"There are other priorities now."

His thumb rubbed my knuckle, and he offered me a small smile. "Finding Chronos will kill two birds with one stone." He removed his hand and picked up the map. "I had already considered the possibility that Daniel's skill is beyond normal. This map is incredible."

"But it's just a map. It doesn't *do* anything."

"Not for us, but it may for Daniel, or for the intended recipient."

"As your watch only keeps you alive, no one else?"

He nodded. "It must be magic. How else could he have raised the lines? And why else would you feel warmth when you touch it?"

"You think my...magic is responding to his?" It felt odd associating the word with myself. I didn't feel magical; I felt ordinary. My upbringing had been ordinary, my parents were ordinary, my story up until the point of my father's death had been ordinary.

Yet a voice in my head echoed Matt's. Evidence pointed to me possessing a small amount of watch magic.

"I do." He stretched his long legs under the table and once again studied the map. "Does the kidnapper want both Daniel and the map? Or is abducting Daniel merely a means to finding the map?"

"And why would Daniel keep the map from whomever is after it?" I asked. "He gave it to the one man he thought could protect the map—his police commissioner father—knowing it was safest with him. Yet he told Munro nothing about its magical properties."

"Perhaps because he suspected Munro wouldn't believe him. He strikes me as a skeptical man."

"Who can blame him for not believing in magic? I'm not even sure that I do."

Matt's wry smile held a hint of wickedness. "You believe, India. I know you do. It's only stubbornness that prevents you from wholeheartedly embracing the idea of magic."

"It is not," I said crisply. "It's years of thinking logically and believing in only what I can explain and replicate."

His smile didn't waver, as if he thought he knew me better than I knew myself.

"We need to find out who commissioned Daniel to create that map," I said. "If someone did commission him, that is. It might have simply been something he drew for himself."

"In either case, *why*? Why draw it in the first place when there are thousands of other maps of London already in circulation? What's so special about *this* map?"

***

Matt and I drove to the Mapmaker's Guild hall in Ludgate Hill. Cyclops had departed forty-five minutes prior, armed with impeccable references and a bag of coins, the latter to entice a footman to leave his position. Hopefully he would be successful without raising any awkward questions. Matt had decided that we would pretend to be husband and wife. I wasn't sure that was wise. For one thing, it tied us together, and our three pronged attack became two. For another, it meant we had to match our lies. It was easy enough at the bank, where our ruse was short-lived and we weren't separated. It would be harder over a longer period.

"I'm looking for a young mapmaker," he announced upon our arrival at the Mapmaker's Guild hall. He employed a strong American drawl and an air of commanding authority so unlike his personable one that I glanced sideways at him.

The ancient footman stood in the recessed doorway of the Ludgate Hill building and surveyed Matt with a critical, albeit watery, eye. He didn't spare me so much as a glance. "And you are?"

"Mr. Prescott, of Stanford and Prescott, out of Boston. Bankers," he clarified. "I hear there is an apprentice cartographer purported to be excellent at his craft, possibly the best. I need the best to produce a map for me, something special, unique. Well, man? This is the Mapmakers' Guild, is it not? You must know who I'm referring to."

"You'd better come in." The footman shuffled backward. He was so stooped that Matt almost doubled his height.

"Thank you," I said when Matt simply strode past him without a word. He may be playing a role, but that didn't mean I had to be rude too.

The blue and white tiled floor of the porch gave way to a more modern black and white checked tile inside. It was a simple style, designed not to draw the eye away from the large globe perched on the shoulders of a bronze statue of a bent old man. The globe glinted in the gaslight thrown out from the dozen lamps attached to the walls. There were no windows, and once the door closed, no natural light filtered through. It could have been the middle of the night rather than the middle of the afternoon.

The footman indicated a room off the hall. "Wait in there. Someone will see you presently."

Matt, however, didn't go. He was too busy pacing around the globe, studying it. "Look at this, my dear," he said to me. "Such fine work. The names of countries and oceans have been engraved. Mountain ranges are raised and valleys depressed. There are little symbols too."

"I see a mermaid." I pointed to a girl with long flowing hair in a river. "And a crown over London. How charming."

"How expensive." Matt caressed the globe with as much gentleness and attention as a lover. "Art like this ought to be in a secure bank vault, not on display."

"Through here, if you please," the footman repeated with less patience.

"We'd like to inspect this globe longer," Matt said without looking up.

"No." We both glanced at the footman. He pointed a gnarled finger at the door. "Wait in there."

I took Matt's arm. "We'd better do as he asks."

Framed maps of all shapes and sizes adorned the sitting room walls, and another less elaborate globe sat proudly on a table near the sofa. I sat but Matt paced, his hands clasped behind him.

"Is everything all right?" I asked. He didn't look particularly tired, but perhaps he had to use his watch already. It would trouble him to need it so soon after the last time.

"Yes," he said gruffly without breaking stride. "I'm busy and wish to get on. That's all."

Ah. He wanted to remain as his character in case someone walked through the door. I ought to do the same. I sat with my hands folded in my lap, with what I hoped was a demure expression. A wealthy banker's wife would not be the sort of woman to buck her husband's authority.

I forgot all of that when Cyclops walked in, dressed in the same coat tailed livery as the ancient footman. I beamed at him. He did not smile back, or acknowledge me in any way, and Matt didn't acknowledge him. I swallowed my smile and pretended he wasn't there, as I'd noticed Lady Rycroft, Matt's aunt, do to her footmen. Cyclops set down a tray on the table in front of me.

"Tea, madam?" he intoned in a perfect English accent.

"Yes, thank you." I accepted the cup but didn't meet his gaze. I didn't want to start giggling, even though no one else was present.

Cyclops left, only to be replaced by a smiling gentleman with a short gray beard and a droopy left eyelid. He held a large blue book to his chest. He shook Matt's hand and introduced himself as Mr. Onslow, the guild's treasurer. A cherub-faced youth followed behind, his curious, open gaze taking us both in.

"You're lucky you caught me here," Mr. Onslow said. "My apprentice and I were just about to leave. How can I help you?"

"I hear there is an apprentice cartographer purported to be excellent at his craft, possibly the best," Matt said. "I need the best to produce a map for me. A special map," he added, infusing a sense of mystery into the word "special."

"An apprentice? No, no, you're mistaken." Mr. Onslow laughed, but only his good eye crinkled at the corner. The droopy one remained droopy. "An apprentice is too new, his skill too raw. You want an experienced man."

"I want the best. I hear this apprentice is the best."

Onslow sobered. "By whose claim?"

"That's irrelevant. The lad's name is Daniel Gibbons."

The apprentice gasped. Onslow glared at him, and the youth pressed his lips together and bowed his head.

"You know the lad I speak of." Matt underpinned his statement with a hint of menace that only a brave man would ignore.

Still, Onslow hesitated before finally acquiescing. "He's apprenticed to Mr. Duffield, the guild's master, but has gone missing."

Matt feigned surprise, so I did too. "Missing?" Matt demanded.

Onslow shrugged. "He left work and didn't arrive home, apparently. The police made inquiries, but... It's all very sad."

"Did he run away?"

"Hard to say." Onslow brightened. "But he was just an apprentice. There are many experienced mapmakers in the guild who can produce a fine piece for you. What type of map, and of what region?"

"I'll go to Duffield," Matt said, ignoring him. "I assume the best apprentice works for the best cartographer, and he is the guild's master, is he not?"

The apprentice's cherubic lips flattened. In disappointment? Envy?

"He's not necessarily the best," Onslow said tightly. "Quality is subjective. Duffield's specialty is the sub-continent. He traveled there extensively in his youth. Unless the map you wish to commission is of India, or one of the neighboring countries, I wouldn't go to Duffield. That's my humble opinion, of course."

"It is of India," Matt said without missing a beat.

"Oh." The bridge of Onslow's nose wrinkled. "In that case, you'll find him at his shop in the Burlington Arcade. Now, we must go. I shouldn't be away from my shop for too long. If you find Duffield's manner not to your liking, come and see me. I have an excellent grasp of the sub-continent myself. You'll find me on Regent Street. Good day, sir, madam." To his apprentice, he said, "See them out."

Mr. Onslow left, and the youth indicated the door. Now that he was separated from his master, I wondered if he might be more inclined to talk about Daniel.

"What's your name?" I asked.

He looked up sharply, perhaps startled that I addressed him directly. "Ronald. Ronald Hogarth."

"It's a pleasure to meet you, Ronald. Am I correct in guessing that you know Daniel, the missing apprentice?"

His apple cheeks pinked. "I only met him twice. Both times here, at meetings. We weren't invited to the meetings, of course, they're just for full members, but often the apprentices come along and take part in the dinner afterward."

"You spoke to him?"

"A little."

"How did he seem?" Matt asked. "Anxious? Troubled?"

Ronald lifted one shoulder. "I suppose you could say that, but only recently. The first time I met him, he was a regular chap, nice enough. The second time, he couldn't sit still. He startled easily, especially when someone new walked in. He kept looking over his shoulder, too, like he expected someone to sneak up on him."

"Did he seem more anxious when his master was in the room?"

"No." Ronald looked owlishly from Matt to me and back again. We'd alarmed the poor lad. "Why do you want to know? Is this about his disappearance?"

"We just want to find him so he can make a map for me," Matt assured him.

I took Matt's arm, hoping he would see it as a sign to ease back on his questions. Ronald was too suspicious.

"He was good," Ronald mumbled. "But not as much as everyone says."

"You saw his work?" Matt asked.

"No, but I just know he couldn't have been all that good. He was only a first year apprentice. The customer who commissioned him must have realized and wanted his money back, that's why he argued with Daniel."

I felt Matt's muscles tense beneath my hand. "How do you know they argued?"

"I heard Mr. Duffield tell Mr. Onslow and some others, a week or more ago."

Before Daniel went missing, then. "Do you know what they argued about?" I asked.

"No. Mr. Duffield couldn't hear them."

"Thank you," Matt said. "Hopefully the lad turns up after he finishes having a lark at everyone's expense."

Ronald nodded sadly. "I hope that's all it turns out to be. He was a pretentious sod but I don't like thinking something bad happened to him."

We climbed into our waiting carriage, and Matt knocked on the ceiling once we'd settled. Bryce drove off in the direction of Clerkenwell.

"We didn't learn much," I said with a sigh.

"On the contrary." Matt removed his hat and ruffled up his hair. "We learned that Duffield specializes in the subcontinent, so that's something I can use when I speak to him. We also learned that Daniel argued with a customer. I'd wager the customer is the same one who commissioned him to create that map. Perhaps they argued about Daniel not giving it back to him."

"It does seem likely." The brougham lurched around a corner and I put my hand on the seat beside me to steady myself. "We were very lucky that Ronald was prepared to speak to us. We didn't even know he'd be there."

"That's the thrill of clandestine work. You never know who you'll encounter or what information will turn up. It keeps me on my toes." He did look rather invigorated by the encounter. His eyes looked brighter than they'd been all day, and a small, satisfied smile touched his lips.

"You're rather suited to it," I said. "I'm impressed that you maintained your character for so long, even when no one was looking."

"You did well yourself."

"My nerves were stretched to their limit the entire time. I hate to think how frayed they would have become if Onslow suspected us of lying."

"He didn't have a clue." He grinned. "We make a good team."

I wasn't so sure. He hadn't needed me at the guild, nor at the bank. It seemed more and more likely he had asked me along to justify the expense of my wages. A small twinge of guilt pinched my gut, but I set it aside. I wanted to work, and I wasn't asking for more than I would have earned as a shopkeeper's assistant. Besides, if his lack of concern over the growing number of people under his care was anything to judge by, Matt could afford my wages and much more.

The factory district of Clerkenwell was thoroughly working class. Few gentlemen's carriages ventured down its dreary, narrow streets. Sunlight and color seemed to have abandoned the rookery, and hope too, by the looks of the miserable faces. The factories were more like workshops than large manufacturing premises. Most were owned by craftsmen who'd managed to scrape together enough capital from investors to scale up their efforts. Years ago, my father had been approached by a watchmaker who wanted him to invest in such a venture. He offered my father part of the profits in exchange for some initial money up front, but Father had been a conservative man, and he hadn't wanted to invest in a scheme that might not produce results. He preferred to keep his workshop at the back of his shop so he could come and go as he pleased.

Matt assisted me down the carriage steps and we entered the brick building with the sign WORTHEY, MANUFACTURER OF FINE CLOCKS painted across its façade. The rhythmic clank of machinery echoed throughout the vast space, underpinned by the whirring of hundreds of small gears and the occasional chime. Four men dressed in leather aprons sat at a long bench, sorting parts into small boxes. Another two stood by the machines, turning cranks and feeding the coal, and four more sat at tables, assembling the clocks.

A whiskery fellow sat in an office. He looked up from his paperwork and saw us at the same time we saw him. He greeted us and, taking in our good clothes, smiled. It was fortunate that Miss Glass had insisted I buy new outfits more suited to being her companion than the dull gray and brown dresses I'd worn my entire life. I still felt a little uncomfortable in the conspicuous blues and greens of my new gowns, but she said I looked "much improved" in them.

"Good afternoon, sir, madam," the man said, shaking Matt's hand. "Welcome to Worthey's. My name is Archibald Worthey. How may I help?"

"We're looking for a specific watchmaker," Matt said. "Perhaps he works here, or you know him."

The man's smile slipped a little. It was the standard response whenever we said we were looking for someone and not in the market for a new watch or clock.

One of the workers approached the office, his attention on the small carriage clock in his hand. The casing was open, and he tinkered with the mechanisms.

"I'll be with you in a moment, Pierre," Worthey said. To Matt, he said, "Your accent. Is it American?"

The worker went very still. He didn't look up from the clock, but he no longer gave it his attention. The tool went limp in his hand.

I turned back to Matt. "It is," he said. "I met the watchmaker in America, as it happens, although he was English. That was five years ago. I'm now searching for him. Do you know of an exceptional watchmaker who may have been out of the country at that time? He would be old, with white hair."

Worthey shook his head. "Can't think of anyone. Pierre might know. He's old and well traveled." He chuckled. "Pierre? Do you... Oh. He's gone."

I spun round, as did Matt. The workman had indeed left, having set the clock down on the table near the door. I strode out of the office and scanned the other men on the factory floor. None wore the same blue cap as Pierre, and the spot at the end of the long bench stood vacant.

Beside me, Matt's breathing became heavier, more erratic. I took his arm. "He had a white beard," I said quietly. "But I couldn't see his face."

"Where the devil did he go?" Worthey said, hands on hips. "It's not time for his break."

I picked up the carriage clock Pierre had been working on, but let it go with a gasp. "It's warm."

Matt took off at a run.

CHAPTER 3

Matt searched for the man named Pierre on foot, while I had Bryce drive slowly through the streets of Clerkenwell. I shouted up at him to stop no less than eight times, and got out to inspect every white-bearded man I spotted. None wore the same blue cap as Pierre, and all gave me blank looks when I questioned them. It was possible they were lying, however. Since I hadn't seen Pierre's face, I had no way of knowing what he looked like.

After two hours, I ordered Bryce to return to the factory. Matt wasn't there, so I marched into Worthey's office. "That man who was here earlier," I said. "Pierre. What's his full name?"

"Excuse me, Mrs....?"

"Miss Steele. I'm the daughter of—" Telling him that I was Eliot Steele's daughter may not work in my favor. "Never mind." Few watchmakers had treated me without fear or reservation since my father's death. While I didn't know Mr. Worthey, that didn't mean he hadn't known my father.

Worthey sighed and returned his pen to the inkstand. "Pierre DuPont. Why? What's your interest in him?"

"He may be the man my employer seeks. Is he French?"

He nodded. "From Marseilles. He came to England a few years ago."

"Does he have a French accent?"

"Yes, a strong one."

So he wasn't Chronos. Matt said the magical watchmaker had a middle class English accent and had worked in London. I rested my hands on the chair back in front of me and lowered my head. We should have questioned Worthey before chasing after Pierre.

But if he wasn't Chronos, why had he run away when he heard Matt's American accent? And why had the clock felt warm?

"How long has he worked here?" I asked.

"Three months."

A clock on the mantel chimed. Worthey checked his watch before slipping it back into his pocket. "Excuse me." He strode to the office door and rang the bell hanging there.

Like automatons, the men at the long bench set down their tools and rose. The ones at the machines pulled levers and the cogs ground to a halt. An eerie silence settled over the factory floor.

"Do you mind if I speak to your men briefly before they go?" I asked Worthey. "They might know something about Pierre that could help us."

He held out his hand. "Be my guest, but you'll have to be quick. Nobody likes to stay here longer than necessary."

He escorted me down the steps as the men plucked their coats off hooks ranged along the wall.

"Before you go, men," Mr. Worthey bellowed, "Miss Steele would like to ask you some questions about Pierre. Who among you knew him well?"

Blank eyes stared at me.

"Does anyone know where he worked before he came here?" I asked.

They shook their heads.

"What about friends and family?" I asked.

More head shaking.

"He had no kin," Worthey told me. "I always ask for next of kin for each of my men, in case the worst happens. He told me he had none."

"Where did he live?"

"I don't know. He turned up every morning and collected his wages from my office on payday. It's no concern of mine if he slept under a broken old cart every night. He was a good watchmaker, a solid worker who required no training, and kept to himself. I can't ask for more than that."

My heart sank. As the men filed out, I felt as if all hope went with them.

I waited another hour in the coach for Matt to return and was more relieved than I cared to admit when he came around the corner. Dusk cast his face in shadow until he reached me at the open door of the brougham. I already knew from his slumped shoulders that he'd not been successful in finding Pierre, but I wasn't prepared for the exhaustion flogging him. Dark circles rimmed his eyes, stark against his pale skin, and deep lines bracketed his mouth. He stumbled as he stepped into the cabin, and I caught him by the shoulders. His weight and momentum propelled him into me, however, pinning me to the seat.

"Christ," he muttered, picking himself up. He touched his jacket pocket at his chest as he plunged onto the seat opposite. He lowered his head into his hands and kicked his hat, now on the floor, away from the door. "My apologies, India."

I swallowed the lump rising up my throat and called out to Bryce to drive us home. I shut the door and sat again. "Matt." When he didn't respond, I drew his hand away from his face. He lowered the other one and regarded me through thick lashes. I wanted to ask if he was all right, but I could see that he wasn't, and I didn't want to offend his masculine pride by alluding to his illness. "I don't think that man was Chronos."

He lifted his head to look at me properly. "Why not?"

"According to Worthey, he was French with a strong accent."

"He could be pretending in order to escape notice."

"True." I sighed. "I wish I'd seen his face so I could describe him to you. I only saw his white beard."

"That's more than I saw," he bit off. He lowered his head again. I ached to stroke his hair, to offer him some comfort. I wasn't sure if it would be welcome, however. "We'll return and ask more questions tomorrow."

"I questioned Worthey and the other factory hands," I said.

He straightened. "What did you learn?"

"Apparently his name is Pierre DuPont. He's originally from Marseilles but has lived in England for a few years now. He came to Worthey's three months ago. He has no family, and Worthey has no address for him. He kept to himself and made no friends among his co-workers."

Matt tipped his head back and closed his eyes. "I'd still like to return tomorrow. He might come into work as if nothing were amiss."

I knew from his tone that he didn't hold out much hope.

His breathing suddenly quickened, became more ragged, and a trickle of sweat dripped from his brow.

He looked ghostly in the dim light. I moved to sit beside him and touched his forehead.

"You're burning."

His eyelids fluttered. Was he asleep? Or...?

"Matt?"

No answer.

"Matt!" I shook him, and he slumped against me.

"Mmmm?" His finger fumbled with his jacket pocket. I helped him pull out the magic watch and remove his glove. I folded his fingers around the device, leaving my hand over his, and stretched my other arm across the back of his shoulders. He rested his head beneath my chin.

I couldn't see his veins turn blue from that angle, but I knew from his even breathing that the magic flowed through him, rejuvenating him, although not healing him entirely. He would need to sleep when we arrived home.

I pushed aside thoughts of his illness and simply enjoyed the feel of him in my arms. Not every spinster was fortunate enough to hold a strong, handsome man like this, and I planned on relishing every second, committing each hard muscle to memory.

We were passing the large colonnaded houses of Mayfair when Matt finally sat up. "I'm sorry," he muttered without meeting my gaze.

"Don't apologize." I clasped my hands tightly in my lap. They seemed to want to reach for him again. "You forget that I've already seen you like that before. And worse." The day he'd been arrested, when his watch had been left behind, had seen him nearly die. Just thinking about it made me sick to my stomach.

"That doesn't mean I want to repeat that performance."

I suddenly felt awkward and didn't know where to look. He hated me seeing him weakened, yet I already had and would again, if we maintained this close working relationship.

Neither of us spoke as we arrived home and were met by a strange man dressed in a formal suit and white gloves at the front door.

"Who are you?" Matt asked.

"The new butler. Bristow, at your service." The clean-shaven slender man, with a full lower lip and thin upper one, bowed. "Are you Mr. Glass?"

"I am, and this is Miss Steele."

Bristow straightened and stepped aside. "Welcome home, sir, madam. Miss Glass and Miss Johnson are in the drawing room, getting acquainted with the other new staff members."

Matt's brows lifted. "That was fast."

"Indeed, sir." Bristow took our hats and gloves then retreated to the cloak room to hang them up.

Matt put out his hand for me to go ahead. "It seems they've been busy while we were out."

He still looked very tired, and I bit my lip to stop myself ordering him upstairs to rest. I doubted he would take kindly to me fussing.

"There you are," Miss Glass said upon our entry into the drawing room. She sat like a queen on her throne, surrounded by her courtiers. In this case, the courtiers were dressed like servants. One, a young man, wore footman's livery, and two middle aged women and a girl of about nineteen wore aprons over black uniforms. I'd seen the outfits in the livery cupboard below stairs.

Willie marched over to Matt, hands on hips. "You look like you've been run over by an iron horse," she said quietly.

"Don't," Matt growled, low.

"Go upstairs and rest. This can wait."

"No, it can't." He pushed past her and greeted his aunt with a peck on her cheek.

Willie glared at me. "You should've taken better care of him," she hissed.

I dearly wanted to spit back a retort, but I couldn't think of one. She was right. I should have been more aware of how long he'd searched for Pierre DuPont and how that would take a toll on his health. But I'd forgotten, in the excitement of finding a magical watchmaker.

Because DuPont was definitely magical. I'd felt the warmth of his magic in the clock he'd been working on.

Miss Glass introduced us to the new staff. The housekeeper turned out to be married to the butler, and the young maid was their daughter. All the staff had come from the household of Miss Glass's old neighbor. Their employer recently passed away and his house closed up until the heir, a nephew living in New Zealand, either returned or sold it.

Miss Glass watched the new staff file out of the drawing room with a satisfied smile. "What good fortune that old Mr. Crowe died when he did."

"Not for him," Willie said.

"All he did was lie in bed all day and complain to poor Mrs. Bristow. That's barely living. It's such a worthy thing to give the staff a new home here. They're all quite grateful."

"It's only until we leave. Don't let them think it's permanent."

Miss Glass put out her hand, and Matt helped her to her feet. "Now that we have adequate staff, we can receive callers."

Willie groaned.

"We shall have proper meals, thanks to Mrs. Potter's cooking, and dinner parties too. We'll employ a temporary footman and extra kitchen staff for more grand affairs." She patted Matt's arm. "It's a shame this house can't fit more, or we'd have another six permanent staff at least."

Willie counted on her fingers, her lips moving as she did so. "There are more servants than us now! We'd be laughed out of California if our friends back home caught wind of these hoity ways."

"You didn't have staff in America?" Miss Glass clicked her tongue. "Such a wild, uncivilized country. Well, that's in the past. Now, you can live as you were born to, Matthew."

"Don't expect entertaining on a grand scale, Aunt," he said. "You're welcome to have friends come calling, but I'm afraid I won't be joining you. I'm very busy."

"Of course you'll join me, and of course there'll be dinner parties. How else are you supposed to meet your bride?"

Willie guffawed, rocking back on her heels and slapping her thighs. "Him marry a limp English rose that'll wilt at the first hint of the Californian sun?" She snorted.

Miss Glass's mouth pursed so tightly her lips disappeared altogether. She cupped her hands around Matt's arm, anchoring him to her side. "He's a Glass. He can't marry a wild, prickly..."

"Cactus?"

"Tumbleweed."

"They ain't prickly."

"This conversation is moot." Matt extricated himself from his aunt's clutches. "Marriage is the furthest thing on my mind." He fixed a glare on Willie, causing her smug smile to fade. "I have more important things to do, right now."

"Nonsense," Miss Glass snapped. "Nothing is more important than your future."

"Now *that* we agree on," Willie muttered.

Matt sighed and rubbed his forehead. "Thank you for hiring the staff. I admit to being surprised you two got along well enough to act so quickly."

"Mrs. Bristow will whip this house into shape in no time." Miss Glass peered at Matt's face. "You do look peaky. Are you unwell?"

"I'm fine."

"Perhaps you ought to rest," I said. "You look as though you're coming down with something," I added for Miss Glass's benefit.

She frowned. "India is wise. Listen to her and rest. Lewis can bring your supper up in a little while. Indeed, he can act as your valet as well as performing his footman duties."

"I have no need of a valet."

"Every gentleman of quality has need of a valet. It's the way things are done here." She shooed him toward the door.

Matt put up his hands. "I'm going. I'll come back down later."

"Is there any need?" I asked. "You ought to have a solid, uninterrupted rest. Otherwise you won't be at your best tomorrow, and I think it's going to be another full day."

"India is right," Miss Glass said.

"I need to discuss the day's events with the others," he said.

"I can do that." I gave him a reassuring smile.

He sighed. "I feel superfluous."

"You ain't," Willie said. "You're just not needed."

Matt glanced at each of us in turn and shook his head. "I see that the odds are stacked against me. I know when to retreat."

Once he was gone, Willie turned to me, hands on hips. "Why does he do what you want him to do, and not me? When I told him to rest, he refused. You tell him to go and he's all agreeable."

"That's because you don't have a delicate feminine touch," Miss Glass said.

"Huh?"

"If you want a man to do what you want, you have to subtly suggest it, not order him. You have to show him the benefits of doing what you want, as India did when she reminded him that he'll be busy again tomorrow and wouldn't want to feel unwell. She's a marvel at subtle suggestion."

"I am?" I blinked. "I've been told I can be rather forthright."

"Willie is forthright. You are simply good at manipulating, at least where Matthew is concerned. I'm quite at a loss as to why you're unwed, my girl."

I laughed and looked to Willie to laugh along with her. But she simply shrugged.

"I'd wager the ranch it's because she's too choosy," Willie said, regarding me with a critical eye.

"Hardly," I said. "If you met Eddie Hardacre, you'd wonder why I wasn't choosier."

"Maybe you scared off all the others. What do you think, Letty?"

"I quite agree," Miss Glass said. "You're too clever for a woman, India, and you have a tongue to match it, on occasion. No man wants a wife more intelligent than he, and he certainly wouldn't like one who'll remind him of that fact in front of his friends."

Willie nodded and gave me an apologetic shrug. "It's not too late for you, if it's marriage you want."

"I...I don't know," I said numbly. How had this conversation come about? I felt all at sea, unsure whether to stay and listen to their frank appraisal or walk out and make a show of being offended.

"Mark my words, India, the world's a cruel place for an unwed woman," Miss Glass said, her voice heavy. "A widow has a certain freedom and independence, but a spinster does not. If you can marry, you should."

"It ain't that bad," Willie said, her back rigid. "In California, a woman like me can do as she pleases."

"But India is not a woman like you. You are...unique. Hardly a woman at all, really."

"You ain't the first person to say that."

Miss Glass took my hand and patted it. "Don't fret, my dear. I'll find you a nice man who isn't put off by your brain. Not too young, of course, but a man who needs a wife. Perhaps he'll be a widower with little ones."

I pulled my hand free. "It's quite all right, thank you. I can find my own husband, if I decide I need one."

She *tsk tsked*. "Don't leave it too long. Time is of the essence." She left the drawing room.

I sat on the sofa, the wind knocked out of me. It was how I often felt when contemplating my future. One day, Matt would return to America and take his friends and family with him. I was neither, and my home was London. Unlike Miss Glass, I had no family to keep me occupied, and although I'd earned four hundred pounds by helping to catch the Dark Rider, the reward money wouldn't last forever. I needed to work, for financial reasons as well as for company. A long, lonely life stretched before me if I didn't work or marry.

Yet Eddie had taught me that being beholden to a man through marriage wasn't something I wanted. I couldn't give up my independence, my four hundred pounds, or even my body, to someone who would treat them with contempt. Perhaps I ought to move to America, after all, and act like a man as Willie did.

***

"You're not supposed to screw up your nose like that when you have a bad hand," Willie said, dealing out everyone's last card.

I scooped mine up and added it to the rest of my hand. "Perhaps I'm screwing my nose up so you'll *think* I have a bad hand."

"You ain't that good at hiding your emotions."

Duke placed two matches in front of him. "You need to keep your face straight."

"I thought I was." I looked to Cyclops.

He shook his head. "Don't take it to heart, India. Poker's only a game, and we're not playing for ranches."

Willie flicked a match onto the table.

I shuffled my cards but they still only made a pair of sixes. Since everyone knew from my expression that I had little to go on, I folded. "I think I'll read instead."

I joined Miss Glass on the sofa, unintentionally waking her. She blinked rapidly and patted the gray curls at her nape. "What time is it, India?"

"Three minutes to ten."

"Time to retire."

Everyone stood and bade her goodnight. As soon as she was gone, Cyclops closed the doors.

"Finally!" Willie threw down her cards, face up. "I thought she'd never leave."

"You had nothing?" Duke showed his cards. "I would have beat you."

"Here, take my matches. I don't care." She pushed her considerable pile toward him. "There ain't no point playing unless real money's involved. This..." She waved her hand at the card table. "This is pathetic. We're pathetic. Christ, I need to smoke."

"Not inside," Duke quipped.

"The dragon's not here to see." Willie pulled out her pipe from her pocket and set about packing it with tobacco from her tin.

"What did you learn at the guild today, Cyclops?" I asked, eager to get on.

"That Daniel wasn't well liked by the other apprentices." He sat and stretched his long legs out toward the fire. "He was a skillful mapmaker but he knew it. He liked to lord it over the apprentices, telling them he'd been picked to be apprenticed to the master of the guild without any previous training."

"Sounds like a right little prick," Duke said.

"Was there any talk of him being magical?" I asked.

Cyclops shook his head. "They thought he was lying about not having any formal training. Everyone thought he was too good to be a first year apprentice. I'll continue making inquiries tomorrow."

"Be subtle. We don't want to raise anyone's suspicions."

"He knows what he's doing." Willie shook the match to put it out and puffed on the pipe. "He ain't a green little miss now, is he?"

"I take it that's a barb meant for me."

She lifted one shoulder. "Take it however you like." She grinned around the pipe. "Don't mean I don't like you. You won't always be green, if you keep in our company."

I wasn't sure how to take that, so I said nothing.

"What happened with you today?" Duke stoked the fire to reveal hot coals beneath the ash. "Why was Matt so tired when you returned home?"

I told them about our visit to Worthey's and the French factory worker who'd run off. The hope on their faces was plain as day.

"It's something," Willie breathed, expelling a cloud of smoke through both her nose and mouth. "Thank the lord."

"We have to find him before we'll know if he's any use to us," I said.

"And he don't want to be found," Duke added. "Why?"

"Because he must be Chronos, and Chronos knows that magicians are being badly treated by their guilds," Cyclops said. "He panicked when he recognized Matt. Magicians are supposed to be a secret, but Matt knows he's a magician. Dupont will be worried."

"Perhaps," I said. "But Worthey was adamant that he was French, not English, and we know Chronos is English. It could be that he was simply a timepiece magician and suspected we knew it."

"What does he think will happen to him if people learn he's magic?" Duke asked. "He doesn't own a watch shop, so it don't matter that the guild won't have him as a member."

"Maybe it's more than that." Cyclops's dark eye pinned Duke. "Maybe the guilds want all magicians dead."

I gasped. The three of them looked to me. "No one has attacked me," I said. "Even though Abercrombie and the other Watchmakers' Guild members seem to suspect that I...that I have some magical ability."

"It's only a theory," Cyclops said in his reassuringly deep voice. "I'm sure Daniel will be found safe, and Pierre DuPont's behavior can be explained."

I nodded and smiled, but my heart continued its mad rhythm. I would be watching over my shoulder at every turn now. "Even if you're right, and DuPont is Chronos, he must know Matt doesn't want to see ill befall him. Assuming he is Chronos, then he saved

Matt's life. Surely if there's anyone he *can* trust, it's Matt."

"When a person is hunted, they don't trust no one. Not even people they used to trust, and especially if they're with a stranger, no matter how pretty and finely dressed she is."

I got the feeling from the way the others bowed their heads that Cyclops was speaking from experience. I hated thinking of him as being a hunted man. He was a gentle, friendly soul.

"All of this is assuming DuPont is Chronos anyway," I said. "I'm still very uncertain."

"Who else would he be?" Duke asked.

"Mirth."

"I s'pose. Maybe Mirth, Chronos and DuPont are all the same man."

"Mirth were in a home for the old," Willie said thoughtfully. "That man today must have been able bodied if he evaded Matt."

She had a point. None of it made sense, and there were too many possibilities and no certainties. One thing I did know for sure—we had to find DuPont and Mirth.

"Now what?" Duke asked.

Unfortunately none of us could think of anything beyond watching Worthey's factory to see if DuPont returned. Duke and Willie assigned themselves to the task. In the mean time, Matt, Cyclops and I would continue to look for Daniel, until Wednesday when Matt would wait at the bank for Mirth to show up. If we didn't see Pierre DuPont again, perhaps Mirth would know something about him that could help. They quite possibly knew one another, at the very least.

We four studied the fire in silence until the clock on the mantel chimed ten-thirty. I was about to retire for the evening when Willie pulled her pipe from her mouth and drew her legs in. She sat forward and regarded me. "Magicians inherit their magic, yes?"

"So we've been told," Duke said.

"My father wasn't magic," I pointed out.

"We don't know that. He may have hid his magic, because he wanted to keep his guild membership and his shop."

It was a possibility I had considered over and over. Where had my magic come from? Father's watches and clocks were excellent pieces but entirely worldly. I'd not felt any warmth in them after he touched them. That left only one other possibility, one that I didn't want to contemplate. My father wasn't my real father, and my mother may not have been my real mother either. I wasn't truly a Steele at all. So who were my parents? And why did the guild members suddenly begin to suspect me around the time of Father's death? Who had given them an inkling of my magic when I didn't even know about it myself?

So many questions and not a shred of an answer. It all felt so wrong, somehow; as if it ought to be happening to someone else, not plain old me. My life had been uneventful to date, with loving parents and a safe, happy home. It was impossible to think they weren't actually my mother and father. Quite impossible.

"What are you getting at?" Cyclops asked Willie. "What's India's family got to do with Chronos?"

"Not Chronos," she said. "Daniel. Who did he get his magic from? Not Commissioner Munro, I'd wager."

"His maternal grandfather was a mapmaker," I said. "Daniel must have inherited the skill from his mother, and she got it from her father."

"Then that's where you need to go tomorrow. To visit the mother and grandfather, and find out why they let him be apprenticed to the guild's master when Daniel's magic needed to be kept hidden."

CHAPTER 4

The visit to Daniel's grandfather had to wait, as Matt wanted to meet Jeremiah Duffield first. We walked to Burlington Arcade, since it wasn't far, while Cyclops returned to the Mapmakers Guild hall, and Willie and Duke took turns to watch Worthey's factory. Our walk through the spring sunshine gave me time to apprise Matt of the theories we'd discussed in his absence the evening before. He agreed that we ought to speak to Daniel's family to learn more about his magical skill.

We nodded at the beadle at the arcade entrance, dressed in his traditional uniform of frock coat, gold buttons and gold braided top hat. "You English have some odd customs," Matt said once we were out of the beadle's hearing.

"You think their clothing odd? You ought to see the beefeaters at the Tower."

He grinned and patted my hand, nestled in the crook of his arm. "Come, my dear. Let's find this mapmaker so we can get on with our shopping."

I smiled, relieved that he was his cheerful self again. His ability to throw off his troubles was remarkable—that or his ability to hide them.

We found Duffield's shop between a jeweler and toyshop. A fine globe occupied prime position in the window on a brass stand, surrounded by a display of items that an intrepid explorer may need—a compass, maps of India, water pouch, goggles, traveling writing desk complete with paper, ink and pens, and a pistol in its holster.

A man looked up as we entered. He was alone in the shop. "Good morning," he said brightly, coming out from behind the counter. "Welcome. Pleasant morning, is it not?"

"Very pleasant," Matt said.

"How may I help you today?"

"Are you Jeremiah Duffield?"

"I am. You've heard of me?" His smiled widened. He was younger than I expected, perhaps about forty. His black hair had begun to recede, leaving a widow's peak at the front, but it sported no gray. He held himself straight and tall, standing almost to Matt's height. With his broad shoulders and direct blue gaze, he was quite a striking figure.

"My name is Prescott," Matt said, "and this is my wife. I want you to create a map for me."

The smile turned hard. "You're the American who visited the guild yesterday."

"I am."

"You made inquiries about Daniel, my missing apprentice."

"I heard he was the best, and I want only the best to create this map for me. It's very special."

"You're mistaken. He wasn't the best, he was merely an apprentice. I am the best."

"That's quite a bold statement." Matt sounded amused, like he was goading Duffield.

It seemed to throw Duffield off. He glanced from me back to Matt, as if he were hoping my reaction would help him understand my "husband." As a shopkeeper, it was important to get the customer's measure. It was easy to sell to a man who wanted to be seen as the purveyor of fashion among his friends, but less so to a man who cared little for appearances. Mr. Prescott was proving a challenge to pin down, and I, Mrs. Prescott, wasn't going to assist him in any way.

Duffield indicated the plaques accompanying a display of two maps and a globe on a nearby table. "I have the awards to prove it."

"Awards mean little to me," Matt intoned. He wandered around the shop, picking up items, giving them cursory inspection, then returning them. He behaved like the sort of customer shopkeepers disliked yet needed. He had little respect for the wares and a disdain for the shopkeeper himself. Gentlemen like that usually had more money than manners. It was worth ignoring their rudeness to keep their custom. "However, since your apprentice is missing, it seems I must settle for your services instead."

"I'll try not to disappoint, sir."

Matt continued his slow walk around the small shop. "I'd like a map of India. A region in the north east, to be precise."

"Then you've come to the right place." Duffield indicated his window display, and several framed maps hanging on the walls. "I'm an expert on the sub-continent. I've visited India many times. Have you been, sir?"

"To India?" Matt's gaze flicked to me. "Not yet."

My face flamed, and Matt's lips curved into a curious little smile.

"You plan to visit?" Duffield asked.

"Hence the map."

"Yes, of course. It's a fascinating place, so vibrant and complex. One could visit every year for the rest of one's life and never grow tired of it."

"I don't doubt it."

"Would you like one of my existing maps of the area, or do you require something more personal?" Duffield opened a long, flat drawer behind the counter and pulled out a stack of maps. He set them on the counter.

Matt spent some time going through them. I stood by and watched, waiting. I felt as if we'd gotten precisely nowhere so far, and I couldn't think what Matt was getting at by not asking more probing questions. The silence stretched on, and I couldn't bear it any longer.

"Tell me about the guild that you're master of," I said to Duffield. "My husband's country doesn't have guilds, you see, although I've explained the system to him. I found the Mapmakers' Guild rather fascinating on our visit yesterday. There's something I don't quite understand, however. Map shops seem to be rare in London, so what is the point of the guild?"

"Shops are indeed rare," Duffield said. "This is one of only four in the city. We're not a very large guild, but we do have more than four members." He spoke slowly and deliberately, as if I were hard of hearing or a simpleton. "Many cartographers don't have shops at all, but use stationers to sell their maps on commission. Others are employed by the government, railway companies and various private enterprises."

"Fascinating. The process of making maps seems quite involved."

"Oh, it is. They originate as drawings, penned by a cartographer's own hand after extensive surveying. Do you know what surveying is, Mrs. Prescott?"

Oh, good lord. Did he not credit me with any brain at all? "I think so. Do go on. This is fascinating."

"The drawing is then refined, embellished and improved upon until the cartographer is satisfied. This is where the process may end if the map being commissioned is a one-off piece for a private customer."

"As with my friend who commissioned your apprentice," Matt said, paying attention now.

Duffield swallowed. "Your friend?"

"You must remember him. He commissioned a rather elaborate map of central London. Unfortunately, he never received it." Matt shook his head sadly. "I heard the apprentice refused to give it to him, although I can't think why."

Duffield suddenly looked rather hot and uncomfortable. "Nor can I."

"It doesn't make your business look very professional."

"I can assure you that won't happen in your situation. The apprentice in question is no longer here, as you know. He was a very wayward lad, highly skilled but not at all suited to shop work. I've promised to let Mr. McArdle know as soon as the map turns up. I'm sure it will, sooner or later."

McArdle! We had a name. Now all we needed was an address. Duffield must have some way of contacting him if he promised to return the map to him. I eyed the ledger lying open on the counter. Most likely his details were in there.

"Please tell me more about making maps," I said to Duffield. "It's so interesting." I angled myself toward the counter, with Duffield between it and me. That meant his back was to Matt and the ledger. I didn't need to look at Matt to convey my intention. He leaned back against the counter and scanned the ledger's page, upside down. "Why do some customers want to commission a map when there are so many already available at relatively low cost?" I asked.

Duffield's eyes gleamed as we returned to the safer topic. "The uniqueness adds value, you see, and that's all that some customers want. Value and a thing of art."

"Like the globe in the window?"

Matt quietly turned the ledger's page and continued scanning it.

I moved to the window display and Duffield followed with an eager smile that held a hint of shyness. "You're correct, Mrs. Prescott. I made that for display only, although it's for sale if the right offer is made." He went to glance back at Matt, so I feigned a coughing fit. Duffield fussed over me with a frown until it passed.

"Thank you," I said, accepting his handkerchief and dabbing my brow. "You're very kind. Please, tell me more about mapmaking. What happens to a map once it's finished if it isn't given directly to the private customer? Do you bind them together in a book?"

"I have a printing press at another premise. I reproduce my maps on the press and sell them here in the shop."

Matt turned another page of the ledger. How far back did he need to go? I couldn't discuss maps for too much longer.

"What about the ones bound in guides and atlases?" I asked.

"Those are usually commissioned by the publishers. Once my map is finished, I send it to them and they bind it with others and the author's text. I've had several published, you know."

"All of the sub-continent?"

He nodded. "It's my favorite place."

I smiled. "Does your wife like India too?"

"She's never been." His faced soured. "She doesn't like the heat."

"Fortunately the heat doesn't affect me," Matt said, joining us. "I'm rather looking forward to my journey." He smiled at me with undisguised triumph. He must have found McArdle's address.

"Will you go too, Mrs. Prescott?" Duffield asked me.

"I'm seriously considering it, if Mr. Prescott can endure my presence," I added with a little laugh.

"Of course, my dear," Matt said. "I'd travel to the end of the Earth with you. You're excellent company."

I resisted the urge to roll my eyes. He had a habit of laying on the compliments too thickly when he played a role.

"The map of India, Duffield," Matt said. "I'll purchase one of your regular maps of the region rather than commission something new. While I enjoy art as much as any gentleman, a more functional map will suit me on this occasion."

"Very good, sir." Duffield returned to the counter and selected one of the maps from the stack he'd pulled out of the drawer. "This is a good general one of the area, but I suggest a guide book for the cities and villages. Their maps are more detailed."

Matt bought both a map and guidebook, and we thanked Duffield. He walked us to the door, and I could see he wanted to say something more but held himself in check.

"What is it?" Matt asked, noticing too.

Duffield cleared his throat. "When you encounter your friend, Mr. McArdle, please reiterate how sorry I am that my apprentice turned out to be so duplicitous. I would appreciate it if he didn't speak of this to anyone else. My reputation, you know..."

"I understand."

"Of course, if the map isn't found, I'll refund his money."

"I think he'd rather the map."

Duffield's lips flattened. "I'm afraid it's likely lost."

Did he know about the burglaries at Daniel's house and the missing maps? "You ought to ask the family if you can look through the apprentice's things," I said. "Perhaps the map is among them."

"I tried, but the grandfather refused me entry. He never liked me."

"You know him?"

"He's a mapmaker too, but of little repute." He sounded apologetic. "Later, I heard that many of Daniel's maps were stolen. Terrible business. I can't think who would have an interest in them, aside from Mr. McArdle, of course."

Matt offered me his arm and we headed out of the shop. "Come, my dear. I want to take you shopping."

We walked idly past the other shops in the arcade and pretended to take an interest in their displays. "Did you get an address for McArdle?" I asked.

"He's in Chelsea. I must congratulate you on diverting Duffield's attention. Very well done. We'll make a poker player of you yet."

"Hardly." We walked a little more, but I didn't really notice any of the wares in the shop windows. My mind was still on Duffield. The more I thought about it, the more I couldn't believe how well the encounter had gone. He hadn't suspected a thing. "He laid the blame for the break-ins at Daniel's house squarely at McArdle's feet," I said.

"He did. McArdle does seem like the most obvious suspect. He commissioned the map, Daniel refused to give it to him. They argued and McArdle kidnapped him to get it back. When he discovered Daniel didn't have it, he searched the house."

"The question is, what did he do with Daniel?"

We walked on in heavy silence until Matt stopped outside a milliner's. He nodded at the window where several colorful hats sat upon spikes. "See anything you like?"

"You can end the ruse now. We're well away from Duffield's shop."

"Who said anything about a ruse?"

I let go of his arm. "Stop it, Matt."

"You're right. You need a new evening gown rather than a hat." He glanced along the arcade and nodded at a dressmaker. "I think I've lost the argument with Aunt Letitia. We must resign ourselves to the occasional dinner party."

I stared at him, feeling somewhat out of my depth. "You mean for me to attend these dinners?"

"Of course."

"But I'm not..." Important. I didn't say it and merely shrugged.

"You're as much a part of the household as Willie or even Aunt Letitia."

"I don't think companions or assistants attend things like formal dinners in Mayfair mansions."

"How do you know? Have you ever been a companion or assistant before? Or attended a dinner in a Mayfair mansion?"

I narrowed my gaze. "You're mocking me."

"No, India, I am not." He took my hand and tucked it into the crook of his arm. "If I have to endure the damned dinners, so do you. Don't force me to face both Aunt and Willie alone in my weakened state."

I smiled and shook my head. "You're incorrigible."

"Does that mean you're agreeing?"

"If I must, but you'll have to get your aunt to agree too."

"She will." He sounded quite sure, but I suspected Miss Glass would not acquiesce as easily. She was quite a stickler for the proper way of doing things, and social order was paramount. "Let's see what the dressmaker can do for you now."

"But we're busy. We have so much to do."

"We can spare a few minutes."

"Clearly you've never been to a dressmaker's shop before."

An hour and a half later, I'd been measured, poked, spun around and judged by Madame Lisle and her two assistants while Matt watched on. Despite my protests, silks for two evening gowns were chosen, one in sage and ivory, and the other a deep rosy pink. Madame Lisle drew some preliminary ideas based on the latest House of Worth collection in *The Young Ladies Journal* that she thought would suit my figure. Matt paid a deposit and I insisted on paying him back using the reward money later. The first dress would be available early the following week.

"What if Chronos is found before then?" I asked him.

"I'll cross that bridge when we come to it."

Is that all he had to say on the matter? I was about to press him further when he steered me toward a confectioner's shop near the arcade entrance.

"What do you like?" he asked, surveying the array of colorful sweets in jars behind and on top of the counter. "Peppermint drops? Bulls eyes? Brandy balls?"

"You're not buying me sweets."

He regarded me with a frown. "You're being particularly stubborn today."

I folded my arms over my chest and realized too late that doing so only proved his point. "I am not."

"Actually, the sweets are for my aunt. I only wanted your opinion."

"Oh." My face heated. I felt like a spoiled brat, and an utter fool. "In that case, nothing too hard."

"Good thinking."

He ordered a bag of marshmallows, another of chocolate drops and a third of mixed boiled sweets. "Pity they don't sell fudge," he said. "Now *that's* a treat."

"She won't like boiled sweets," I said as we left.

"Those aren't for her." He pocketed two of the bags and opened the third. "Go on. Take one."

I selected a red and white Gibraltar rock. "Why are you being so nice to me?"

"I'm not allowed to be nice to the woman who saved my life?"

I looked down at the sweet as we headed into the wan sunshine. I didn't like being reminded of him almost dying in the Vine Street Police Station cell. If I hadn't been able to get his watch to him... It didn't bear thinking about.

"It makes me feel awkward," I said, popping the sweet into my mouth.

"You'll become accustomed to it."

We walked home, sharing the sweets, and Matt joked about manufacturing fudge in England. The confection sounded quite delicious, as did the chocolates he'd tasted on the Continent in his youth. He spoke of those days wistfully, without too much sorrow. I wondered if he thought of his parents at such times, or if he no longer thought of them at all. They'd died fourteen years ago. My father had been dead only a few weeks, and while I thought of him every day, the terrible pain in my heart had eased somewhat. It was still there, but it didn't sting quite so much. Keeping busy helped.

Miss Glass was in the midst of receiving her first callers upon our return. In fact, according to Bristow, who met us at the door, they were Matt's cousins and other aunt, Lady Rycroft. I veered off to the stairs to head for my room, but Matt grabbed my arm.

"Oh no you don't," he said. "I'm not facing a room full of Glass women without reinforcement."

I laughed. "It could be worse. Willie could be with them."

He winced. "Please, come with me. Protect me."

"You don't need protecting. Your cousins will adore you, just like your Aunt Letitia does."

"According to Aunt Letitia, they're all as bad as their mother. My request still stands."

"Oh," I said with mock innocence. "If it's only a *request...*"

His gaze narrowed.

I grinned. "Come on, then. The sooner you meet them, the sooner the meeting will be over."

I headed into the drawing room first, and bore the full brunt of five frowns. Clearly my presence wasn't expected—or wanted—by any of them. I felt a little bruised at Letitia Glass's disapproval. I thought we'd become friends, in a way. It would seem she didn't think I should meet her nieces.

"There you are, Matthew," she said, accepting Matt's kiss on her cheek.

"Good morning," Matt said breezily. "Aunt Beatrice, I didn't expect to see you again so soon after our last meeting."

"Nor did I." Lady Rycroft surprised me with her quick quip. The last time we'd met her, Matt had admonished her husband in his own home, in front of his servants. Lady Rycroft had been rude to her sister-in-law, and to me, and disdainful of Matt's mother. Seeing her sitting with her hands in her lap while her three daughters perched on the sofa opposite was quite a turnabout. "I hope we can get off on a better foot today. I have no wish to be enemies."

"Nor do I," he said. "We're family, after all."

She gave him a tight smile. To be fair, it may have been tight because of her turban, not because she disliked the idea of being related to him. The turban slanted her eyes and smoothed the skin on her forehead. It didn't affect the grooves carved deeply around her mouth, however. "Allow me to present my daughters to you."

The girls were arranged in a pattern, from tallest to shortest, darkest to fairest, prettiest to plainest. And, as it turned out, youngest to oldest. I guessed them to be aged from about twenty to twenty-five.

"Miss Patience Glass, my eldest." Lady Rycroft indicated the brown-haired girl whose face resembled her mother's ,with lines drooping from the corners of her mouth although not yet as deep. "Miss Charity Glass," she said, pointing out the girl in the middle, whose dark brown hair fell across a ponderous brow. "And finally, Miss Hope Glass." Lady Rycroft clearly favored her younger, pretty daughter with the midnight black hair and milky skin. And it was clear from the scowls of the older girls that they knew it.

Matt bowed over each girl's hand in turn and welcomed them to his home. "Tell me, do you all resemble the traits of your given names?" he asked.

Hope laughed. "Quite the opposite, I'm afraid. Patience cannot abide waiting, Charity is kind enough when someone is watching, and I'm quite the hope*less* romantic, according to Mama."

Matt laughed.

"Hope!" her mother scolded. The elder two girls' scowls deepened, but none of it had any effect on Hope. Her smile turned somewhat wicked. I'd wager her mother had her hands full with that one. It was unusual for the two older girls to be unmarried at their age. Unlike me, they had something to offer a husband aside from an education. Their father was a landed gentleman and would no doubt settle an adequate dowry on the girls. The pretty younger one, Hope, shouldn't have much trouble finding a husband at all, but she may be forced to wait until the oldest was married first. Some families worked that way.

"Aunt Beatrice, you recall my assistant, Miss Steele," Matt said, indicating me. It was very obvious from the mere fact that he had to introduce me that Lady Rycroft didn't plan on acknowledging my presence.

"Yes," she said, flatly.

"Pleased to meet you," Hope said. "Tell me, Miss Steele, what sort of things do you do for Cousin Matthew?"

I glanced at Miss Glass, but she seemed not to be listening. I wondered if she'd fallen into one of her vacant episodes where she seemed to forget that she was in company. "I attend meetings with him, take notes, that sort—"

"Matthew, there's no need for your assistant to stay," Lady Rycroft said. "I'm sure she's busy."

Matt stiffened. "She's staying." He'd gone from amenable to growling in the space of a heartbeat, catching all the guests unawares. Lady Rycroft and her daughters gasped.

"Of course she should stay, Mama," Hope said with a nervous laugh and glance at her mother. "She seems like a pleasant sort of person."

Her mother's jaw hardened. "We're here to discuss family business. She is not family."

"But she attends to all my affairs," Matt said, his voice low. "She stays." He indicated I should sit in the only remaining chair while he stood.

I hesitated, unsure if I wanted to be involved in their squabbles. In the end, I only sat because I didn't want Lady Rycroft to win any sort of argument, even a small, insignificant one like this.

"I see this isn't a private call then," Matt began. "So you'd better get on with it, Aunt."

"Oh, but it is a private call," Miss Glass said, rousing. "Isn't it, Beatrice? The girls wanted to meet you, Matthew."

"We did," Hope said quickly. "Our maids said you were the most dashing gentleman they'd ever spied after your visit the other week."

"That's enough, Hope," Lady Rycroft snapped. She drew in a deep breath and put up her hands. "Let's begin again. Letitia is correct, and this is a private call. I wanted to introduce my girls to you so you could choose."

Matt cocked his head to the side, as if he hadn't heard correctly. "Choose?"

"To marry, of course."

CHAPTER 5

"Marry!" Matt spluttered a laugh, but no one joined in.

I suddenly wished I hadn't remained. This was indeed family business of a nature that I didn't want to get involved in.

"You don't have to choose now," Lady Rycroft told him, her face perfectly serious. "Get to know them better first."

Matt sat on the arm of my chair, very close to me. It didn't go unnoticed by a single person in that room. Five scowling faces once again turned to me, as if it were my fault. He shook his head, over and over. "Are you sure that's what you want?"

Why had he not laughed them out of his home already? He couldn't truly be considering it. Could he?

"It's what both Lord Rycroft and I want, yes. Most assuredly."

"But my uncle dislikes me. He dislikes everything about me."

Lady Rycroft's gaze slid to her hands. "There are the girls' futures to consider."

Ah, now I understood. Matt was the heir, and the girls were unmarried. The entire estate would one day turn over to him, risking the wellbeing of the daughters if they weren't happily settled. It would seem settling the older two in any kind of situation at all, happily or not, wasn't looking likely at their age and with their sour countenances.

"This is so awful," Hope muttered, pressing her gloved hand to her glowing cheek.

"I quite agree," Matt said. "Aunt Letitia, surely you don't approve of this shameless parade."

She spread out her hands. "It had to be done, Matthew. Better to get it over with. I'd like you to remember, however, that there are far more fish in the sea than these three."

"Letitia!" Lady Rycroft gasped in horror. "You should encourage him to choose one of your nieces. It's the right thing to do."

"The right thing for whom?" Miss Glass snapped. "Not for Matthew, I can assure you."

Lady Rycroft bristled. "My girls are good, decent, well-bred ladies. They would make fine wives."

"Not for Matthew."

"Why not?"

"I'd rather not discuss that in front of them."

Hope lifted her chin, and her eyes flashed. Her two older sisters studied their clasped hands resting in their laps.

"I feel as though I've walked into a stage show. Make that a farce." Matt rubbed his forehead. "Let's make one thing clear. I am in no hurry to marry, but when I do, she'll be a woman of my own choosing."

"I am giving you three perfectly fine choices here!" Lady Rycroft's face turned redder and redder, matching her turban.

Her daughters all looked as if they wanted to sink into the sofa. Not even Hope met Matt's gaze.

He sighed. The first signs of tiredness began to show around his eyes and in the slope of his shoulders.

"Think of my girls," Lady Rycroft said. "Think of your *family*, Matthew. Would you see them suffer?"

"How will they suffer by not marrying me?"

"By being thrown out of their home!"

"I won't throw anyone out of Rycroft. Besides, my uncle seems to be in good health. I doubt he'll fall off the perch any time soon."

She waved her hand, as if the health of her husband was inconsequential to the discussion. I happened to agree with Matt; Lord Rycroft could live for another twenty years or more. "You would see my daughters become homeless urchins?"

I smothered a groan. The girls might be rendered poor by their own standards, if their father died before they married, but they would hardly be urchins. They didn't know the meaning of poor. None of them did and never would.

Matt nudged me with his elbow, and I got the feeling he was trying not to laugh too. He kept a straight face, however, as he regarded each of the girls in turn. Only Hope met his scrutiny with a calm countenance that I couldn't help but admire.

"Hasn't Uncle Richard settled a sum on them all?" Matt asked.

"Ye-es. But their home..." Lady Rycroft's lower lip wobbled. She pulled out a handkerchief from her reticule and dabbed at the corner of her eye. "Rycroft Estate is everything to them."

"Then it's settled. When I inherit, they can live there, and I'll live elsewhere."

"Assuming you haven't married one of us," Patience said.

Hope glared at her sister. Patience shrugged innocently.

"Don't you want to live there?" Charity asked him.

He met her gaze. "No."

"Why not? What's wrong with Rycroft?"

"It'll be a noose around my neck, just as much as it was for my father."

Both Patience and Charity stared at him aghast, their mouths open like unhinged trapdoors. Hope's sharp eyes softened, however, as she regarded Matt.

"This is beastly," she said. "I can't bear it. We only just met him and here we are discussing marriage as if we were bargaining chips and he the prize."

"The discussion couldn't be put off any longer," her mother said with a sniff.

"You promised you wouldn't be so forthright about it all, Mama. You've embarrassed us in front of our cousin."

I cleared my throat, but she paid me no mind. Clearly she didn't think it a problem to be embarrassed in front of me.

"There's no time for delicate negotiations," Lady Rycroft said. "He might return to America any day."

"He's not leaving England," Miss Glass announced.

Everyone looked to her.

"Aunt Letitia," Matt said quietly. "We've been through this." He abandoned the rest of his gentle lecture. No matter how many times he'd said it, it never seemed to sink in.

"I don't want to live in America." The eldest, Patience, pouted. "It's so *wild*."

"It appears we've whittled down the number of candidates to two already," Hope said, with a wicked gleam in her eyes. "That ought to make your choice easier, Cousin. Oh, why don't I make it even easier. I withdraw from the race."

"Hope!" Lady Rycroft blurted out. "Stop being so obstinate and snide. It's most unbecoming in a lady."

"The point I'm trying to make is, I'd like to get to know Matthew as my cousin, without this drama hanging over our heads." She gave Matt a weak smile. "I do apologize. I hope it won't color your perceptions of us. We're not all bad."

He smiled. "I can see that."

I blinked up at him.

"Tell me, Aunt Beatrice," he said, sounding quite cheerful all of a sudden. "Did you tell your daughters what *trade* my mother's family are in?"

The blood drained from her face. She continued to dab at her eyes with renewed vigor.

"What trade is that?" Hope asked, glancing from one to the other.

"The illegal kind. My mother's family are mostly outlaws."

"Oh." Hope bit her lip. "That's, er, interesting."

"It is, isn't it? Does it make you want to withdraw from the race too, Charity?"

"Quite the contrary," the middle sister said, shifting forward. "It sounds very intriguing."

Hope giggled, only to smother it with her hand when her sister jabbed her in the ribs with her elbow.

"Your mother's family is irrelevant," Lady Rycroft snipped.

They hadn't been a mere week ago.

"Don't let Willie hear you say that," Matt said.

"I think it's time we left." Lady Rycroft stood and instructed her girls to rise with a lift of her hand. "We look forward to seeing you again, Matthew. Please call upon us at your earliest convenience. Perhaps I'll host a dinner in your honor."

Matt bowed. Each of the girls curtsied as they filed past.

Hope, however, didn't immediately follow her mother out. "She hasn't given up." She grinned, changing her face from pretty to remarkable. "You must remain on your guard at all times, Cousin."

"Hope!" Lady Rycroft screeched.

"Coming, Mama." She winked at Matt. "Until next time, Cousin. It was lovely to meet you. Oh, and you too, Miss Steele. You were so quiet throughout that exchange. I feel as if we hardly got to know you."

"That was the point, wasn't it?" I said, hating the strain in my voice and the way my heart wouldn't stop pounding. It was just a silly conversation, after all. "For me to sit quietly by and listen without interrupting?"

Matt frowned at me.

Hope's smile wilted. "Well. It would seem you have a sting, after all." She followed her mother.

Matt went to see them out, and I remained in the drawing room with Miss Glass. I wanted the chair to swallow me up. Why had I snapped at Hope like that?

I knew why. And I didn't like it. Not one little bit.

"Horrible girls, all of them," Miss Glass said with a wrinkle of her nose. "So like their mother. Don't be fooled by Hope's friendliness. She's clever, that one. Too clever, if you ask me."

I sighed. "A clever girl can't possibly be a good thing, can it?"

"I'm not referring to you, my dear." She got up and offered me her hand. "You're a sweet girl. Your cleverness is an entirely different sort to Hope's."

I took her hand. I couldn't blame her for her earlier coolness toward me. After all, she must be worried that I was a distraction for her nephew. I ought to reassure her that I was not a player in the game and never had been. "I have no idea what you mean, Miss Glass, but I appreciate the sentiment nevertheless."

Matt strode in and took in our linked hands. "India? What's wrong?"

"Nothing."

"It's not nothing. You seem upset. Don't let it affect you. They're not important."

I withdrew my hand and smoothed down my skirts. I couldn't meet his gaze. He saw too much when he looked at me with that intensity. It was far too unnerving, and I already felt unnerved enough after the exchange with Hope. "Are we going out again before lunch?" I asked.

"No."

"Then I'm going for a walk."

***

A stroll through Hyde Park cleared my head and settled my nerves. By the time I returned to the house, a lunch of cold meats and salads was spread out on the dining room table.

"I can get used to having servants," Duke said, helping himself to the sliced beef.

"Did you see DuPont?" Matt asked.

Duke shook his head. "Worthey was furious, too. Says you can't trust a Frenchman's word, and if the man dares show his face, he'll find himself without a job. Willie's going to stay the rest of the afternoon, in case."

Miss Glass walked in and took her seat. "We'll do our best to avoid them, but it may not always be possible, particularly if you receive a dinner invitation."

We all stared at her. "Pardon?" Matt asked.

"Your Glass cousins." She looked at him as if he were slow.

"What about them?" Duke asked.

"They were here with their mother," Matt told him. "The intention is for me to choose one of them to marry."

Duke grinned. "Willie'll be sorry she missed that conversation. Did you pick one?"

"No!"

Miss Glass shuddered. "Thank goodness you have good sense, Matthew."

Duke chuckled. "Did you warn them that the lucky bride will have to live in California?"

"He did no such thing," Miss Glass said with a sniff, "since he's not leaving England."

"I told them I'm not looking for a wife." Matt sipped his wine and went to return his glass to the table, but changed his mind and drank the lot.

"When can I expect you to be home, Matthew?" Miss Glass asked. "I must invite callers, but there's no point if you're not here."

Matt eyed her over the rim of his glass. "You're not giving up, are you?"

"I only have your best interests at heart. A gentleman ought to marry or he becomes selfish and idle. And he ought to marry well, not for love. Love matches never work out after the first bloom withers and dies. I wouldn't want you to make a mistake that you'll regret later."

"My parents married for love and that turned out rather well."

She stuffed a large piece of chicken into her mouth and didn't meet his gaze.

Matt looked as if he would argue the point, then he suddenly turned to me. "Ready, India? I find myself in rather a hurry all of a sudden."

***

"I'm sorry for the way my cousins and aunts treated you," Matt said in the carriage as we headed for Daniel's house.

"You don't need to apologize."

"They'll get used to you."

I tightened my grip on my reticule but remained silent. I was in no mood to discuss his cousins, aunts, or his future wife. It would seem that he was, however.

"The thing is, I can't tell them why I cannot consider marriage at present. But you understand, don't you? I can't consider marriage until my health improves. It would be unfair on my bride if I were to die soon after the wedding."

"I understand."

He tapped his fingers on the window sill. "Good."

"But until they're told, your aunts will continue with this...game."

He groaned. "I'm not sure I have the patience for being an English gentleman of means. I prefer being a poor American with criminals for relatives. It's more liberating."

"Then the sooner you return home, the better. I will miss you. All of you," I added, in case he thought I was flirting with him.

The coach lurched to a stop and I suddenly found Matt sitting beside me. "That wasn't fair of me," he said quietly. "It was thoughtless and selfish. I'm a fortunate man, and I shouldn't whine like a petulant child."

"You're out of sorts today. I understand."

"Stop being so understanding!" He dragged his hand over his face, down his chin. When it came away, I was shocked by the tiredness tugging at the corners of his eyes. Had he not slept before lunch? "Tell me I'm being a turd."

"A gently-bred Englishwoman doesn't use that word."

One side of his mouth flicked up, as I hoped it would.

"But you're, right," I went on. "You're being a turd. But since you apologized, I forgive you."

"One of these days I'm going to say something to really upset you. Something unforgiveable."

I doubted it.

We arrived at Daniel's home in Hammersmith and introduced ourselves to the maid who opened the door. We'd decided not to play roles with Daniel's family. We would get more direct answers to our questions if they knew we were searching for him.

The maid took us through to the sitting room where a woman sat. Matt repeated the introductions. "Commissioner Munro sent us," he finished.

The woman bristled. Her light blue eyes widened ever so briefly. She was in her mid forties, and well dressed in a neat waistcoat over a black and green striped dress. She would have been beautiful in her youth, with her heart shaped face, high cheeks and lovely figure. Even now, she was lovely, despite evidence of recently-shed tears.

"Are you Miss Gibbons?" I asked.

She hesitated then nodded. "Mary, fetch Mr. Gibbons and bring in tea." To us, she said, "My father will want to meet you."

"And we want to meet him," Matt said.

"Are you a detective?" she asked, her gaze sliding to me before returning to Matt.

"A private inquiry agent. Commissioner Munro came to us after his men failed to make progress. He's very keen to find Daniel."

"Did he inform you of his...relationship to my son?"

Matt nodded.

She bowed her head and clasped her hands in her lap, the picture of a demure, sensible woman. She wasn't at all how I pictured her to be. I thought she'd be vibrant and genial, the sort of woman to have liaisons with gentlemen out of wedlock. It was wrong of me to judge her without knowing the situation, and I felt bad for it now.

A man marched in and I was immediately struck by the similarity between him and the commissioner. Both tall, robust men of a similar age, he had a direct gaze that immediately took in the situation and made an assessment. I'd wager he prided himself on control and order within his domain. Discovering his daughter was having a child to a married man must have come as quite a shock; particularly as that daughter seemed obedient and docile, not wayward and flirtatious.

Matt repeated the introductions. At the mention of Munro's name, Mr. Gibbons' nostrils flared.

"It's about time he did something," he growled.

"He has been trying, Papa," Miss Gibbons said quietly yet earnestly. "You know he has."

"Yet he has failed at every turn."

She lowered her head once more.

"Munro informed us of the burglaries here," Matt said. "We believe they're related to Daniel's disappearance."

Gibbons grunted. "If that's all you've discovered then you're wasting Munro's money and my time."

Matt remained remarkably calm. He was far less ruffled by Gibbons' abruptness than his aunts' matchmaking. Questioning suspects and witnesses, and playing a role to sniff out criminals, came naturally to him. Sipping tea in drawing rooms with ladies did not.

"It's not all we've discovered," Matt went on. "Indeed, we learned something remarkable about Daniel. Something he inherited."

Miss Gibbons sucked in a sharp breath. The maid took that moment to enter with a tray. Miss Gibbons dismissed her and poured the tea herself. She handed a cup to me. "What did you discover?" she asked in a whisper.

"Judith," her father snapped.

She pressed her trembling lips together.

"We don't know what you're referring to," Mr. Gibbons said.

"Of course you do." Matt ignored him and turned to Miss Gibbons. "Don't be afraid. We're not here to persecute you. We simply wish to find your son. It's looking more and more likely that his disappearance is related to his magic and a particular magical map he made for a customer."

Mr. Gibbons met his daughter's gaze. He no longer appeared confident; rather, he seemed like a man out of his depth. Clearly he wasn't used to discussing magic with strangers. Considering how the guilds treated those with magical ability, it wasn't surprising. As a mapmaker himself, he would have kept his own magic a secret for years to avoid notice.

"We know Daniel inherited his magical gift from you," I said.

Mr. Gibbons shook his head at his daughter, warning her not to speak.

"Papa, we can talk to them. If we don't..." She swallowed. "If we don't, we may never find Daniel."

Mr. Gibbons looked as if he would snap at her to be quiet, but then the hard lines of his face softened. He nodded.

"It's not a gift." Miss Gibbons dabbed at her eyes with her handkerchief. "It's a curse. And he didn't inherit it from me."

"He got it from me," Mr. Gibbons said. "My daughter isn't magical."

"It skipped a generation?" I blurted out.

Mr. Gibbons inclined his head. "What do you know of magic?"

"Very little."

"As do I. But I do know that while it is an inherited trait, it's common to miss a generation or two before it reappears."

"You keep your magic a secret from the outside world," Matt said. "Who knows about it?"

"No one. My father warned me, from an early age, to keep it a secret. He was magical too, and he knew first-hand what happened to magicians if guild members learned of their ability. A friend of his had his membership to the guild revoked. Without membership, he had to give up his shop. He'd been a mapmaker all his life and couldn't find other work in the city. He lost friends, and his children starved, became ill and died. He appealed the decision, over and over, claiming he'd done nothing wrong. Six months later, he was found dead."

I gasped.

"How did he die?" Matt asked.

"Officially, he cut his own throat." Mr. Gibbons shook his head. "But my father couldn't understand why a left handed man held the knife in his right if he was intent on taking his own life."

Oh God.

Miss Gibbons burst into tears. Her father glanced at her and flattened his lips. I moved to sit beside her and placed my arm around her shoulders. It was difficult to comfort her when all I could think about was the magical mapmaker being murdered, perhaps by his own guild.

"Surely that sort of thing wouldn't happen nowadays," I said, appealing to Matt.

He nodded and gave me a small smile, which didn't reassure me in the least.

"If you think so, then you're very naive, Miss Steele," Mr. Gibbons said. "The guild is a nest of vipers, just waiting to strike at those better than them. They want to maintain their positions, their customers and reputation, and to do that, they must eradicate all the magicians. After all, who would go to a plain mapmaker when they can go to a magician who'll create a responsive map?"

"Responsive?" Matt echoed.

"A magical map reveals places or routes, but only for the man who commissioned it and the magician who instilled the magic in it, and only for a brief time."

"Did anyone at the guild know that Daniel was magical?"

"I never told them, nor could he have done so. He didn't know that he was."

"You should have," his mother spluttered, tears streaming down her cheeks and dripping off her chin. "You should have warned him, as your father warned you. This is *your* fault."

Mr. Gibbons' face turned ashen. "I only wanted to protect the boy. I thought it would be safer for him to go into a different trade, perhaps join the police, as his father wanted. When I discovered that he had inherited my magic, I kept all maps and mapmaking tools away from him. I expected him to simply develop other skills." He lowered his head. "But he didn't, and I didn't learn that he'd been making maps in secret until it was too late. When he said he wanted to be apprenticed to a mapmaker in the guild, I refused. His father, however, insisted." His lips twisted into a sneer. "Munro is a fool."

"He didn't know the dangers because *you* never told him about Daniel's magic," Miss Gibbons wailed. "Or yours."

"He wouldn't have believed me. Men like Munro don't believe. They deny and ignore, even when the evidence is presented to them. Telling Munro would have achieved nothing but derision and ridicule. This family has endured enough of that at his hands. No more, Judith. No more."

"It might have saved Daniel," she said weakly.

"I doubt it," I said. "Daniel clearly loved creating maps. It was in his blood. His skill would have been discovered by the guild members sooner or later."

"You think they did this, don't you? You think they've taken my son?" She pressed her handkerchief to her nose as sobs racked her.

"We don't know."

"Did the guild know that you were magical?" Matt asked Mr. Gibbons.

"I kept it from them," he said, "as my father told me to. I've never used my magic to create a map. Never. If I had, I could have created the most beautiful pieces, like Daniel. But I didn't dare risk it."

"Tell us about the magic maps only working for a brief time," I said, intrigued that time featured in a map's magic. I caught Matt looking at me and turned away. He knew why I asked and I didn't want to see disapproval in his eyes. He didn't want me to discuss my magic with anyone.

Mr. Gibbons shrugged. "There's nothing to tell. My father told me that magic is fleeting. The maps come to life to show a hidden route or location, but only for hours or perhaps a few days. After that, it never happens again."

Unless a watchmaker's magic was infused with it, perhaps. Matt's watch possessed both Chronos's magic and that of the doctor who'd saved his life. The time magic extended the life of the doctor's magic. It might work that way for any type of magic combined with that of a watchmaker's.

"Do you know any other magicians?" Matt asked.

Both Mr. and Miss Gibbons shook their heads.

"May I look in his room?"

"If you must." Mr. Gibbons led us up the stairs to Daniel's room. "The police have already searched it, as have we. You won't find anything."

It wasn't a large house, but it was comfortable enough and I suspected better than a mere mapmaker could afford. It was certainly better than the home my father and I had, above our shop. Perhaps Commissioner Munro saw to their wellbeing to enable his son to have a good home.

The bedroom was tucked away into the roofline. Matt had to duck to enter. We checked under the bed, in cupboards, drawers, beneath the mattress and rug, the undersides of chairs and desks. We found nothing suspicious or of interest.

"Did he mention anything about the customer, McArdle, who commissioned a special map from him?" Matt asked as we returned downstairs.

They both shook their heads. "Do you mean he was commissioned directly?" Mr. Gibbons asked. "Or through his master?"

"Directly."

Father and daughter glanced at one another. "How did he find out about Daniel's magic?" Miss Gibbons asked, pressing her fingers to her trembling lips.

"A bloody good question," Mr. Gibbons said. "And another question...how did Daniel learn to make magic maps? He didn't learn from me."

"It may have been Mr. McArdle himself," I said. "Or someone he knows."

"Have you questioned him?

"We're about to," Matt said.

Miss Gibbons clasped Matt's arm with one hand, and held the handkerchief to her cheek with the other. "Find my son, sir. Please. I beg you."

"We'll do our best, Miss Gibbons."

We headed outside to the waiting carriage and Bryce drove us to the address in Chelsea not far away.

"It was a mistake not to tell Daniel about his magic," I said. "He ought to have known so he could protect himself."

Matt merely watched me carefully from beneath half-lowered lashes webbed with red spidery lines.

"I know," I said on a sigh. "I'm aware that my father didn't tell me, even though he most likely knew."

"We can't be sure about that."

"Even if he wasn't magical, his father or grandfather must have been, and he'd probably been told at some point, in case he—or I—developed the skill. He should have told me."

"Don't blame him entirely," Matt said gently. "If he didn't show any magical ability, his father might have put it to the back of his mind. Perhaps he planned on telling your father when he had children, but his untimely death prevented him."

"I suppose." I rubbed my forehead. "It's all so strange, Matt. I don't want to be magical if it comes with danger. Thank goodness mine is very slight."

"Is it?"

I glanced up. "What do you mean?"

"Your watch shocked a man, temporarily incapacitating him. Another clock you worked on swerved to hit a man in the head. Those are remarkable feats, and so far, none of the magical people I've spoken to have reported such a thing."

I tried to laugh but it was half-hearted. "I cannot imagine a map killing anyone."

He smirked. "The guild's bronze globe could do some damage." He reached across the gap and rested his hand over mine. "No harm will come to you, India. I'll make sure of it."

"Thank you."

"But you must keep your secret just that, a secret. Abercrombie and the other guild members may suspect that you're magical, but that doesn't mean you have to prove it to them."

"I'll only tell people when it's necessary."

"Or not at all." He squeezed my hand. "Now let's reprise our roles as Mr. and Mrs. Prescott and see what we can learn from McArdle."

***

McArdle rented rooms in a tidy red brick Chelsea house from Mrs, Dawson, a widow in her sixties whose clothing would have been the height of fashion twenty years ago. Unfortunately he'd paid his rent in full and departed only the day before, taking his belongings with him.

Matt looked like he'd explode with the most colorful language learned in the Wild West, so I quickly spoke first. "What can you tell us about him?" I asked the landlady.

Mrs. Dawson lifted her chin in the same way Miss Glass did when she dug her heels in. "Why?"

Matt pulled some coins from his pocket. "Answer the question."

She put out her hand and he dropped the coins onto her palm. "He kept to himself," she said. "He went out every day, but didn't tell me where, and I didn't ask."

"Did he ever mention maps or mapmakers?"

"No."

"Did he mention an argument?" Matt asked.

"He came home one afternoon in a foul mood, muttering about an upstart lad."

"How angry did he become?" I asked. "Did he hit things, throw things?"

"He wasn't a violent man. He was pleasant enough, merely kept to himself."

"Where was he from?"

"He was British, of course." She pressed a hand to her bosom, a horrified look on her face. "I only allow decent Englishmen to board in my house. Foreigners are not welcome."

"We Americans need not apply?" Matt asked, laying his accent on thickly.

She gave him a tight smile. "I might make an exception for a gentleman such as yourself." She made a point of glancing at his pocket where he'd kept his money.

"What part of England was Mr. McArdle from?" I asked. "Did he have an accent?"

"Not that I detected. He mentioned no cities, counties or villages to me. I don't know where he was from." She glanced past us then stepped closer. "There is one other thing. Something he left behind. As his landlady, I would feel terrible if he wrote to me and asked me to send it on and I couldn't find it, but sometimes, small things go missing."

I didn't understand. Did she have it, or didn't she?

Matt passed more coins to her. She checked the quantity then pocketed them and signaled for us to follow her up the stairs. I stared at her back, somewhat aghast at her duplicity. She may dress and sound toff, but she was as desperate as, well, as I had been for a brief few days before going to work for Matt.

She led us into her small sitting room and opened her sewing kit. "I found this on the floor under the dresser in his bedroom. It must have rolled there." She dropped a small, round metal object onto Matt's hand.

He inspected it, turning it over, twice. "It's a gold button," he said flatly. "I did not pay you to give me one of McArdle's buttons."

She merely shrugged.

"May I see?" I asked.

He placed the button in my hand and I sucked in a ragged breath.

"What is it?" he asked, frowning.

My gaze connected with his. "It's warm."

CHAPTER 6

We took the button with us and inspected it in the carriage on the way home. "It's certainly magical warmth," I said. "Not from human touch or the sun. I'm beginning to learn the difference."

The old metal had dulled considerably and some of the pattern worn off it with time. The edge didn't look as if it had ever been perfectly round, but beaten into a circular shape with a crude tool. A small shank of a different metal had been attached to the back, and was clearly not part of the original button.

"There's an inscription," I said, holding it up to the window for better light. "But I can't read it. There's also an image, but it's not clear."

Matt leaned closer to get a better look, pressing his arm against mine. "I can't make it out either."

"So we have a button maker magician somewhere too."

"Or a metal worker. He or she is most likely dead. That button is old."

I dropped it into my reticule. "I wonder what magical buttons do."

"Button up clothing without the need of human hands?" he said airily.

"I can see how that would be useful. I could fix my hair while my jacket does itself up. It would save, oh, seconds of effort."

"Saving several seconds in one's day is a useful thing, particularly for someone who likes to keep busy and account for every minute in her day."

I blinked at him. "Are you referring to me?"

He lifted one shoulder, but the wicked gleam in his eyes gave me the answer.

"I do not need to account for every minute in my day, thank you. Although I do like to keep busy, I'll grant you that."

"You check your watch a lot, you know."

"No more than anyone else."

"If you're near a clock, you'll check that instead."

"Now you're being silly. I am not obsessed with the time."

He said nothing, but his smirk widened.

"I'll prove it to you." I opened my reticule and handed him my watch. "You may keep it for a day. It doesn't bother me."

"Very well. And I'll turn all the clocks around at home."

I watched him tuck my watch into his pocket and tried not to worry. That watch had saved my life. Should I be parted from it? What if I were attacked again?

"I'll take good care of it," he said. "And you'll be with me the entire time, so you won't need its magical properties to save you."

I twisted my fingers together in my lap. "If you lose it, I'll tell Lady Rycroft that you have your heart set on marrying her daughter."

"Which one? Please say Charity. She seems like the sort of girl who could thrive in California with my family."

I laughed and nudged him with my elbow. His smile faded a little and his gaze turned serious as it held mine for a moment longer than appropriate. Then he yawned.

Bristow handed Matt a note when we arrived home. Matt's face, already looking a little gray, paled more. He stared at it a long time then folded it up and tucked it into his pocket.

"Is something wrong?" I asked.

"It's from Munro, asking for an update on our investigation."

"If that's all it is, why do you look so worried?"

He suddenly smiled. "I'm not. Just tired."

I didn't believe him for a moment.

To Bristow, he said, "Please turn all the clocks in the house around to face the wall."

Bristow didn't flicker so much as an eyelash at the strange request. I, however, rolled my eyes. "It doesn't bother me in the least that I won't know the time."

"Good."

"You can stop smiling so smugly now."

"I will, tomorrow, if you prove to me that I'm wrong and time is unimportant to you."

"You're an impossible man."

"If that's the worst you can lay at my feet, then I'm content."

I stalked off, not sure whether I was angry with him or wanted to laugh at my own expense. He was truly baffling at times.

Matt rejoined us for dinner after a rest, as did Cyclops, Duke and Willie, back from their set tasks. With Miss Glass present, we refrained from updating each other until she went to bed. She finally bade us goodnight at...at somewhere between nine and half past. Perhaps.

"DuPont hasn't returned," Willie told us, settling in the armchair in the sitting room with her pipe. "I don't think he will."

"Damn," Matt muttered.

Duke opened a window and glared at Willie. "Miss Glass can smell the smoke in the morning, you know."

She puffed out a smoke ring in his direction.

"Cyclops?" Matt asked. "Have you got anything to report?"

"Aye. There's something strange going on at the guild."

Matt leaned forward. "What sort of strange?"

"Hard to say. The treasurer was back again today, when he didn't need to be."

"Mr. Onslow." I nodded. "We met him, along with his apprentice, Ronald Hogarth."

"The apprentice now works for Duffield," Cyclops said. "Onslow was grumbling about it to the old footman. Apparently Duffield stole him from Onslow this afternoon."

"How do you steal an apprentice?" Duke asked.

"Pay him more money. Onslow whined that he couldn't afford to match what Duffield offered, and the lad jumped at the chance to work for the guild's master. That's not the suspicious part." Cyclops swirled the brandy around his glass and stretched his bare feet toward the fire. "He met a man at the guild today. The man gave no name to the footman but Onslow clearly knew him. They spoke in whispers in the entrance hall then disappeared into an office with instructions not to be disturbed. When I disregarded orders and disturbed them, they were pouring over the treasury ledger. A ledger that I later discovered never leaves Onslow's hands. According to the servants I asked, no one else looks at the ledger, not even the guild master. Apparently he trusts Onslow and has no interest in figures."

"What do you think he's up to?" I asked.

"Stealing from the guild's treasury, most like," Willie said.

"It's easy enough to do," Duke said.

Cyclops nodded. "Especially if no one else sees the ledger, but even then, money can be hidden in plain sight."

I blinked at them in turn. "You sound as if you have experience in such matters."

Duke and Cyclops didn't meet my gaze while Willie flashed a grin around her pipe. "We ain't got no halo like you," she said. "Don't take offence, India."

I returned her smile. "You do have a halo. I've seen it. Only you pretend it's not there. Don't take offence, Willie."

She grunted but her smile remained.

Matt cleared his throat. "I wonder if the fellow Onslow met is a customer."

"Or if he has anything to do with Daniel's disappearance," Duke added. "Maybe he's paying for a magic map too, but unofficial like." His face brightened and he half rose from his chair. "Maybe Onslow kidnapped Daniel and is keeping him somewhere, forcing him to make magic maps for special customers who'll pay big."

It was a sound theory, and going by the nods of agreement, I wasn't the only one to think so. "We should investigate Onslow and perhaps follow him," I said. "If he is keeping Daniel somewhere, he must be visiting him from time to time."

"I'll follow him," Duke said.

Matt shook his head. "I need you and Willie to share duties at Worthey's factory, at least until we're completely sure that DuPont isn't coming back."

"I'll follow Onslow," I said. "There's no need for you and I to investigate together. We might as well split up and—"

"No. We are not splitting up. If something happens to you..." He sliced his hand through the air in a cutting motion. "We're not splitting up. Don't suggest it again."

I straightened and squared my shoulders. "Is this because I'm a woman? Do you think I'm incapable of following someone without being noticed?"

"No. I think you incapable of protecting yourself against someone who wishes to do you harm."

"Would you like to add 'no offence' to that to soften the blow?"

He winced. "I'm sorry, India, but no. I don't care if that offends you or not. I'm responsible for you, now that you live and work here."

I was about to argue that he wasn't responsible for me when Willie cut in first. "It ain't because you're a woman. It's because you can't fight like a man. And you don't carry Mr. Colt like I do."

"I could carry a gun if I wanted to."

"But you wouldn't use it."

She had me there. With a sigh of resignation, I nodded. "Very well. We'll work together."

Matt watched me a moment longer then finally said, "Good. Cyclops, continue at the Mapmakers' Guild, but be careful. Let me know if anything else happens, or if you discover that man's identity."

We told them what we'd learned from Daniel's family and showed them the button from McArdle's landlady. They couldn't think of a use for a magical button either. There seemed to be no point to it, particularly if it only lasted a brief time, like other magic.

"Do you think your time magic can work with it to extend its magic?" Cyclops asked, handing the button back to me.

"I don't know," I said. "Not that it matters, since I don't know how. Even if I did, why would anyone want to do such a thing for a button?"

"By the same token, why would anyone want any magical object if the magic is fleeting?" Matt said, touching the pocket where he kept his watch. "As far as I can see, most magic is useless without longevity."

"Except for map-making magic. Even if the magic only lasted a few minutes, the hidden route would still become visible long enough for someone to memorize it."

He nodded thoughtfully.

"We have to find Daniel," I said heavily. "His poor mother is so upset. Munro too, I imagine."

"We'll start afresh tomorrow by following Onslow." He stood and bade us goodnight.

I glanced at the clock on the mantel, forgetting that it had been turned to face the wall. He noticed and smiled. If I were a child, I would poke my tongue out at him. Instead, I raised my chin.

"Anyone want to play?" Duke asked after Matt left. He pulled the cards and matches out of the card table drawer.

Willie pulled a face. "Not me. It ain't no fun when the stakes aren't real."

"What are you going to do instead? Read a book?" He snorted.

"I might." She pulled out her pipe. "India, what's a good one?"

I handed her *The Three Musketeers* which I'd borrowed from Matt's library but hadn't yet begun. "Try this. I hear it's quite fun."

"Does it have battles and lots of blood?"

"I do hope so. We innocents need to get our fun somehow."

She chuckled.

"India?" Duke asked. "You want to play?"

"I think I'll retire. Goodnight."

Instead of going directly to my room, I headed for Matt's and knocked lightly on his door. He opened it and I swallowed heavily, forcing my gaze to meet his and not look at his bare chest. It was not an easy task.

He stepped aside and indicated I should enter.

"No, thank you," I said in a prim voice. I winced. I sounded exactly like the naive prude Willie accused me of being.

He leaned his forearm against the doorframe and crossed his legs at the ankles. "This must be important," he drawled. "Come to see what time it is?"

"Very amusing. You do know that I can simply turn one of the clocks around if I want to."

"But you won't because you're an honorable person."

"Not *that* honorable. I won't do it because I suspect you'll catch me if I do. You have a tendency to sneak up on people."

He grinned a positively wicked grin. He didn't care in the least that he was half naked. I should have known he wouldn't, based on prior experience. Despite having seen his impressive physique already, I did not tire of it. This time, however, I resolved not to succumb to temptation and gawp. It was unladylike to let him know I liked what I saw.

"I do wish you wouldn't smirk like that," I said, holding his gaze hard and not looking down.

"I'm not smirking, I'm smiling. I'm smiling because you look like you're trying not to blink."

I blinked.

"I can't think what you have against blinking," he went on. "Are you sure you won't come in? I promise to put a shirt on."

I lifted a shoulder. "I don't care if you do or not. You seem to be under the impression that your nakedness affects me. It does not. I'm hardly a sensitive chit."

His lips twitched. "Is that so? Then why won't you look below my chin?"

"You have a nice chin, and I have no need to look below it. I happen to prefer meeting the gaze of the person I'm speaking to. Stop smirking!"

He didn't. "Well?" he asked.

"Well what?"

"You came to my room for a reason. Or was it simply to catch me in a state of undress?"

I had the distinct feeling I was losing a battle I hadn't known I was participating in until it was too late. "I came to ask you about the note from Munro."

The smirk vanished. He lowered his arm and crossed them over his chest. "What about it?"

"What was in it?"

"I told you. He wanted me to update him on our progress. I'll visit him tomorrow in person."

"I'll join you."

"No."

"I thought we were going to remain together during our investigation," I said, throwing his words back at him.

"You can remain here while I go out. I'll pick you up when I'm finished."

"Matt, what else was in that note? Don't lie to me," I said before he could speak.

His brows crashed together. "I don't think I've ever lied to you."

"Perhaps not lie, but I know you'll certainly avoid trying to answer. As you are now. Well? What was in that note?"

He looked away.

"Allow me to read it."

He squared his shoulders. "Are you giving me orders now? I seem to recall *I* employ *you*."

"I saved your life. I think that gives me certain privileges."

He laughed. "You're a formidable woman."

Other men might consider that a negative trait, as Eddie certainly had, and my friend Catherine Mason's brothers. But it amused Matt. It was nice to be liked for being myself and not have to hide my forthrightness under a polite façade all the time.

"You'd better come in after all," he said.

"But someone may see." I glanced up and down the corridor. No one was about, but someone might come up the stairs at any moment and see me heading into or out of his rooms. I teetered on the edge of respectability by living in Matt's house as it was, but at least his aunt didn't think anything sordid in the arrangement. I didn't want her opinion of me to sink.

"You do know that I could ravish you in the carriage when we're alone together if I wished."

"Why do you think I keep the curtains open?"

He laughed. "Wait here, then."

I smiled at his back. Not just because I liked admiring the straps of muscle across his shoulders and the V shape of his upper body, but also because I enjoyed his company when he was like this. He might be lightly teasing me, but I didn't mind, and I liked to think I served it back to him in equal measure.

"I knew it," he said, turning and catching me staring. "I knew you secretly wanted to look at my nakedness."

"I had to look at something, since your face was averted. It was a battle between your back and the floor."

"And my handsome back won."

"I should have chosen the floor," I said, accepting the note. "It's not so arrogant as to think it's a distraction." I read the note as he waited, arms crossed over his chest again. I had to read it twice because I didn't take it all in the first time.

It was indeed from Commissioner Munro, and it did ask for an update on our investigation. However, it went on to mention that a man claiming to be an American sheriff visited him and warned him against trusting Matt. Munro didn't say whether he believed the man or not, but I thought it a point in Matt's favor that he was informing him at all.

I folded the note and gave it back to him. "This must be the sheriff you recently learned had followed you here."

"Payne. He's corrupt, and that makes him more dangerous than most of the outlaws in America, because he can literally get away with murder. He wants me dead because I'm the only one who knows he's corrupt."

"The other lawmen don't believe you?"

He shook his head. "Not even the good ones who employ me. Payne has covered his tracks well. For every crime I've accused him of, he's countered with a valid reason to explain his actions."

"Why would he come all the way over here to get you?"

"I have fewer friends here, particularly on the police force."

"You'd better watch out for people following you." I shivered, remembering the problems we'd had with the Dark Rider. The outlaw had followed us here, broken into the house, befriended me, and tried all manner of tricks to hurt Matt. It would seem it was about to start again.

He took my hand and squeezed. "He won't be as blatant as the Dark Rider," he said gently. "It's too risky, and he doesn't like risk. He stays low, and uses more subtle methods to achieve his ends. That's how he's managed to avoid the notice of the honest lawmen."

"He may be more subtle, but you're still in danger." I placed my other hand over his, trapping it. "You must be extra careful."

"So must you. We've been spending so much time together..." At my frown, he added, "The Dark Rider assumed you were special to me. Sheriff Payne might too."

"Oh. Yes, of course. But that doesn't give you an excuse to leave me behind and continue the investigation without me."

"I wouldn't dare."

"I don't think you should be on your own right now. Safety in numbers."

"Yes, ma'am."

"Matt, I'm serious."

He leaned forward and kissed me on the forehead. It was a light, chaste kiss, over in less than a second, but it jangled my nerves nevertheless. "I appreciate your concern."

The kiss quite stole my breath so I couldn't respond, just stand there like a fool, with his hand trapped between mine.

"Goodnight, India." He glanced down the corridor to the staircase. "You should go to bed." He pulled his hand free, gave me a wan smile, and closed the door.

"Goodnight, Matt."

***

An invitation to dine with Lord and Lady Rycroft arrived the following morning, but only for Matt and Miss Glass. The only person it bothered was Matt. I was quite content not to sit through another social engagement with the Glass girls and their parents.

"I'm not attending unless we're all invited," he told his aunt when she presented it to him.

Miss Glass folded the thick cream card in half and ran her thumbnail along the fold. "Don't be absurd. This is England, Matthew. Whether you like it or not, we do things a particular way here. There's no cause to be put out. India and Willie aren't."

"You don't even like your brother's family," he declared. "Nor do you wish me to be tied in matrimony to any of your nieces. Why do you want me to go at all?"

"Because we're family."

He looked as if he'd protest again, then shut his mouth and sighed heavily.

"Just be sure not to fall for the girls' charms," Miss Glass said.

Willie snickered. "They have charms? The way you described them, Matt, they didn't sound charming."

"Hope has a certain way about her that some men like," Miss Glass said. "But she's a devious minx and cannot be trusted. If you find yourself seated next to her, you must converse with the person on your other side, no matter who that is. Understand?"

"I'm quite sure I said I'm not going," he told her.

"We both know you are."

Willie snorted as she and Duke put on their hats. "I'm sorry I'm going to miss it now," she said. "Might be fun to see you drowning in dull conversation."

Matt appealed to me. "Can you think of anything that would save me?"

The only thing that may save him would be his health, but he didn't want his aunt to know about his illness. I shook my head. "Shouldn't you be going? It's getting late."

He pulled my watch from his pocket and flipped open the cover with slow, deliberate moves that were no doubt meant to tease me. "It's still early. But you're right, I ought to see Munro. Enjoy your morning, ladies." He shot me a smile as he returned my watch to his pocket. "Have a lovely *time*."

I narrowed my gaze at him, which only made his smile brighter.

He headed out with Duke and Willie. Cyclops had already left to go to the guild's hall. I tried to read in the sitting room with Miss Glass, but found it difficult to concentrate. The clock on the mantel beckoned me to turn it back around. I eyed Miss Glass, sitting on the sofa with embroidery in her lap. Would she tell Matt if I peeked at the time?

I was saved from my dilemma by callers. "Mrs. and Miss Haviland, madam," Bristow announced. "I've put them in the drawing room."

Miss Glass dropped her embroidery and clapped her hands. "The Havilands! How delightful. I haven't seen my old friend in an age. Thank you, Bristow. We'll be down in a moment."

"We?" I echoed.

"You are my companion when you're not being Matthew's assistant. Come along."

Two women who were clearly mother and daughter, going by their similar oval faces and blue eyes, rose from the sofa. "Letitia," said the mother smoothly. "How lovely it is to see you again. When I heard you were living here with your nephew, I knew I had to call upon you."

Did she mean she wanted to see Matthew or Miss Glass? Or both?

Miss Glass greeted Miss Haviland and introduced me. I was offered polite smiles and given only cursory glances. The gazes of both ladies slipped past me to the door.

"Is he here?" Mrs. Haviland asked.

"Harry is overseas at the moment," Miss Glass said.

My heart sank. Miss Glass was confused again, thinking Matt was his father. The Haviland women glanced at one another.

"Mr. Matthew Glass is out," I told them.

"Oh." Mrs. Haviland glanced at the door again. Looking for an escape?

"Bristow is bringing tea."

"Are your family good friends of the Glasses, Miss Steele?" Mrs. Haviland asked.

"I met Mr. Glass a few weeks ago when he was looking at watches in my father's shop."

Mrs. Haviland's lips pursed. "A shopkeeper? Oh. How...interesting. Letitia, do you know when Matthew will return? We've got a busy morning making calls, but I did so want to meet him."

"He'll be home soon," Miss Glass said. "I'm sure he would like to meet you too."

Bristow arrived with tea and cake. Miss Haviland reached for a slice of cake only to whip her hand back when her mother glared at her. She sipped her tea instead and looked utterly bored—and hungry.

"How pretty you are, Miss Haviland," Miss Glass said. "You were only a little girl when I last saw you."

"I don't like to seem boastful," Mrs. Haviland said, "but my Oriel is very accomplished." She smiled at her daughter. Oriel Haviland returned it. "She can sing, play the pianoforte *and* the harp, draw, paint, sew, and is an excellent horsewoman."

"Goodness. It's a wonder a gentleman hasn't snapped you up already." I couldn't quite discern whether Miss Glass was being serious or sarcastic. "Matthew will be very pleased to make your acquaintance, I'm sure. He does appreciate a well accomplished young lady, particularly a pretty one."

"How long will your nephew be in London, Miss Glass?" Mrs. Haviland asked.

"He won't be returning to America."

"Is that so? We've heard conflicting reports."

"Reports?" I echoed. "From whom?"

"Everyone," Oriel Haviland said, speaking for the first time. "He's quite the topic of discussion wherever we go, isn't he, Mama?"

Miss Glass sat a little taller at this news. "Of course he is. My nephew is a fine gentleman. He's tall, charming, clever, good natured, and very handsome."

The Haviland women glanced at the door but, when nobody entered, sighed into their teacups.

We stumbled through polite conversation for what I gauged to be less than half an hour, thank goodness. Any more would have been painful for all of us. The Havilands clearly weren't interested in Miss Glass, only Matt. Discussion frequently returned to him, sometimes steered there by Miss Glass, and other times, by Mrs. Haviland. Her daughter mostly stayed silent, although I frequently caught her looking at me.

Finally, Mrs. Haviland finished her tea and glanced at the clock on the mantel. "Goodness, is that the time? We must be going."

I looked at the clock, but it still faced the wrong way. Miss Haviland, seeing my smile, blushed.

"Please tell Mr. Glass we're disappointed that we missed him," her mother said. "You must call on us,

Letitia, with your nephew, of course. You'll both be most welcome. Make it soon. Oriel will be on tenterhooks until she meets your intriguing nephew, won't you, my dear?"

"Yes, Mama."

Miss Glass tugged on the bell pull and Bristow arrived to see the Havilands out.

"What a charming girl," Miss Glass said once they were out of earshot.

"How do you know?" I said. "She hardly opened her mouth."

"That's precisely what made her so charming. No one wants to listen to the chatter of silly young girls. I wonder if she's as accomplished as her mother claims. She can't possibly be, surely. No one is good at *everything*."

"I hardly call music, art and horseriding everything. What of her wit? Is she well informed? Can she have an interesting discussion?"

Miss Glass made a scoffing noise. "Honestly, India, you do like to be difficult sometimes. It would be unfortunate for Matthew if you were choosing a bride for him."

"I was under the impression he would choose his own bride. Actually, he said he's not looking for one at all at the moment."

She waved her hand as she sat. "All men say that, and yet all men marry, don't they? Come. Read to me while I rest my eyes."

I read to her for what felt like an age, until Bristow announced another caller. This one, however, had come to see me.

"Catherine!" I hugged my friend tightly. "It's so good to see you. I've missed you terribly." It wasn't until I said it that I realized how true it was. Ever since going to live with Matt, I felt as if my life had been split into two distinct parts: before Father died and after. Before his death, I'd lived a carefree, happy and uneventful existence. After, I'd been chased, accused of theft, discovered I may be magical, almost been killed, and seen first-hand how cruel London's elite could be. Catherine was a link to my old life, a place where I'd felt safe, welcomed and loved. Although I liked Matt and his friends, I didn't really belong in his home or his life. My melancholy thoughts brought tears to my eyes and I quickly looked away.

Not before Catherine saw them. "India, what's the matter? Is everything all right?" She glanced at Miss Glass, sitting serenely on the sofa. She had not risen, and seemed unaware of Catherine's presence. Mine, too, I'd wager. She'd fallen into her own world again, where her beloved brother still lived.

"Everything is well," I assured Catherine. "Seeing you makes me a little homesick for my old life, that's all. I miss my father."

She hugged me again. "I know. It's been so difficult for you lately." She took my hand and steered me to the window, away from Miss Glass. "Are you quite sure Mr. Glass treats you well?" she whispered.

"Very well. Everyone here has been kind to me. Don't worry." I took her hands and squeezed. "Tell me your news."

"Well." She perched on the window sill and fixed her wide blue gaze on mine. "Mr. Abercrombie from the guild came to visit my father yesterday."

My stomach rolled at the mention of the Watchmakers' Guild master. I despised him as much as he despised me. At least I had good reason—he'd falsely accused me of theft and blocked my entry into the guild.

"Do you know what he and your father discussed?" I asked.

"I listened in." A wicked gleam lit up her eyes. Catherine was mostly a good girl, and certainly immature, but she had a lot of spirit. The prospect of an adventure lured her more than it did me. "He warned Papa to keep you at a distance."

I groaned and slumped against the window frame. "Why won't he leave me alone?"

"He even went so far as to say that our friendship should not be encouraged. Can you believe such a man! Who is he to say who I can and cannot be friends with?"

I clasped her hands. "How did your father respond?"

"He said he'll warn me, but that I'm often willful and do as I please. Abercrombie told him a father ought to control his children, not let them run wild." She bit her lip, and her gazed darkened. "India, he also told Papa that you need to be kept out of the watch and clock trade."

I had a horrible feeling about this. "Why?"

"That's the odd thing. Papa didn't ask for an explanation. He told Mr. Abercrombie that you were a good person, and that this wasn't your fault. I don't know what he was referring to. Do you?"

"No," I said with as much conviction as I could muster. But I *did* know.

"Papa told him he has no authority over you, and that he can't stop you from seeking work in the watch trade. However, he assured Abercrombie that you're now employed here, and have nothing to do with timepieces. India, it was the oddest conversation. What could it be about?"

I shook my head. "Was there anything else?"

"He changed direction entirely and mentioned something about the Mapmakers' Guild."

I sucked in a breath and held it. "Go on."

"I lost interest so didn't listen after that. I was still mulling over what he'd said about you. All I heard him say was something about another being found in the Mapmakers' Guild."

Another.

"Whatever it means, it's not important to your situation. Oh, India, why is he being so beastly toward you?"

I didn't answer. I simply stared at her sweet, innocent face. She was the same age as Daniel, the "another" Abercrombie must be referring to. Another magician, besides me. So he *did* know what I was—it was a certainty now. But how did the master of the Watchmakers' Guild get involved with the affairs of the Mapmakers'?

More importantly, was he involved in Daniel's disappearance?

CHAPTER 7

"India?" Catherine touched my cheek. "You look pale. Are you all right?"

I nodded. "Yes. Yes, I'm fine." I took her hand and led her to an armchair then I sat alongside Miss Glass on the sofa. I needed to divert the conversation before Catherine asked some pointed questions. "Tell me the things you've been doing of late. Tell me about your Mr. Wilcox."

"Is he your paramour?" Miss Glass asked, suddenly alert. "I do love hearing about paramours from you young things. Tell me, is he handsome? Charming?"

Catherine's lips flattened and her hands twisted in her lap. "He's neither of those."

I'd hoped she would prattle on, like she often did when discussing one of her conquests, so that I didn't have to think too hard, but she fell into silence. "Is something the matter, Catherine?"

She sighed. "The more time I spend in Mr. Wilcox's company, the more I can see you were right, India."

"Me?"

"He's respectable, steady, and kind."

"He sounds admirable," Miss Glass said.

"But you don't want respectable, steady and kind," I said quietly. "Do you, Catherine? You want exciting and interesting."

"I do want kind, most assuredly. But, yes," she muttered into her chin, "a little bit of excitement wouldn't go astray. Oh, India, I feel awful for saying so, but I want someone who'll take me to a show on his day off rather than suggest a walk. I want a man who'll laugh at my silly jokes, not look at me like I'm mad."

"Don't feel awful," I told her. "If that's what you want in a suitor, then you should wait for him. The right man will come along. What does your mother say?"

"I haven't discussed it with her. She wants to see me settled with a sensible man, and Mr. Wilcox is very sensible."

"Why not talk to her? She'll understand."

"I will, but I wanted your opinion first. Sometimes I think you know me better than my parents do. You're my best friend, India, and I feel as though I can tell you anything."

"More so than your parents," I muttered. I'd been like Catherine in that regard. Despite loving my father, I hadn't confided in him much. Would I have taken my mother into my confidence, had she survived into my adulthood? I wasn't sure. Children often didn't confide in their parents, preferring their friends.

Perhaps Daniel Gibbons had too.

"You ought to introduce Miss Mason to Duke or Cyclops," Miss Glass said to me. "They're interesting men, worldly, and they laugh at Willemina's jokes and those are some of the silliest I've heard."

"Cyclops is the big one-eyed coachman, isn't he?" Catherine asked, turning up her nose. "He looks rather frightening."

"He's not," I assured her. "Nor is he the coachman anymore. Mr. Glass employed proper servants. Cyclops is Matt's friend, as is Duke. Although I'm not sure Duke is available." There was something between he and Willie, although neither may not yet know it.

Bristow appeared and bowed. "Would you like a fresh pot of tea, madam?"

"That would be lovely," Miss Glass said.

"Not on my account." Catherine rose. "I must be going. I'm only supposed to be at the market. Goodbye, Miss Glass."

"Goodbye, my dear. Good luck with your Mr. Wilcox problem. Let the poor fellow down gently."

Catherine drew in a fortifying breath. "I will." She turned to go, but spotted the clock on the mantel. "Why is the clock facing the wall? Doesn't it work?"

"It's perfectly fine," Miss Glass said before I could speak. "Matthew tells me that India mustn't check the time for an entire day. It's a small wager between them."

I narrowed my gaze at her. "Did he ask you to spy on me?"

She patted my arm. "Don't worry, dear. You haven't succumbed to temptation once, so I have nothing to report. You're a very strong willed woman, and I admire you for it."

"She has your measure, India," Catherine said with a smile.

I kissed her cheek and walked her to the front door. "Let me know if you hear anything else about either the Watchmakers' or Mapmaker's Guild."

"Why the Mapmakers?"

I shrugged. "I'm merely curious."

***

"It's definitely Payne," Matt said, kicking off his boots and leaning back in the chair. We sat in his office, he at the mahogany desk and me in the armchair by the unlit fire. We'd wanted privacy, away from Miss Glass and the servants, to discuss the morning's events. I'd not yet told him what I'd learned from Catherine.

"What did he say to Munro?"

Matt took out his watch and clasped it in his fist. The purple glow crept along the veins in his hand, up under his sleeve and re-emerging at his collar. When it reached his hairline he finally deposited the watch back in his pocket. He looked healthier, his face not quite so pallid, but the tiredness didn't leave his eyes altogether. I'd grown used to seeing it there and almost never noted it anymore. I'd never known Matt in full, complete health, but I did know that he couldn't live like this. He ought to be enjoying his prime.

"Munro wouldn't say much, only that Payne told him I should not be trusted, as my family are law breakers."

"Did you tell him that Payne is corrupt?"

He nodded. "He said he'll send a telegraph to California. I told him it won't do any good, since no one there believes me." He sighed. "It remains to be seen what Payne will do next, but I assure you, India, he's not the sort of man who'll come after you to get to me."

"Thank you, that is somewhat reassuring, but I don't like the idea of him targeting you specifically very much either."

"He'll be subtle, whatever he chooses. He can't risk coming under suspicion, either here or at home. He's gone to great pains to hide his duplicity there, and it's worked."

"So far."

He gave me a weak smile. "I like your optimism." He hunched forward, elbows on knees, and dragged his hands through his hair.

"I'll leave you to rest, but first, I need to tell you something. Catherine Mason came by this morning and told me of a conversation Abercrombie had with her father."

He glanced up. His hair stuck out from his head in damp, bedraggled spikes thanks to the rain. I resisted the urge to smooth it down. "What the hell did he want?"

I told him what Catherine had told me. "I'd like to pay Abercrombie a visit," I finished. "With you, of course."

"No."

I'd been prepared for that response. "Matt, we have to confront him about Daniel."

"We need to stay clear of him. He's afraid of your skill just like the Mapmakers' Guild is afraid of Daniel's. Your existence threatens his livelihood."

"But I'm not even making watches."

"Not now, perhaps, but one day."

Neither of us spoke for a minute, or perhaps two. I glanced at his clock on the mantel, but he'd even turned that around. Damn him.

"There's one other thing," I said. "Something struck me as I spoke with Catherine. She talked to me about her suitor, you see, rather than discussing him with her mother. It made me realize that people don't always confide important things to their parents, but sometimes discuss them with their friends. I think we ought to visit Daniel's friends. I wrote down their names when Commissioner Munro first came to us."

Matt went around to the other side of his desk and picked up the notepad. "There's two. We'll visit them this afternoon." He slapped the notebook against his hand. "Good thinking, India. Where would I be without you?"

"You'd be able to look at all your clocks, for one thing."

He smiled. "How is your challenge progressing?"

"Excellently. I haven't thought about the time once. You can ask your aunt, if you like, since you enlisted her to spy on me."

"I knew she'd crack and tell you."

I smiled back. "I don't mind that she spied for you."

His smile vanished. "Why? What are you up to?"

"Nothing." I got up. "But do get some sleep so you're refreshed for dinner tonight with the Rycrofts. It's a pity Miss Haviland won't be there. I told your aunt how she's precisely the sort of girl you'd like. Obedient, placid and very accomplished. I think Miss Glass is planning on holding a soiree here so the girl can display her talents."

He groaned. "You're wicked."

"I prefer clever."

I strode to the door, glancing at the mantel again out of habit, forgetting that the clock had been turned around.

"I saw that," he called after me. "You'll succumb before the day is out."

I shut the door on his chuckle.

***

Daniel's two friends boarded in the same house not far from Daniel's home in Hammersmith. Their sitting room didn't entirely lack feminine touches, as one would expect of bachelors. While the leather armchairs, writing desk and tables were solid, simple pieces, the pretty floral curtains and cushions cheered up the room. I guessed the two men to be younger than me but older than Daniel by three or four years. The fair, slender one, Mr. Connor, worked as an office clerk, and the darker, stockier Mr. Henshaw labored in a shoe factory. Being Saturday, neither was at work.

"We'll do everything we can to help you find Daniel," Mr. Connor said. He seemed the more outgoing of the two. He answered our questions first and possessed a confident air. The quieter Mr. Henshaw only spoke when pressed. "We're extremely concerned about him, aren't we, Thomas?"

Mr. Henshaw nodded.

"But as we told the police, we don't know where he is. He didn't stop here on his way home. Sometimes he does, but not that day." Mr. Connor flicked his blond hair back off his forehead with a jerk of his head.

"You may not know his movements," Matt said, "but you may have other information. Did he ever discuss things with you that he wouldn't tell his family?"

"What sort of things?"

"Anything."

"A girl, perhaps," I clarified, since Matt was doing a terrible job.

The two men glanced at one another. Mr. Henshaw's left eyebrow quirked and Mr. Connor's frown deepened. It seemed as if they were silently communicating with one another, but I couldn't fathom what the signs meant.

"Did he have a particular female friend?" I asked. "Someone he met in secret and didn't tell his family about?"

"No," Mr. Connor said. "Nothing like that."

"But there is something," Matt pressed. "You must tell us. We need to know everything if we're to find him."

The men glanced at one another again and Mr. Henshaw nodded. "You mustn't tell his family," Mr. Connor said. "Daniel's grandfather would be furious if he found out he was selling his maps. Daniel didn't know why the old man was so against it. He's very strict."

Mr. Henshaw tapped his temple. "He's mad."

"This is between us," Matt said. "Mr. Gibbons won't be told anything."

Mr. Connor looked relieved. "Daniel became frustrated that his family wanted him to stop drawing maps. Daniel couldn't stop. It was like a compulsion. He had to do it."

"When he tried to stop, he became moody," Mr. Henshaw added. "He wasn't someone you wanted to be around at those times." He looked to his friend.

Mr. Connor nodded. "So we suggested he draw them in secret, which he did here." He opened the top drawer of the writing desk. "He kept his pencils, rulers, papers and other tools here. He made his maps on this desk." He skimmed his hand over the surface as if he could still see Daniel's maps there.

Mr. Henshaw placed a hand on Mr. Connor's shoulder.

"But drawing them wasn't enough for Daniel," Mr. Connor went on. "He wanted to make money. They were bloody good, begging your pardon, Miss Steele. I've never seen anything like what he did. His maps were beautiful works of art, and incredibly accurate, too."

"So he got himself a small cart and sold his maps from them," Mr. Henshaw said.

"On the streets?" Matt asked.

Mr. Connor nodded. "At first, he simply wandered up and down the main shopping thoroughfares on his days off, but he discovered that Oxford Street was more lucrative. Not just anyone buys maps, see. Daniel realized he needed to be where the better class of gentleman shopped, somewhere he could be found again. One customer even sought him out after hearing of his reputation."

The guild wouldn't have liked that at all. "Did his master, Mr. Duffield, find out that he was selling maps without a license?" I asked.

"Not that we are aware," Mr. Connor said, perching on the edge of the desk. "Daniel only sold existing maps from his cart, ones that he'd drawn here. He didn't take commissions for new ones. He insisted that anyone wanting to commission him approach Duffield and go through the correct channels. He didn't want to upset his master or the guild."

Yet he would have done so simply by selling from his cart. I knew all too well how the guilds liked to control the sale of products that fell under their jurisdiction.

"Daniel may have led you to believe that he didn't take commissions without Duffield's knowledge," Matt said, "but he might not have told you everything."

"He did." Mr. Henshaw's eyes flashed as they bored into Matt. Matt didn't so much as blink. "He kept no secrets from us."

Matt produced Daniel's map from his inside jacket pocket. "Then he would have told you who commissioned this map and why."

The wind left Mr. Henshaw's sails. He glanced uncertainly at Mr. Connor, but the blond fellow kept his gaze firmly on the map.

"Where did you get that?" he asked.

"That's not important," Matt said. "But since you don't know the answer, it proves that Daniel did not tell you everything. What do you know about it, gentlemen?"

Mr. Connor shrugged. "Nothing, really. He mentioned that a gentleman approached him on Oxford Street after hearing of his reputation. He commissioned

Daniel to make a special map of inner London. That may be it. "

"Special?" I said.

"He didn't clarify, and I admit to not being interested enough to ask. I didn't think it important. Is it important, Mr. Glass?"

"I don't yet know," Matt said. "Did Daniel tell the gentleman to go through Duffield's shop?"

"As far as I am aware, yes. *Is* that the map?"

"I'm not sure," Matt said. "What I do know is that Daniel later argued with the man who commissioned the special map you speak of. Did he mention an argument to you?"

Mr. Connor shook his head and glanced at Mr. Henshaw. Mr. Henshaw shrugged. "Could be that day he came here all foul-tempered and wouldn't say why."

"Could be," Mr. Connor agreed. "I wish we'd pressed him, now. Do you think the fellow he argued with, the customer, is the one who caused him to go into hiding or...or has taken him?"

"It's too early to say," Matt said.

"There's one other thing," Mr. Henshaw said in his quiet, uncertain voice. He looked to his friend, who nodded for him to go on. "Remember when Daniel said he was going to get some money?"

"That could be linked to the special map," Mr. Connor said thoughtfully. "Daniel told us he would get more money than he'd ever seen in his life. Enough to take the three of us out of London and go live somewhere in the country together, away from our families."

"All from one commission?" I asked. While I could believe that a man who knew the rarity of a magical map would pay a high price for one of Daniel's, it seemed unlikely that Daniel knew his own worth. His grandfather thought he hadn't even been aware that he was magical, but *someone* had told him and helped him learn spells to create a magical map.

"Oxford Street is a long street," Matt said. "Is there a particular part that Daniel frequented?"

"Not many of the traders liked him being outside their shops," Mr. Connor said. "Many ordered him to move on if he lingered too long. Only the old toymaker near Baker Street was kindly. He let him stay out front as long as he wanted."

"Thank you," Matt said, rising. "You've been very helpful."

"Please let us know as soon as you find him," Mr. Connor said, shaking Matt's hand. "We're very worried. This isn't like Daniel."

"No," Mr. Henshaw chimed in. "He wouldn't leave without getting word to us. Something's happened to him."

"At least someone is doing something about it. I thought his father had given up, yet here you are."

"And we're following every path until we find him," I assured them.

***

Some of the shops on Oxford Street had already closed for the day, but most were still open, including the toyshop. Abercrombie's Fine Watches And Clocks had not yet shut either. Its grand corner position on the other side of the street dominated the smaller premises nearby, much like Abercrombie dominated those beneath him in the guild ranks.

"You don't have to leave the carriage," Matt said.

"I'm not worried about Abercrombie. He won't try to have me arrested again. He knows you're friends with the police commissioner."

"Munro's involvement is the least of Abercrombie's worries if he tries anything," he said darkly as he climbed out of the carriage. He folded the step down and held out his hand to me.

I didn't dare ask him to elaborate; I suspected I might not like the answer. Matt's past had been colorful, to say the least. After his parents died, he'd lived with his mother's family, most of whom were outlaws. He must have learned some of their criminal ways before he betrayed them. I wasn't foolish enough to think he was a saint who never sought retribution against those who harmed people he cared about. To think that I was one of the people he cared about, however, was as intoxicating as a glass of brandy. Two, in fact.

"Come now, Mrs. Prescott," Matt said with a genial smile. "Let's purchase some English toys for our niece and nephew back home in California."

"An excellent idea, Mr. Prescott."

I placed my hand on his arm and allowed him to lead me into the small shop with the bright red door and matching window trim. I would have loved to come into this shop as a child, but a watchmaker's daughter didn't usually shop for toys on Oxford Street. Her clever father made them for her out of spare parts.

"Oh, look," I said, pointing to an automata of a mother with her children having tea. "My father made me one just like it. You turn the crank that winds the gears beneath the floor, making all the parts work at different intervals."

"I had soldiers like these," Matt said, picking up one of the red coats. "Kept me occupied for hours."

The toys were clearly made for the children of wealthy parents. There were gleaming rocking horses with long manes, pretty dolls, dollhouses furnished with perfect miniature furniture, and even a Bing clockwork train set.

"I've only heard about these," I said, crouching to get a better look. "I've never actually seen one. Do you know these work on the same principles as timepieces?" I picked up the engine to inspect it, but the shopkeeper looked anxious so I put it down.

"Good afternoon," he said with a bright smile. He looked just like a toymaker ought, with rosy red cheeks, snowy white hair and friendly eyes. I was so pleased that he fit the mold that I smiled enthusiastically.

"Good afternoon," I said. "My husband and I are looking for something for our niece and nephew. What do you recommend?"

He showed us around his shop, winding up some of the automata so we could see them work. It was utterly fascinating, and I told him so. "Your shop is delightful," I said. "Isn't it, Mr. Prescott?"

"Yes, my dear," Matt said, eyes twinkling with good humor. It would seem the shop had lifted his spirits too.

"Do you see anything your niece and nephew would like?" the toymaker asked.

"Everything," I said with a laugh.

"The train set," Matt said.

I was about to protest that it was too expensive, since we weren't actually in need of toys, but we were supposed to be wealthy, and wealthy people didn't worry about expense.

"Your nephew will cherish it for years," the toymaker said, plucking the engine off the table.

"As will our niece," Matt said. "We'll also take the zoetrope."

We joined the toymaker at the counter as he gently wrapped up the gifts. "Do you know of any good map shops nearby?" Matt asked idly. "I had heard of a lad who sold his maps out the front, but he doesn't appear to be here today."

"Daniel, his name is," the toymaker said without looking up. "He usually comes on Saturdays but I haven't seen him today. Must have found something more important to do in his spare time, eh?"

"Do you know where I can find him?"

"No, I'm sorry."

"Did you ever see Daniel's maps? Are they as good as my friend, McArdle, claims?"

"They're very fine. Your friend doesn't exaggerate. Daniel's maps are a work of art in themselves. I'm surprised only the one fellow has come here specifically asking after him. You're the second, of course."

Only one? "That's our friend," I said. "Mr. McArdle."

"The archaeologist?"

Matt hesitated a second before saying, "Is that how he introduced himself to you?" He chuckled. "McArdle likes to make himself sound more interesting than he is."

The toymaker slid the wrapped train engine and carriages to me and set to work on wrapping the zoetrope. "His hobby explains why he and Daniel fell into a discussion about Roman hoards."

Matt went very still. I leaned forward. A Roman hoard meant treasure, and Daniel had told his friends he would come into a lot of money soon.

"McArdle is always on about hoards," Matt said with a laugh and shake of his head. "He's obsessed with them. Was he commissioning Daniel to make a map of an area known to contain a hoard?"

"I wouldn't know, sir. I didn't hear the entire conversation, just a little, in passing, as I was outside cleaning the window." He passed the package to me with a smile. "That'll be one and eight, sir."

Matt paid him and we took our parcels to the carriage. As soon as we pulled out from the curb, we turned to one another and grinned.

"Daniel's map must show McArdle where to find the hoard," Matt said. "Although I'm not sure how. If he commissioned Daniel to draw a map of the location of the hoard, doesn't that mean he already knows where it is?"

"Perhaps he does. Perhaps he's not trying to find the hoard but hide it again after finding it."

"Then why the map, if he already knows?"

I sighed. "It doesn't quite make sense, does it?"

"Don't be disheartened. I think we're onto something. I do know one thing—we need to find out everything we can about Roman archaeology in London, specifically hoards that might be buried beneath the modern city."

"Do you know anything about hoards in general?"

"Archaeology is all the rage in Italy, and my mother had a keen interest. She took me on a dig when I was twelve. We didn't find a hoard, but the archaeologist said he'd once found a large bowl full of coins, buried in what had probably been the garden of a wealthy merchant's villa."

"What did you find on your dig?"

"Walls and a few coins, but not hoards."

Hoards. Coins. I pulled out the button from my reticule and inspected it again. "Perhaps it's not a button but a coin," I said, showing Matt. "The shank is certainly a modern addition."

He plucked it from my palm and inspected it. "I think you're right. Perhaps it's a Roman coin from McArdle's hoard."

"A magical Roman coin."

CHAPTER 8

Miss Glass eyed the packages in Matt's hands. "What have you got there?"

"Gifts," he said, setting one down on the table and holding out the other.

"For me? Oh, Harry, that's so like you. I knew you'd bring me something from your travels."

Matt no longer batted an eye when his aunt experienced her episodes. He simply handed her one of the packages. "This is for you." He pecked her cheek. "The train is for India."

"Me!" I blinked at him. "Why?"

"You showed an interest in its mechanisms. I thought you might like to pull it apart to see how it works."

"Oh. That's very generous of you." I accepted the package and sat heavily on the sofa. What did he expect in return?

"Don't look so troubled," he said with a sly grin. "Consider it my lost wager. You haven't looked at a watch or clock all day."

"I suppose."

"A zoetrope!" Miss Glass said with a girlish giggle as she unwrapped it. "I love these. What does it show?" She spun the drum and peered through the slits at the spinning images. "What a lovely little toy. Thank you, Matthew. It's been years since anyone gave me a toy."

"My pleasure, Aunt. Are the others back?"

"Not yet." She set the zoetrope down. "Now, before we dress for dinner, I wanted to speak to you about the Haviland girl."

Matt's gaze slid to me. I gave him an innocent shrug. "What about her?" he asked darkly.

"She's a lovely girl," Miss Glass said. "Very pretty."

"So you told me. And extremely accomplished, too. But can she converse? Is she intelligent?"

Miss Glass's lips pressed together. She glared at me. "Have you two been colluding?"

"What do you mean?"

"Never mind." She stood. "I'm going to dress for dinner. You ought to too."

"It's hours away," he said.

"Nevertheless." She left clutching her zoetrope.

He threw himself into an armchair with a deep sigh. "It's going to be a long evening."

"You should rest a little before you leave," I said. "And use your watch."

"Speaking of which." He pulled out my watch and gave it back to me. "Congratulations. You are one hell of a mule-headed woman, as we say back home."

"I prefer to use the term iron-willed."

He smiled. "What are you going to do tonight? Play poker? Read?"

"Play with my train."

***

Without Miss Glass present, I didn't bother dressing for dinner. Duke, Cyclops and Willie only changed when they felt like it, and none did tonight. They'd managed to report to Matt before he left with his aunt to dine with the Rycrofts. According to Willie and Duke, DuPont hadn't returned to the factory, and according to Cyclops, neither Onslow nor the mysterious gentleman had been to the guild hall. We dismissed Bristow after he served supper, and I informed them of what we'd learned from Daniel's friends and the toymaker.

"So what do we do now?" Willie asked, putting her booted feet on the spare chair beside her.

"We want to visit an archaeology expert," I said, cradling my wine glass. "Not only to find out more about the coin and hoards but also to find McArdle. I suspect the archaeology field is small and they all know one another."

"McArdle seems like he may be the key," Cyclops said. "Wonder how he heard about magic if he ain't magic himself."

"And how did he find out about Daniel specifically?" Duke asked.

That was a good point. It was somewhat alarming to think that Daniel's reputation had gathered momentum so quickly that a man like McArdle would seek him out.

"Maybe magic ain't as secretive as we think," Willie said. She pulled her pipe from her pocket and patted her other, looking for matches.

"Not in the dining room," Duke grumbled.

She made a rude gesture at him but tucked the pipe back in her pocket.

"Willie may be right," Cyclops said. "Seems to me that most magicians know about it from family stories. How many magicians are there? Dozens? Hundreds? Thousands?"

"And then there are people like McArdle," I said, "who aren't magical but are happy enough to pay for it."

"Don't forget worms like Abercrombie," Willie said. "People who know about magic but aren't letting on."

"From the way most of the Watchmakers' Guild members looked at me with fear in recent weeks, they must all know that I am..." I studied my glass, swirling the contents in slow circles. "That I possess..."

"Magic, India," Willie said. "You can say it. It ain't a cuss word."

"But it's a despised one, in some circles."

"Despised or feared?" Cyclops said.

"I wish Matt would confront Abercrombie over his comments to Mr. Mason," I said. "He seems to know something about Daniel, and we ought to discover what it is."

"Aye," Cyclops said.

"Matt's being too careful. It ain't like him," Duke agreed.

"He wants to keep India away from Abercrombie."

"Why?" Willie asked. "What can Abercrombie do to her now that Matt's warned him off? He won't try that trick of getting her arrested again. Besides, we only want to talk."

Willie and I looked at one another. I lifted my brows. She nodded. We both smiled and turned to the men.

"The four of us will visit Abercrombie tonight," I said, setting down my glass.

"No." Duke shook his head. "Matt won't like it."

"Matt ain't our master," Willie said. "Cyclops? Will you come?"

The big man nodded. "You two will go anyway, and I ain't going to face Matt and tell him I let you go alone. Besides, you need some muscle."

"Then there's no need for you, Duke."

Duke stood and buttoned up his waistcoat. "I'm coming to keep you from doing anything foolish."

"I won't do anything foolish," I said, also standing.

"Not you. Willie." To her, he said, "Maybe you shouldn't take your gun."

"You just try and take it off me." She pushed back her chair, an air of anticipation in her movements. "Least this'll be more interesting than wagering matches at poker."

***

Cyclops drove the brougham to the Watchmakers' Guild hall in Warwick Lane in the hope we'd find Abercrombie there. I knew he spent much of his spare time at the hall instead of home. My father had once joked that Mr. Abercrombie did everything in his power to avoid the two Mrs. Abercrombies, his wife and mother, who both lived with him. Father said the women bickered incessantly and he almost felt sorry for the man.

Duke peered up at the coat of arms and let out a low whistle. "It's almost as big as the door itself. What does the writing mean?"

"Time is the ruler of all things," I said, blinking up at Old Man Time and the emperor. "It's in Latin."

"Truer words..." Duke murmured, perhaps thinking of Matt's predicament.

"Aye," Cyclops said, equally somber.

We all stared up at the coat of arms, brightly lit by the two lamps mounted on either side of it. The passing of time weighed us all down, as well as the worry over our lack of progress in finding Chronos.

"The Mapmakers' Guild have an old man holding up a globe in their coat of arms too," Willie said, hands on hips. "Why all the old men? Why not have a young muscular brute holding up the globe, or wearing that cloth around his waist? Be easier to look at."

"Because guilds are run by old men," I said, knocking on the door. "And old men don't like to be reminded of what they once had but lost."

"Muscles?"

"Youth."

She snorted. "Hair and teeth, too. Smooth skin."

"A memory," Duke added. "Women falling at their feet."

"We're talking about real life, not your fantasy."

The door was opened by the same footman who'd let me in the last time I'd confronted Abercrombie at the guild hall. I pushed past him before he recognized me and shut the door in my face. He spluttered a protest but didn't bother trying to stop the others from entering.

"You!" he blurted out. "You're not welcome here."

"Is Mr. Abercrombie present?"

"Get out!" He pointed at the door.

Cyclops closed it and stood with his feet a little apart and his hands clasped loosely in front of him. He looked like a pirate anticipating a brawl.

"Is Mr. Abercrombie present?" I repeated.

"I'm here."

I spun round to see the tall figure of Abercrombie approach. He held his pince-nez in one hand and a candlestick in the other. "Good evening, Mr. Abercrombie," I said. "Is there somewhere we can speak privately?"

"Here will do." He didn't advance any closer than the end of the entrance hall, some six or seven feet away. "I cannot imagine you have anything to say that I want to hear."

The footman strode up to his master and whispered something in his ear. Abercrombie nodded and the footman disappeared into the shadows behind him. I guessed we had only a few minutes before constables arrived.

"You have nothing to fear from me," I said. "No one here wishes to harm you."

"Then why is your friend resting her hand on her gun?"

Willie lowered her hand and the flap of her jacket once again obscured the Colt she'd tucked into the waistband of her trousers. I tried to catch her attention to warn her to keep the gun holstered, but she was too intent on glaring at Abercrombie to notice.

"What do you want, Miss Steele?" he said. "I'm a busy man and I don't have time for your games."

"What do you know about Daniel Gibbons?"

The candle's flame flickered with his expelled breath. "Who?"

"Don't play me for a fool. You know about the mapmaker's apprentice. You know he's...special."

"I've never heard the name."

"Did you have anything to do with his disappearance?"

"I beg your pardon? Are you accusing me of something, Miss Steele?"

I approached him slowly, Duke and Willie flanking me. Abercrombie backed away. "It's a simple question, Mr. Abercrombie. Did you have something to do with Daniel's disappearance?"

"How can I when I don't know him?"

"That's a lie."

He backed into the long case clock, throwing the pendulum off its rhythm. It chimed once. "Be careful, Miss Steele, or I'll set my lawyer onto you for slander."

"Your threats don't scare me."

His oiled mustache twitched. "They should. I see that your employer, Mr. Glass, is not here. Is that because you know he won't always be able to save you? He may have friends and influence now, but he won't always. He's not infallible."

"What does that mean?" Willie snapped.

I put out my hand to stay her arm in case she decided that the only way to get him to answer was by shooting. "If you had anything to do with Daniel Gibbons's disappearance, your lawyer won't be able to help you," I said. "Not in the face of his father's ire."

"He doesn't have—" He cut himself off.

I smiled.

"Through here." The footman returned with six thuggish brutes in tow. They looked as if they'd come straight from the docks or an East End tavern. They certainly weren't constables.

I tightened my grip on Willie's arm as I felt it twitch. Duke moved in front of us, arms out at his sides. Cyclops joined him.

"It's time for you to leave, Miss Steele." The smug look on Abercrombie's face made my blood boil more than the presence of his thugs.

"Coward," Willie spat. "Turd. Son of a whore."

I pulled her arm hard and backed toward the door.

"Let me use my Colt," she hissed, trying to pull free.

I was saved from ordering her to leave by both Duke and Cyclops backing up, forcing us to retreat. I opened the door and rushed outside, dragging Willie with me.

Cyclops hurriedly untied the reins from the bollard and threw them to Duke as he sat on the driver's seat. Cyclops joined him while Willie and I climbed into the carriage. She pulled down the window and shouted obscenities at the guild hall as we drove off, not even stopping after we'd turned the corner.

"Willie! Enough!" I cried, rubbing my temples.

She slammed the window shut, *humphed*, and slouched into the corner, arms folded across her chest. We'd almost reached home by the time her scowl cleared and she spoke again. I was grateful for the silence in which to think.

"What did he mean, Matt's not infallible?" she asked. "Does he know about his illness?"

"I don't know. Even if he's aware of the existence of magic, how would he know that a watchmaker's magic and doctor's magic have been combined in Matt's timepiece to keep him alive?"

She kicked the seat beside me with her boot. "Then what's he talking about?"

"I don't know," I said again, even though a thought had occurred to me. Matt had gotten Abercrombie to drop his accusation of theft against me by telling him about his connection to Commissioner Munro. Perhaps Abercrombie was referring to that connection being broken if Matt failed to find his son.

No, that couldn't be right. Abercrombie didn't know who Daniel's father was.

Willie kicked the seat again. "We didn't achieve anything," she grumbled.

"Nonsense. We did. We now know that Abercrombie knows Daniel. When I mentioned Daniel's father's ire, he almost replied that Daniel doesn't have a father."

"It ain't enough."

"Did you expect Abercrombie simply to blurt out that he'd been involved in Daniel's kidnapping?"

"He would have, if you'd let me draw."

"And if he hadn't? Would you have shot him? No, you wouldn't, and if you had, you would have been foolish to do so since the footman had seen us enter. We'd all hang."

"I weren't thinking of murdering him, just shooting off his little toe or something else he don't really need but will hurt like the devil."

I closed my eyes and tipped my head back. Matt had my utmost respect for the way he handled Willie. How he'd managed to keep her out of jail thus far was a miracle.

"He's going to kill us when he finds out, you know," she said.

I opened my eyes. "Abercrombie?"

"Matt. When he learns that we went to visit the guild without him."

"Then don't tell him."

***

"It was just as I expected," Matt said at breakfast. "Painful. My uncle clearly didn't want me there, and Aunt Beatrice wouldn't stop talking about the girls' charms and accomplishments. Twice Aunt Letitia forgot where she was, and who I was, which made Charity laugh. Hope sat on one side of me, and Patience on the other, but Aunt Letitia glared at me every time I conversed with Hope. I tried to engage Patience in conversation but she's so shy she wouldn't look up from her plate. I spent the entire evening talking to her left ear."

"That must have upset Hope," I said.

"If it did, she's gracious enough not to mention it. We finally managed a conversation when the gentlemen rejoined the ladies in the drawing room. Hope wanted to know why Aunt Letitia disliked her so. I couldn't think of an answer so I feigned innocence. Now she thinks I'm an unobservant fool."

Willie snorted. "If she knows men then she'll think you're normal."

Why did he care what Hope thought of him?

"What about the food?" Cyclops asked. "Did you dine like a lord?"

"Always thinking about your stomach," Willie said with a shake of her head.

Cyclops shoveled two entire rashers of bacon into his mouth and nodded.

"The food was good, although Mrs. Potter is better," Matt said.

"Glad we weren't invited then," Duke said from the sideboard where he helped himself to sausages. "We had a quiet evening here, playing poker, and went to bed early. Didn't we?" he said, turning around with his full plate.

Willie glared at him over her cup of tea. Cyclops concentrated on his breakfast, shoveling in more bacon. Matt frowned.

"Did you and Hope talk for long?" I asked quickly, latching on to the first topic I could think of. I wished I hadn't. I wasn't interested in hearing more about the pretty and gracious Hope.

"A good half hour. Aunt Letitia interrupted us a few times, but Aunt Beatrice kept luring her away again so that I could be alone with Hope and 'get to know her better,'" he mimicked. "Hope and I laughed about it."

I sipped my tea and glanced at him over the rim of the cup only to see him already watching me with an indecipherable frown.

Willie set her cup down with a clatter in the saucer, drawing everyone's attention. "Forget her," she said. "Letty says that girl's cunning, and I believe her."

"You've never met her," Matt said.

"I trust Letty's judgment. She's known her nieces their entire lives."

"She also thinks a knight saved her from a dragon once."

"Hope won't want to move to the States, Matt."

"Is that what this is about? You think I'll stay here because of a woman?"

"Can't say I haven't thought about it." Willie tore off a corner of toast. "We all have, haven't we?"

Duke and Cyclops didn't look up from their plates.

"Cowards," Willie muttered.

Matt set his knife and fork down and rested his palms flat on the table. "Let me put all your minds at ease. I am not considering marrying Hope, or any of her sisters. I'm not considering the Haviland girl or anyone else my aunts dredge up. I am not marrying. Not until I know I have a future. Is that clear?"

The three of them nodded. I felt like an interloper, eavesdropping on a conversation not meant for my ears. Until Matt turned his gaze squarely on me.

"India?" he said, a little gentler.

I nodded quickly.

He picked up his knife and fork. "Good. So what have we got on today?"

Everyone expelled a breath. It wasn't often Matt grew cross with his friends, and I could see from their uncertain glances at one another that they weren't sure how to react.

"We need to find someone with an interest in archaeology," I said. "The problem is, I don't know how. It's Sunday. Any archaeological societies will be closed."

"We'll go to church," Matt announced.

"You're going to ask God to reveal an archaeologist to us?"

"I'm going to ask Aunt's acquaintances. Archaeology is a gentleman's hobby. One of her friends may know someone we can speak to."

***

There were quite a number of new faces at church, most of which turned to us as we entered. Or, more specifically, to Matt. They followed his progress to his seat then bent their heads together to whisper. It wasn't at all surprising to me, particularly when I noticed that each little group had a girl of marriageable age with them.

"What the hell is going on?" Matt muttered. "Why is everyone staring?"

"It seems you are the latest sensation."

"I've been here almost three weeks. Why now?"

"Your aunt has only just begun sending word out. Aren't you enjoying the attention?" I teased.

"I feel like a tiger in a cage."

"Retract your claws for a little while and smile, for your aunt's sake."

His scowl deepened. "You're enjoying this."

Did I like every woman in church admiring his handsome face and assessing whether he'd be a good husband? Did I like that I sat beside him and not a single one of his admirers even knew I was there? No, I did not. I could see that I'd been quickly dismissed as the companion already confined to the spinster's shelf, an invisible person whom no one considered a threat. It left a sour taste in my mouth and a hollow ache in my chest.

"The Havilands are here," Miss Glass, sitting on Matt's other side, whispered. "Over there. That's Oriel Haviland in blue and white. She's an excellent singer, artist—"

"Tinker, tailor, solider and sailor," he growled. "Yes, you told me. Frequently."

"Look at her eyes," said Miss Glass, not put off in the least. "They sparkle with intelligence and wit, don't they, India? Look, Matthew."

"I am looking," he hissed, following his aunt's gaze.

Mrs. and Miss Haviland nodded and smiled. The gentleman on the girl's other side, probably her father, also gave Matt a nod. Mrs. Haviland waved and Miss Glass waved back. The girl blushed and demurely looked down at her prayer book.

"Such a lovely, sweet natured girl," Miss Glass went on. "Her family is very respectable. Her mother's side is related to the earls of Quinley."

"Thank God," Matt muttered.

I thought it was a strange thing to say following on from Miss Glass's description of the Haviland family until I saw the vicar enter.

After church, Matt made his aunt happy by asking to be introduced to Mr. Haviland.

"I knew you'd fall in love with Oriel the moment you set eyes on her." She nodded and smiled as acquaintances filed past but did not engage any in conversation. More than one mother appeared put out by it, and their daughters did too.

"I have not fallen in love with her," Matt whispered while simultaneously smiling politely at two young women who nodded at him as they passed. They hurried off, giggling into their fans.

"You will," his aunt sang. She spied the Havilands and waved.

Mrs. Haviland waved back and pushed her daughter toward us. The girl stumbled a little before regaining her balance. She turned on a smile then bobbed a curtsy for Matt. Miss Glass made the introductions.

"It's very nice to meet you," Matt said, shaking Mr. Haviland's hand. "I haven't seen you here until now."

"We usually attend the service at Christ Church," Mrs. Haviland said. "But we felt like a walk today. It's such a lovely day to be out."

Matt glanced at the sky. It was gray and threatened rain. Mr. Haviland chuckled. "My wife wanted to see *you*," he said with a knowing smile. "To get your measure."

"Mr. Haviland!" his wife cried. "How you do exaggerate. Not at all. Although I am glad to have met you, Mr. Glass. You're everything your aunt described and more."

"Really?" Matt drawled in a strong accent.

"My wife is a quick judge of character," Mr. Haviland said with a hearty laugh. He turned his smile onto me and thrust out his hand. "And you are?"

"Miss Steele," Matt said with an admonishing glance at his aunt who should have introduced me, since the Havilands were her acquaintances.

"Delighted," Mr. Haviland said. "Are you related to Mr. and Miss Glass?"

"She's the companion," Mrs. Haviland said without so much as a glance at me. She nudged her daughter.

The girl sprang to life like an automaton whose key had been turned. She straightened her back and smiled. "What a lovely service. Don't you think so, Mr. Glass?"

Miss Glass looped her arm in mine. "India, would you mind walking with me?"

She steered me away as Matt gave Miss Haviland a polite answer then engaged her father in conversation. No doubt he would soon have the information he needed about archaeologists.

"We must leave him alone so that he can be his usual charming self with the young ladies." Miss Glass's hand tightened. She stopped and forced me to face her. I expected to see a warning in her eyes, but what I saw hurt more. Pity. This woman, a spinster her entire life, knew that I was as unlikely to find myself a husband as she was. "You understand, don't you, India?" she asked gently.

I nodded. Oh, yes, I understood the need for me to stay away from Matt in social situations, lest people come to the wrong conclusion. My constant presence must be a stick in her spokes. It was a wonder she allowed me to come along and sit with her and Matt at all.

That was unkind of me. I knew she liked me; I could see it in her eyes now, and the way she was with me when her friends weren't around. But she'd been born into a system that didn't allow us to be equals, or allow Matt and I to be anything more than employee and employer to one another. I could hardly blame her for it.

"So?" Willie asked, joining us along with Cyclops and Duke. "Is Matt asking that man about archaeologists?"

"Why would he do that?" Miss Glass asked, glancing over her shoulder. She sighed when she saw that Matt had engaged Mr. Haviland in conversation again, and Mrs. and Miss Haviland stood by with twin expressions of frustration on their faces.

"That's the Haviland girl," I told them.

"You mean the one so accomplished that it's a miracle she ain't been hitched to a prince yet?" Willie's cutting remark fell on deaf ears. Miss Glass didn't acknowledge her.

Matt broke away from Mr. Haviland and strode toward us with determined steps and a thunderous expression. What the devil had transpired between them to make him so upset?

"India." Cyclops moved closer to me and placed his hand on my back. "It's Hardacre. Want me to run him off?"

"Eddie?" I peered past Cyclops and my heart sank. My former fiancé had already spotted me and headed our way.

Matt reached us at the same time as Eddie. Between he and Cyclops, I felt quite safe. Not that I ever felt danger from Eddie. His cruelty was verbal, not violent.

"There you are, India," Eddie said, a hesitant smile on his face as he glanced at each of the men flanking me. "Mr. Glass, what a pleasant surprise to see you again."

"Is it?" Matt said, a sharp edge to his tone.

"What do you want, Eddie?" I asked.

"To see you." He tried on a brighter smile, but it didn't reach his eyes and quickly faded when he saw that I didn't return it. "You look well. That dress suits you."

"Save your flattery for a woman who'll fall for it. I no longer do."

He cleared his throat. "Yes. I'll get to the point, then. When we parted, you mentioned you'd made notes regarding some of the timepieces in the shop. Since you have no need of them, I thought you might like to give them to me."

"Finding it difficult to fix some?" I asked.

Willie chuckled. She and Duke watched on from behind Eddie. Between the five of us, we'd managed to surround him, and Eddie had only just noticed. His face paled and he fingered his tie. Miss Glass had wandered off to speak with friends, for which I was glad.

"Some of your father's clocks and watches are unique," Eddie said. "His methods were not always conventional. The notes you made to fix them would help a great deal."

"They're *my* notes, Eddie, and they are not part of the inheritance. You're not getting them."

"It's a shame to see such fine pieces go to waste." He sighed. "I'd have to throw them out or sell them at bargain prices if I can't get them to work. Pity."

"India made her position clear," Matt said. "She's not giving you the notes."

Eddie inched away from Matt. "India?"

"You're wasting your time," I said. "Good day."

I went to leave, but his hand whipped out and caught my arm. Matt and Cyclops stepped forward and Eddie let me go. He swallowed. "I also want to give you a warning, India. Considering our history together, I think it only fair that I advise you to stay away from Abercrombie."

Out of the corner of my eye, I saw Matt turn to me. I couldn't quite see his expression, but I knew that he was waiting for me to deny it. "India hasn't been to see him lately," he said.

"She went last night." Eddie sounded like he was giving a victory speech, he was so smug. "That's the thing with India, Mr. Glass. You have to keep your eye on her or she does and says things no gently-bred woman ought to do and say. God save us from women with a mind of their own, eh?"

His chuckle died on his lips as Matt turned his icy glare onto him. "Go away."

Eddie backed off, hands in the air. Willie and Duke parted and he slipped through the gap between them. He turned and hurried up the street.

"India," Matt growled, gripping my arm hard. "Why in God's name did you visit Abercrombie without me?"

I jerked free and squared up to him. I was tired of Eddie ordering me about and tired of Matt doing so too.

"We went with her," Cyclops assured him.

"That's supposed to make me feel better?"

"Don't, Matt," I said, keeping my voice low. "Do not tell me what to do. I'm capable of making my own decisions, and I decided that I was in no danger from Abercrombie. We had to find out what he knew about Daniel."

"I beg to differ about the danger. The man tried to have you arrested! Don't do anything like that again without me."

I marched off. I was in no mood to listen to him. Eddie had left me with frayed nerves and deep-rooted anger over my stupidity in thinking he'd loved me. Matt's domineering attitude only fueled that anger.

I pushed through the members of the congregation still lingering on the pavement, only to be stopped by a man blocking my path.

"Excuse me," I said.

He crowded closer and caught both my elbows, pinning them to my sides. I gasped and peered up, but most of his face was obscured by the hood of his cloak. He smelled of ale and sweat, and a curved white scar sliced through the stubble on his jaw. He was huge, taller than Matt and more solid.

I shivered. "Wh—what do you want?"

CHAPTER 9

"Let me go," I snapped, struggling.

My plea only made his fingers dig in more, cutting off the blood flow at my elbows. "Cease your search for Daniel Gibbons," he hissed, "or you and those you care about will come to harm."

He let me go and ran off. His long strides took him around the corner and out of sight in mere seconds. I folded my arms and gingerly touched my elbows where he'd held me. Bruises would form soon enough. I was lucky that bruises were all he'd given me. He could have done worse. If his threat was to be believed, he *would* do worse unless we ended our investigation. Despite willing it to settle, my thundering heartbeat reverberated through my entire body.

"India? What is it?" Matt followed my gaze down the street. "Did that man bother you?"

"He...he threatened me."

"*What?*"

"He told me to stop searching for Daniel or...or someone would be harmed."

"Willie, stay here with India. Duke, Cyclops, with me." He hadn't finished speaking before he sprinted off. Duke and Cyclops followed but couldn't catch him.

"What is he doing?" Miss Glass shook her head and clicked her tongue. "Running about like that is terribly vulgar. Everyone is watching."

"Did he hurt you?" Willie asked quietly so that Miss Glass couldn't hear.

I lowered my arms. They ached at the elbows, but I shook my head.

"Do you think he was sent by Abercrombie too?"

"I don't know," I said. "It's quite a coincidence, though. First Eddie and now him."

"Maybe Matt's right. Maybe we shouldn't have gone last night."

"You may think that, Willie, but I do not. We must do everything we can to find Daniel, even if we put ourselves at risk. He's just a lad."

She stared off into the distance where Matt, Cyclops and Duke had disappeared. "I'm not sure Matt will agree with you on that score. Make no mistake, India, he's as noble as can be when it's his own life at risk. But when those he cares about are threatened, he'll back away."

"The thing is, I believe the search for Daniel is linked to magic, and magic is what will save Matt's life. Finding Daniel may help us find Chronos. So I'm not giving up."

She swore under her breath. A moment later, she swore again. "All right. I agree with you about the link." She settled her feet a little apart. "And anyway, I don't back away from a fight. I ain't giving up either."

I looped my arm through hers. "In that case, we may be in for a battle to convince Matt to continue the investigation."

"I reckon between us we'll talk him round."

"Either he continues the search or we'll do so without him. It's his choice."

She snorted softly. "He won't see it as a choice. No matter what he says, India, stay strong. You hear me? We got to do this, for his sake."

The men returned a few short minutes later, looking hot and angry, their hats in their hands. Their expressions made it clear they hadn't caught the hooded man, so neither Willie nor I asked. We simply walked home with them silently. Well, as silently as Miss Glass would allow.

"Why did you tear off like that, Matthew?" she asked. "It was such a sight. Fortunately most people had left, but if someone had seen you exerting yourself, what would I have told them?"

"I thought I saw someone I knew," he said.

After a few minutes of tight silence, she said, "That was good of you to address her father."

"What?" Matt sounded distracted, distant.

"Haviland. You seemed to get along well with him. It was a clever move. Without him on our side, there's no point in courting his daughter."

Matt didn't bother to respond.

"I do wish you'd spent some time meeting other girls, however. Just in case you didn't like Oriel after all. There's nothing wrong with having a spare waiting in the wings."

"Aunt..." He expelled a long breath and peered up at the heavens. He didn't finish his sentence.

We arrived back at the house, and Miss Glass asked Bristow to bring tea into the drawing room. "We should expect visitors," she said, touching Matt's jaw. "Make yourself presentable then join me."

He inclined his head in a nod, although I wasn't quite sure if he'd even heard her. He still seemed distracted.

I went to follow Miss Glass into the drawing room, but he caught my arm in the same spot as the hooded man had held me. I sucked in air between my teeth and winced. His fingers sprang apart and he frowned.

"India?"

"It's nothing," I said, folding my arms again. I'd removed my jacket upon entry. The lace cuff of my dress's sleeves reached a little below my elbows and I wasn't sure if the bruises could be seen below them. I didn't want to look and alert Matt to them.

It didn't matter. He gently drew my arms away from my body and pushed the lace up before I had a chance to resist. A bruise darkened the inside of each of my elbows.

His shoulders rounded. His eyes softened. "India," he murmured. He cupped my elbows and skimmed his thumbs gently over the bruises. "You told me he didn't hurt you."

"Aye," Willie said, her mouth stretched into a flat line. "You did."

I drew away and lowered the lace. "I bruise easily."

Matt's gaze turned flinty. I preferred the softness, yet I didn't want his pity. "My study. Everyone. Now."

I bristled. "Didn't we just have a discussion about you ordering me about?"

"India," Willie hissed. "It ain't the time."

Matt indicated I should walk ahead, probably so he could keep an eye on me and make sure I didn't retreat to the drawing room where he couldn't discuss the matter in front of his aunt. I suppose it was necessary to talk about it, but I felt as if I were participating in a funeral march.

Matt's study wasn't large and the five of us filled it. Duke and Cyclops remained standing while Matt sat behind his desk, and Willie and I occupied the other chairs. I steeled myself for the barrage of questions.

"Did you get a look at him?" Matt asked.

"Not really," I said. "He was tall, hadn't shaved properly, and a small scar trailed through his stubble." I showed them where. "I didn't recognize him."

"And he specifically mentioned Daniel and our investigation?"

I nodded.

"It seems to me that Abercrombie sent him, after your little visit last night."

Duke shuffled his feet. "I didn't want to go," he muttered.

"Shut it," Willie snapped. "We had to go."

Matt turned his icy glare onto her. "I beg to differ. You do realize that Abercrombie now knows we're investigating Daniel's disappearance where before he didn't?"

"Yes," I said. "Does it matter?"

"He could alert Duffield."

"Perhaps, but he doesn't know that we're using false names. If he says a man named Glass is looking for Daniel, it will mean nothing to Duffield." I pressed my hands on the chair arms and dug my fingers into the leather. "If we hadn't confronted him, we would still be in the dark as to whether Abercrombie knew Daniel or not. We can now be certain that he does. We also learned that he's not averse to employing thugs to get his way. That man today may have been paid by him, or he may have been paid by Daniel's kidnapper. I do think the latter more likely, as it happens."

"Based on what evidence?"

"Logic. Abercrombie already sent Eddie. Why would he send someone else?"

"Because Eddie is not effective, or he came of his own volition, not at Abercrombie's urging." A muscle in Matt's jaw pulsed. "India, I don't take threats lightly. In my line of work, threats are usually followed up with action. I can't risk that. I *won't* risk it."

"You don't have a choice, Matt. Willie and I are going to continue the search for Daniel whether you like it or not."

He sat back in the chair and regarded me levelly, assessing me. It was unnerving, but I didn't glance away. "Willie?" he snapped.

"This investigation might help us to find out more about magic," she said. "It might even lead us to Chronos."

"Or it might not."

She rounded the desk and crouched in front of him. "Abercrombie knows about Daniel." This quiet earnestness was most unlike her. "The two guilds seem to share information about magic. If there's a link, we *have* to follow it."

He shook his head. His entire body seemed tightly wound, as if he were barely holding himself back from lashing out. It must frustrate him enormously to be thwarted, not only by the hooded man, but by us too.

"Help us, Matt," I said. "We can do this together."

He flicked his gaze to me then away. Behind the simmering anger, tiredness lurked. The exercise had worn him out.

"I agree with Willie and India," Cyclops said. "We must continue."

Everyone glanced at Duke. He heaved a sigh then nodded. "You know I don't choose to go against you lightly, Matt, but this time, they're right. If there's a chance this leads us to Chronos—"

Matt's fist came down on the desk, rattling the pen in the stand. I jumped then swallowed my gasp. My nerves were more frayed than I realized. "God damn you all," he growled. "Every single one of you'll be the death of me before the watch expires."

I breathed out a long breath. Willie's lips twitched in a smile and she stood.

"So what now?" I asked. "Did Mr. Haviland know of any archaeologists?"

He inclined his head. "There's a society. The president works at the British Museum. We'll visit tomorrow. In the meantime, everyone stays in the house. I'll instruct Bristow not to allow anyone in unless Aunt Letitia knows them." He stood abruptly and jerked his chin at the door. "Now go away before I say something I regret."

"Get some rest, Matt," Cyclops said. "We'll all be fine without you for an hour."

Matt's response was a narrow-eyed glare that didn't alarm the big man in the least.

Unfortunately for me, I was the last one out. Matt took my hand and held me back after the others left. My stomach somersaulted. There was no mistaking his glare for a softening attitude. He was still as furious as ever.

He bent his head to mine and his breath brushed the hair at my temple. It was somewhat ragged and shallow. "I don't like being backed into a corner, India. Particularly by my own friends."

I stepped back, out of his immediate sphere. His power wasn't quite so ferocious with a little distance between us. "And I don't like being told what to do. So it seems we are at a standoff, as you Americans like to say."

I walked off and did not look back.

Later, as I sat in my rooms, Miss Glass's maid, Polly, delivered a bottle of tincture of arnica. "At Mr. Glass's request," she said.

I rocked back on my heels. "Oh. Thank you, Polly." I sat at my dressing table and dropped a little of the tincture on my handkerchief then dabbed it on the bruises. It was kind of him to think of me. I hadn't expected him to remember the bruises; he'd been so riled. The bottle would indicate a truce, but he didn't come to apologize, either in person or via a note.

It was unnerving. I didn't like this tension between us. Even though we were in separate parts of the house, I felt it keenly. I was about to rejoin Miss Glass, in the hope of seeing Matt too, when visitors arrived. From the landing, I spied Bristow opening the front door to a lady with twin daughters in tow. With a sigh, I returned to my room.

I saw Matt at dinner, but we hardly spoke. No one did. Miss Glass carried most of the conversation, discussing each of her callers in great detail, and listing the charms of all the girls who'd visited. Her favorite was still Oriel Haviland. Matt had endured all of the calls in bad humor, according to his aunt's admonishment. He brought that bad humor with him to dinner, and took it away again immediately afterward when he retired early. I decided against knocking on his door and requesting a discussion to clear the air between us. Tomorrow would be better, after he'd had a chance to calm down.

***

He still hadn't calmed down when we drove to the museum the following morning. He ordered the others to remain behind at the house, much to Willie's frustration. Since he didn't address his order to me, I assumed I was to go with him. When I appeared at the door with my hat and gloves, Matt simply indicated I should go ahead of him.

"How long are you going to remain cross with everyone?" I asked as we drove off.

"I'm not cross," he said, thrusting his hand into his glove. "I simply don't feel like talking much this morning."

I leaned forward and peered closely at his face. The tiny lines around his eyes were certainly more prominent than usual for this time of day. "You didn't sleep very well."

He looked out the window.

"Matt, I know you're worried—"

"Don't, India, or we'll only argue again."

I pressed my lips together and checked my watch. I checked it again six minutes later. "This is excruciating. I think I'd rather argue with you than sit in silence."

He slowly turned from the window to look at me. "You do like to tug on dragons' tails, I'll give you that."

"You're not a dragon."

"Are you sure?" He squeezed his eyes shut and pinched the bridge of his nose.

I reached across the gap to touch his knee and offer support, but second thoughts forced me to withdraw. "I'm sure," was all I said.

"I'm sorry, India." He opened his eyes. "I don't want to argue with you any more, either. It seems that neither of us is going to back down from our position, so we must live with our difference of opinion. At least, *I* must live with being in the position you forced me into."

"With that attitude, you'll make a marvelous husband one day." At his fierce scowl I held up my hands. "A joke."

"I'm glad someone finds my predicament amusing," he grumbled, but not with quite so much ferocity. "Aunt Letitia will not give up trying to marry me off, and I don't have the heart to refuse her altogether."

"You're a good nephew. It must be horrid to be paraded in front of pretty girl after pretty girl. No man would wish to be in your position, forced to endure endless cups of tea with women who can't stop staring at him and think every word that drips from his lips is golden."

That coaxed a lopsided smirk from him. "They are pretty," he said with a theatrical sigh. "Also accomplished, well bred, gently-born, and dull as mud."

"Perhaps they will improve on longer acquaintance." The truth of that stung a little. Miss Glass had presented Matt with girls, not women; but girls grew into women and developed their own minds. As soon as those girls were away from their parents, I had no doubt they'd come into themselves and become people he did want to know better.

"We're here," Matt announced.

The stolid structure of the British Museum always comforted me whenever I ascended the steps and passed between the broad portico columns. With few options for entertainment available to me in my youth, I'd frequented the free museum many times. It had been the medieval manuscripts and ancient objects that intrigued me most, not coins.

We inquired after Mr. Rosemont, the head of the Roman antiquities department, and were given directions to his office. We found it tucked behind the Romans in Britain rooms. A snowy haired gentleman didn't look up from the palm-sized stone he was inspecting through a monocle.

"Put it over there," he ordered with a wave of his hand at the corner of the crowded room.

Artifacts of all shapes and sizes covered every inch of every surface, including much of the floor. Very few women must enter Mr. Rosemont's den; my skirts brushed against statues, large jars and table legs. I had to catch a slender statue of a naked Roman gent when my skirts almost caused it to topple. I flushed red when I saw what part of the statue's anatomy I'd caught hold of.

Mr. Rosemont raised his head upon hearing Matt's chuckle. "Oh. Pardon me, I thought you were the delivery lad." His florid cheeks and cherry red nose brightened more as he stood.

"My name is Matthew Glass," Matt said, "and this is my assistant, Miss Steele. Are you Mr. Rosemont?"

"I am." Mr. Rosemont shook Matt's hand then mine, somewhat limply. "How may I help you?"

"We have a coin we'd like you to inspect. At least, we think it's a coin, although it has been used as a button."

I opened my reticule and fished out the coin. I dropped it onto Mr. Rosemont's dusty palm. He pounced on it like a hungry dog on a bone. He turned it over, clicked his tongue at the shank, and turned it again.

"Dear God."

"What is it?" both Matt and I asked.

"It is a coin. A gold solidus, to be exact, from the late fourth century." He pointed to the image outline with his little finger. "It's somewhat worn, but you can just make out two seated emperors holding a globe between them. Behind them is Victory with outspread wings. The reverse would show the head of Magnus Maximus, commander of Britain, later proclaimed western emperor, but the shank covers it. Bloody sacrilege. Pardon me, Miss Steele."

"That's quite all right," I said. "I understand your frustration. Thank you for enlightening us." I held out my hand to receive the coin, but he didn't pass it to me.

"Do you know what you have here?" he asked.

"You just told us," Matt said. "A gold solidus from the reign of Magnus Maximus."

"Oh yes, but this coin is so much more." Mr. Rosemont's tongue darted out, licking his lips.

I held my breath. Could he feel the magic in it too?

"It's extremely rare. It was minted right here in London, during a brief time when the city was known as Augusta. Maximus's short reign was beset with troubles. The mint closed soon after his death. What a marvelous find."

"Is it valuable?" Matt asked.

Rosemont sighed. "It would be, if it weren't desecrated like this. It may still be worth something if the shank can be removed without damaging the coin. You must tell me where you found it. There could be more."

"A friend gave it to me and asked me to take care of it until such time as he could retrieve it."

"Do you know where he found it? In a field? Beneath the foundations of a building?"

"I don't know."

Rosemont's face fell. "Pity. Could you ask your friend to come here and talk to me about it? I'm very interested in its origins."

"If I can find him. My friend, McArdle, has gone missing, you see. I haven't been able to contact him. He's probably off looking for a hoard or some such thing. He's an archaeologist."

"I know the fellow, but he doesn't belong to the London Archaeological Society." Rosemont's lips pursed. He removed his monocle and handed the coin back to me. "I'd hardly call him an archaeologist or antiquarian at all."

He knew him! It wasn't easy to keep the smile off my face, so I took great interest in returning the coin to my reticule.

"I don't want to offend you, sir," Rosemont said. "He is your friend, after all."

"More of an acquaintance. Just between us," Matt said, leaning closer to Rosemont, "McArdle is a braggart when it comes to archaeology. I try to avoid such conversations with him"

"A braggart. An apt description of the fellow, as is treasure hunter, or simply crackpot. The man has no care for true archaeology, for finding answers to questions about our history. He takes whatever he can of value from a dig and sells it to the highest bidder. Then there is the other matter, depending on whom you believe."

"Other matter?"

"Nothing. I shouldn't have mentioned it. Some who've come across McArdle say he's quite mad. I don't know about that, but he certainly has no morals. He's utterly corrupt." He stopped abruptly, as if embarrassed. He tugged on his waistcoat, leaving dusty handprints on the black cotton. "My apologies, Mr. Glass. I've offended you, after all."

"Not in the least. Tell me, do you know where I can find him? I'd like to return the button. Er, coin. He's not at his Chelsea address."

"I wouldn't have a clue."

"Do you know where he's working?" I asked. "A man like him is always in pursuit of the next treasure."

Rosemont returned to his chair and placed the monocle to his eye. "There are a number of treasures he might be in search of. I don't know him well enough to guess where he could be."

"What about coin hoards?" Matt asked. "Are there any here in London that he might be looking for?"

Rosemont's monocle dropped. It swung on its silver chain before settling against his chest. "A hoard here in London? Unlikely. None have ever been discovered in the city."

"What about archaeological digs? Are there any currently being conducted by members of your society?"

"Two, both overseen by Mr. Young, as they're both in the same street. One is actually complete and is being filled in as we speak. The other is active and occupies most of Mr. Young's attention. But McArdle isn't a member of the society and won't be involved."

Our options were thinning. If we couldn't find McArdle, what should we do next? Where should we go?

Matt, however, had not given up. "Nevertheless, perhaps he has appeared at one of the digs in an observational capacity. Your archaeologist may have seen him. Can you tell me where to find Mr. Young's sites?"

"If you insist. But it may be easier if I show you." Rosemont flipped through a stack of papers on one of the desks until he found what he was looking for. "This map shows the sites here."

I hardly took notice of the area he tapped with his monocle. It was the map itself that intrigued me. It covered the exact same area of the city as Daniel's map. I met Matt's gaze. He'd noticed too.

"Why only this part of London?" Matt asked.

"That's the original walled Roman city, as far as we can tell. The entire wall no longer exists, of course, but we have evidence supporting the theory of its location. There was activity outside the walls, but this area intrigues us most. It was the heart of Roman Londinium."

"Thank you," Matt said. "We'll visit the digs this afternoon."

"I doubt you'll find McArdle there, but you're free to visit. The mosaic floor found at the active site is rather beautiful. Not that McArdle would find it so. He's far more interested in his own search."

"For treasure?" I asked.

"Not just treasure, Miss Steele. For magic."

CHAPTER 10

"Magic?" I whispered. Beside me, Matt had gone quite still.

Mr. Rosemont shook his head and sat at his workbench again. "As I said, the man is barking. He once told a fellow antiquarian that he was searching for evidence of ancient magic in Roman artifacts buried beneath London's streets. That resulted in a great deal of laughter, and he never mentioned it again." The eye behind the monocle gleamed with humor. "Beware of that coin, Miss Steele. It may come alive and perform a jig."

Matt laughed, and I followed suit. His sounded genuine, but mine was hollow to my ears. "I had no idea McArdle believed such nonsense," he said with a shake of his head.

We thanked Rosemont and left. I clutched my reticule to my chest as we hurried past the busts of dead men, down the wide stairs to the vast entrance and out into the sunshine. Being a Monday, the museum was quiet, but even so, I bumped into a gentleman striding up the stairs as we headed down them.

He apologized and I smiled, hardly aware that I did so. Matt's hand on my lower back reminded me to keep walking. He steered me along the path at a steady pace and hailed our carriage.

"India?" Matt's face suddenly appeared before mine, all deep frown lines and worry in his eyes. "You seem dazed."

"I'm quite all right."

Bryce stopped the carriage in front of me and Matt assisted me inside. "You look pale," he said. "I'm taking you straight home."

"Let's go past Worthey's first."

"Very well." He called out instructions to Bryce then settled on the seat beside me. He patted my hand. "India, are you sure you're all right?"

"Yes, of course." I touched my temple. "I felt a little overwhelmed for a moment when Rosemont said that McArdle knows about magic. Do you think that means he's magical himself after all?"

"It's possible."

"Goodness. Magicians seem to be popping up all over London. Not only Daniel and his grandfather, but now McArdle."

"We can't be sure yet if McArdle is a magician, or whether he simply is aware of its existence. But you're right. Mere days ago we knew of only you and Chronos, and the dead Dr. Parsons. Now there's Daniel, his grandfather and possibly McArdle. There's not only medical and time magic, but map and coin magic too."

"And goodness knows what else. Your Dr. Parsons implied there was so much more, that it existed in everything." I pulled my watch out of my reticule and closed it in my fist, as Matt did with his watch several times a day. It didn't glow like his, but it warmed to my touch.

I returned it and pulled out the coin. It wasn't as warm as the watch, but I felt its magic tingling my fingers nevertheless. "I wish I knew what to do to manipulate magic and make it useful." I wished I knew how to fix Matt's watch.

"You'll learn," he said. "We'll find Chronos, and he'll teach you."

"What about another magician teaching me? Perhaps McArdle or Mr. Gibbons."

His fingers curled into balls on his knees. "I don't like the idea of more people finding out about you. It's dangerous enough as it is with the guild suspecting."

"Another magician won't harm me or tattle. Mr. Gibbons doesn't strike me as the type to talk about it at all."

"I don't think it's wise until we know if we can trust him or not." He eyed me sideways. "Is my warning going to be heeded or flouted?"

I sighed. "Heeded. For now." Until such time as the situation with Matt's watch became desperate that I must grasp at straws. "Although if you're not willing to trust Mr. Gibbons, what makes you think Chronos will be any more trustworthy?"

"At least Chronos is a time magician and can certainly help you. We're not sure if Gibbons can. The fewer people who know the better, until we understand the world of magic."

I knew he was right, but I wasn't going to tell him so. He might use it against me later when I changed my mind.

***

Pierre DuPont had not returned to Worthey's factory so we headed to Bucklersbury Street. Turning off industrious Cheapside into the curved street felt like we'd driven into a different world on the brink of transition. It couldn't escape its narrow medieval proportions, but both sides saw new buildings in the process of construction. Some were held up by more scaffold than brick. Inside one of these half-built structures we found a gentleman standing on the edge of a shallow pit in the earthen floor. Two laborers crouched in the pit, carefully scraping soil from the blue, white and red mosaic tiles in the pit floor with trowels.

The gentleman didn't look up until Matt cleared his throat. "It's very beautiful," Matt said. "You're a lucky fellow to be in charge of this dig." He held out his hand. "Good morning, Mr. Young. I'm Matthew Glass, and this is my assistant, Miss Steele. We were told we'd find you here by Mr. Rosemont."

Mr. Young gave Matt's hand a quick shake and hardly even glanced at me. "You must be the fellow considering funding our operation."

"I am." Matt's answer was so swift and confident that no one could have detected the lie.

Mr. Young smiled and took Matt by the elbow. "Well then, you'll want to see our operation. Allow me to show you."

"The mosaic is more colorful than I expected," Matt said, allowing Mr. Young to lead him. "What do you think, Miss Steele?"

I'd been left to trail behind, clearly not important for Mr. Young's purposes. "It's lovely," I said. "How old is it?"

Matt's inclusion of me caused Mr. Young to change tack. He suddenly became quite interested in gaining my good opinion. "At least fifteen hundred years, but we won't know the exact date until we can analyze it further, and we can't do that until we uncover more. Careful, Dyer," he said to one of the workers. "He can be something of a clod," Young whispered to us. "Just think, you're among the first people to see this floor in over a thousand years."

"Remarkable," Matt said.

"The Walbrook stream once flowed near here." Mr. Young pointed to the street outside. "We think it was a key area of Londinium, and as such, this floor could have belonged to a government building, or the villa of an important man—perhaps the governor himself. There's evidence of Roman buildings all along here beneath the current structures." Young's enthusiasm for his work was insatiable, and I found it rather infectious. "Unfortunately, we may never see them. The authorities care little for the ruins. They and the builders are far more interested in progress than history." He sighed. "To think, all of this may be lost if we don't quickly work to save it before the new buildings are erected. We've been given only a short window of time, you see."

"How will you save the floor?" I asked.

"By moving it to museums, tile by tile."

"What a painstaking task."

"Very. We're working as quickly as we can, but it's still slow. Another two or three workmen would help us immeasurably."

"And for that, you need funds."

"We do." Mr. Young jumped down into the pit, about a foot below floor level, and held his hands out to me. "Come down here and experience it for yourself."

I allowed him to assist me down, and Matt followed. Mr. Young gave us tiles to inspect and even wanted Matt to take up a trowel himself, but Matt politely declined. We asked the sort of questions a potential investor might be interested in, and generally made ourselves agreeable. Yet Matt did not broach the subject of McArdle. I tried to make eye contact with him, but he was deep in conversation with Mr. Young. I even checked my watch, frequently, but my hints went unnoticed.

It wasn't until Mr. Young asked why we'd decided to invest in archaeology that Matt finally wound up to it. "I have an acquaintance who likes to dabble in treasure hunting. It was his suggestion that I visit Rosemont to learn about the society and any current digs."

"Treasure hunting?" Mr. Young's brows rose. "How intriguing. What's his name? Perhaps I know him." His keen response was quite different to Mr. Rosemont's.

"McArdle."

Mr. Young's lips parted. His whiskers twitched. "I see."

"You know him?" Matt asked idly.

Mr. Young waved his hand. "In passing." He told the men in the pit to break for ten minutes. They exchanged frowns, then set down their trowels and climbed out of the pit. Once they were out of earshot, Mr. Young turned to Matt with a smile. "Tell me, where is your friend working now?"

"McArdle? That's what I hoped to learn here. Rosemont suggested you might know. Have you seen him of late?"

Mr. Young's smile faded. "Not for some time. He stopped by briefly, took a look around, and left. It would seem my mosaic floor doesn't interest him."

"Why not?"

"I suspect he didn't think there'd be anything of value for him here. I still hold out hopes, however. Where there are archaeological structures, there are often small artifacts to be found, some of them valuable."

"By valuable, do you mean something that helps fill in the gaps of our historical knowledge?" Matt asked.

Mr. Young stroked his whiskers with his thumb and forefinger. "Come now, Mr. Glass, there's no need to beat around the bush with me. Mr. Rosemont may pretend that we're all in this for the greater good, and perhaps *he* is, but the rest of us are more pragmatic. While I do enjoy discovering an ancient wall or floor, I get far more excited when a hoard of coins or item of jewelry is unearthed. Since you are acquainted with McArdle, I have a suspicion that you understand me on this point."

"I understand you very well, Mr. Young. Thank you for your honesty. It seems you, McArdle and I are on the same page."

"It's a pity neither of us know where he's currently digging. His ability to keep his whereabouts a secret never ceases to amaze me. You're the first one who's boldly come to me and asked if I've seen him."

Matt's mouth lifted at the corner. His sly smile matched Mr. Young's. "You think he found something interesting and that's why he's hiding?"

"He does have an uncanny ability to find gold objects, so it wouldn't surprise me."

Gold! Well well. I kept my features schooled but my heart leapt. If McArdle's interest lay in gold and magic, perhaps he was a magical goldsmith rather than an antiquarian.

"Perhaps it's gold infused with magic that he connects with." Matt's words dropped like lead weights. He could not have made a more dramatic statement. Mr. Young went quite still, except for the vein throbbing in his throat above his collar. "Perhaps the magic helps him seek out the gold somehow."

I held my breath and waited to see if Matt's gamble succeeded.

"I see you and McArdle have even more in common." Mr. Young's condescending tone told me exactly what he thought of Matt's theory.

"I'm undecided," Matt said. "While McArdle can be quite convincing, I'm yet to see evidence. And you, Mr. Young? What do you believe?"

"I believe in this." Mr. Young spread his hands out to encompass the mosaic floor around us, the tools and mounds of soil. "I believe in what I can unearth from the ground, whether that be tiles or coins. McArdle's luck in uncovering ancient treasure is simply that— luck. Nothing more. I caution you to read too much into it."

"I'll take your advice on board," Matt said, once again assuming the role of friendly gentleman. "Thank you for your time, but we must be going."

"What of your financial backing?" Mr. Young asked as he climbed out of the pit.

He held his hand out to me but, before I could take it, Matt grasped my waist and lifted me up. I swallowed my yelp of surprise and muttered my thanks instead, albeit so quietly I doubted he heard.

"Your work here is remarkable," he said, standing beside me. "We have nothing like this back home. It would be a shame to see all this built over and destroyed."

"Lamentable."

We said our goodbyes and Matt promised to consider investing in the dig. "Miss Steele will be in touch."

Oh? So I was to be a proper assistant in this matter? Or was it all part of his act?

Matt took my hand and helped me pick my way past the equipment and uneven floor to the waiting carriage. I didn't need his help, but thought it best to keep up the ruse until we were safely inside the coach.

"You're very good," I said, settling my skirts as I sat.

"At anything in particular or simply everything?"

I laughed. "No need to be cocky. At acting a part, and changing yourself and your story as the need arises."

"It's like bluffing in poker," he said with a shrug.

"That must be why I'm no good at it. I lose at poker every time."

"You simply need the practice."

"Or perhaps I'm too honest."

"That's not such a bad thing." He frowned. "Did you just imply that I'm deceitful?"

My face flamed. "I, er…"

He grinned and I wished I had something harder than my reticule to throw at him.

"You must find all this running around tiring," I said, to detract from my hot face.

"A little," he conceded. "I wish we had more to show for our efforts."

"We have much to show. We know Daniel's disappearance is linked to a coin hoard, and to McArdle and the map he made for him."

He eyed me warmly. So warmly that it did nothing to soothe my flushed face. "Thank you, India."

"For what?"

"For being optimistic. You have a way of lifting my mood. And God knows, I can be melancholy these days."

He had good reason to be. It was remarkable he was able to smile at all with the dark cloud of his ill health hanging over his head. "We *will* find Chronos," I said. "I'm sure of it. Mirth will lead him to us on Wednesday after we speak to him. I have a good feeling about it."

"As do I, India. As do I."

We arrived home to find Miss Glass receiving a gentleman caller alone in the drawing room. Bristow's mouth turned down as he announced it, and I suspected he disliked the idea of a lady, even one of Miss Glass's age, being alone with a man.

"Who is it, I wonder," Matt said, his lips twitching. "A long-term admirer coming out of the woodwork now that she's free from her brother's clutches?"

"An American, sir, by the name of Payne. Sheriff Payne."

CHAPTER 11

Matt dropped the hat he'd been in the midst of handing to Bristow and sprinted up the stairs, taking two at a time. I hurried after him, lifting my skirts well above my ankles. I was a fair distance behind, however, and arrived in the drawing room just in time to see Matt facing off against the stranger, his fist scrunched in the man's shirt at his collar. So this was the corrupt lawman who'd followed Matt from America, accused him of terrible crimes across several states, and wanted him locked away—or dead.

And he was calmly drinking tea and eating cake with Matt's aunt in her home, smiling back at Matt like the cat that got the cream. I didn't blame Matt for wanting to throttle him.

"Matthew!" Miss Glass's horrified shriek pierced the air, but didn't stop Matt from shouting at the fellow whose shirt suffered in his grip.

He shook Payne violently. "How dare you come here!"

Payne simply kept his hands raised. A sickly smile sheltered beneath his moustache and his hazel eyes gleamed with amusement. He was younger than I expected, perhaps in his mid-thirties; he was tall and lean with a narrow face and high forehead. His slicked back hair and tailored striped suit pegged him as a fashionable city gentleman, not a Wild West sheriff, but the suit looked new so perhaps he'd ordered it as soon as he arrived in London.

"Come now, Glass, this is a free country, isn't it?" Payne drawled in a thick American accent. "Can't a man drink tea with a pretty lady?" He turned his oily smile onto Miss Glass and then me. No woman in her right mind would consider the fellow charming, despite his words. Not even Miss Glass seemed flattered. She looked shocked to her very prim toes.

Matt shoved him toward the door. "Get out! You're not welcome here."

"Matthew!" Miss Glass pressed her fingers to her lips.

I put my arm around her shoulders, and she shrank into me.

"India," she whispered. "What's he doing? Why is Matthew hurting that fellow?"

"He's not a good man," I told her. "Matt will see him out and we'll explain."

Payne smirked. "Got your little wag-tail believing your tall tales too, Glass?"

Matt's fist punched the smirk off Payne's face.

Miss Glass screamed and covered her face.

"Stop, Matt!" I cried. "You're frightening your aunt."

With a snarl, Matt bundled Payne through the door, half marching him, half pushing. Their retreating footsteps didn't quite hide Payne's low chuckle. He had rattled Matt and he knew it. He relished it, perhaps even thrived on the knowledge. I'd known the man a mere minute, and already I didn't like him.

"Miss Glass," I said, "are you all right?"

"I think so." She dabbed at her eyes and patted her hair. "Why did Matthew act like that? That fellow claimed to be a friend of his from America."

"He's not a friend," was all I said. It wasn't my place to tell her, nor did I think it wise to tell her everything. "If he comes here again, have Bristow throw him out."

The front door slammed shut, and Matt returned a moment later. He smoothed down the wayward strands of his hair and tugged on his cuffs. "Aunt, that was a man known as Payne. He...doesn't like me." He shot me a warning look.

I acknowledged it with a slight nod.

"I've warned Bristow not to let him in if he turns up again," Matt said. "But I suspect he won't."

Miss Glass rubbed her arms. "If I'd known he was no good, I wouldn't have taken tea with him. If he's not your friend, Matthew, then he's not mine either." She sounded defiant, but I could still feel her trembles.

Matt sighed heavily. "It's not your fault, Aunt. I'm sorry I scared you."

Polly arrived and took her mistress in hand. Matt must have asked her to collect his aunt and see to her comfort in her rooms. It was good of him to think of her welfare even as he was bundling out an intruder.

"Are you all right?" I asked Matt once Polly and Miss Glass were out of earshot.

"That ought to be my question," he said, hiking up his trouser legs and taking a seat.

"I'm made of sterner stuff than your aunt, and it's not me he wants to send to jail."

He leaned forward, elbows on his knees, and dragged a hand through his hair, messing it up all over again. I half rose before remembering myself and sitting again.

No, I should get up. Matt was my friend and he needed comforting, propriety be damned.

I stood by his chair, unsure where to put my hand. While I wanted to touch his head or massage his neck, I settled it on his shoulder where the touch wasn't so intimate. Or so I thought. It turned out not to be a safe place at all.

He glanced up at me, his eyes smoky. All the anger had disappeared from them, but they were filled with tension and exhaustion. He needed his watch. Hardly aware of my own actions, I undid his jacket button and slipped my hand inside. His body's heat warmed me, his exotic spicy scent filled my nostrils. Being so close to him thrilled me, but my reaction scared me too. I felt so unlike myself. My head clouded with a kind of fog that made it impossible to think clearly, and my heart danced erratically in my chest.

He stared at me from beneath lowered lashes. His throat moved with his swallow. "India," he whispered, his breath brushing my lips.

My fingers found the chain at his waistcoat. I tugged the watch out of the pocket and pressed it into his hand. The magical glow crept along his fingers, across his hand and up into his cuff. It emerged seconds later at his throat and finally spread over his face and disappeared into his hair. He closed his eyes and sucked in a deep breath.

I returned to the sofa and watched, as fascinated as I was afraid. Afraid *for* him. What if the magic stopped working one day?

A moment later he opened his eyes and pocketed the watch. Neither of us spoke for almost an entire minute, and nor did he meet my gaze. I couldn't begin to know the direction of his thoughts. Most likely it was on the matter of Payne, and not me, as was only right for a man with so many responsibilities as well as problems.

"He came here to rattle you," I finally said. "I think he wants you to be aware that he knows where you live."

"I think you're right. It's precisely the sort of thing he'd do. He's too clever to attempt to have me arrested in an unfamiliar city where I have influential family."

"You say clever, I say cowardly."

"He came here, right under my nose, knowing I would show up sooner or later. He's not a coward, India. He's as brazen as they come."

"Perhaps."

He gave me a sideways glance. "Thank you for stopping me when you did. If you hadn't..."

"It was your aunt's influence, not mine. I might have let you strangle the man if she hadn't been present."

He gave a half-hearted smile. "You don't even know him."

"You've painted a picture of a cruel, corrupt man. That's enough for me."

"Considering you hardly know me, you're surprisingly loyal."

I felt somewhat put out. I thought I did know him—quite well, as it happened. "You are my employer," I said snippily.

He blinked, as if my barb hit its mark. "Friends," he corrected. "We're friends, India."

"Even though I hardly know you?"

His smile turned genuine. "Consider me chastised." He gave a deep nod then stifled a yawn.

"Have a rest, Matt. You need it." At his protest, I added, "Payne won't came back, not today. You said so yourself. He made his point. Stop worrying and rest."

"Yes, ma'am."

"Oh, and one more thing," I said as he stood. "What's a wag-tail?"

"Pardon?"

"Payne called me a wag-tail. At least, I think he was referring to me."

His gaze shifted from my face to my shoulder. "It's a type of bird."

"Yes, but is that all?"

"As far as I am aware." He yawned and stretched. "I really need to rest now."

I watched him go, now quite sure that wag-tail meant something other than a type of bird.

***

Cyclops, Duke and Willie all returned to the house for dinner. Miss Glass ate in her rooms, and Matt dismissed Bristow after he carried the dishes into the dining room. I braced myself for their reactions as he told them Payne had visited.

"What!" Willie exploded, pushing to her feet so hard the cutlery rattled. "That low-down mudsill. Where's he staying? I'll gut him like the dirty hog he is."

"Willie," Duke snapped. "Sit down. You ain't helping."

"I don't know where he is," Matt assured her. "And if I did, it would do no good. There's nothing we can do until he commits a crime."

"He has committed crimes!"

"None of which we can pin on him."

She swore liberally and kicked her chair, then kicked it again until it tipped backward. Without even a pause for breath, her colorful tirade continued as she stomped from one end of the dining room to the other.

"Willie!" Matt barked. "Unless you want my aunt coming in here in a panic, I suggest you calm down."

She stopped in front of the sideboard, fists at her sides, body heaving with her breaths. "I hate him," she snarled.

"We all do," Duke said. "But we don't—"

Matt put up his hand and shook his head. Duke dutifully left his sentence unfinished. "The only thing we can do is remain vigilant," Matt told her. "He'll show his hand sooner or later."

She spun round to face us. "It'll be too late by then. We shouldn't be sitting here, waiting for him to make the first move. It'll be too late by the time he lets us know what he's up to. Mark my words, Matt, you'll regret doing nothing."

Matt lowered his gaze to the table. It was Cyclops who spoke in his soothing, resonant voice. "We're stretched too thin as it is. In two days' time, Matt has to be at the bank to see if he recognizes Mirth. In the meantime, you and Duke are watching Worthey's factory, and Matt, India and I are looking for Daniel."

"Forget Daniel," she muttered, all the bluster gone from her sails. She picked up her chair and sat heavily. "I don't think finding him will lead us to Chronos after all."

"We can't forget him," Matt said. "Don't suggest it again. Understand?"

She stabbed the slice of roast beef with her fork and shoved it in her mouth. She nodded but negated it with a defiant look.

"Did you learn anything today?" Cyclops asked Matt.

We told them about our visits to the museum and the Bucklersbury dig, and our new theory about McArdle possibly being a goldsmith magician on the hunt for a hoard of Roman coins. "The button he left behind in his rented rooms is indeed a coin," Matt said. "It holds some magic."

"We think he commissioned Daniel to make a map of a Roman coin hoard, hidden somewhere in London," I said.

"But if Daniel made the map showing the location based on McArdle's information, doesn't that mean McArdle knows where the hoard is?" Duke asked.

"We're not sure why he commissioned the map."

"I wonder if all the coins in the hoard are magical," Cyclops said. "Or just the one."

"What does a magical goldsmith *do*?" Willie asked. She seemed to have calmed down again, thank goodness. "What's the point of magic gold unless it multiplies itself? Now *that* would be worth kidnapping someone for." At everyone's admonishing looks, she merely shrugged. "It were a joke."

"We won't know until we speak to McArdle," I said. "Or Daniel."

"The problem now is what do we do next?" Matt said to no one in particular. "We seem to have come to a dead end."

"I have news about Onslow that might answer that," Cyclops announced as he helped himself to more beef.

"Has he been going somewhere?" Willie asked. "Somewhere that he might be keeping Daniel?"

Cyclops shook his head. "Onslow hasn't been anywhere I wouldn't expect him to go. If he's hiding Daniel then someone else is taking supplies to him. Onslow's been home, to his shop, and the guild hall, but that's it."

"Have you looked around inside the house and shop?" Matt asked.

"How would he get inside?" I asked. When no one answered, I looked to Cyclops. "Well?"

Cyclops shifted his weight. "The housekeeper let me in, thinking I were the gas inspector."

"There are no such things as gas inspectors."

"Good thing not everyone's as bright as you, India, or we'd never achieve anything."

Matt chuckled. "And? What did you see?"

"Nothing," Cyclops said. "No hidden doors, false walls, nothing. If Onslow kidnapped Daniel, he's not keeping him in the house or shop."

"So you learned nothing today," Willie said, pushing her plate away and folding her arms.

"I haven't finished," Cyclops told her. "I found out that Onslow is meeting the secretive fellow again tomorrow at the guild. His name is Hallam, and he's someone's man of business. I don't know whose," he added when Willie opened her mouth. "Want me to listen in during their meeting?"

"I'll do it," Matt said. "I've nothing better to do at the moment."

"How?" I asked. "Onslow knows you as Prescott."

"Then I'll be Prescott, a somewhat bumbling fool who'll happen to walk in on Onslow and Hallam talking."

"And then?"

"And then I'll think of something."

I narrowed my gaze at him. "Your plan contains a few flaws."

Matt stood and lifted the lid on the silver platter in the center of the table. His face brightened. "Flummery! One of my favorite English desserts."

"You're deliberately changing the subject."

He scooped up some flummery with a spoon and handed it to me in a bowl. "Very astute, India. Anyone else for flummery?"

Duke held out an empty bowl. "Duffield was at the hall today too. I didn't speak to him but his new apprentice were talkative."

"Ronald Hogarth?" Matt spooned a generous amount of yellow flummery into the bowl. "Did he say anything of importance?"

"Not really. He told us servants how he's glad to be working for Duffield now. He liked Onslow, but the man wasn't going anywhere, and he wanted an employer who could teach him how to become master of the guild one day."

"That's rather cold of him," I said, "considering it took Daniel's disappearance to make the position available. Did he mention Daniel at all?"

"Aye. Called him precocious and avaricious."

"Them's big words for an apprentice," Duke said.

"For you too," Willie spat.

"Hogarth's whip smart," Cyclops said. "I'll wager he'll make it to guild master, one day."

"So he doesn't like Daniel," Matt said thoughtfully, pushing the flummery around his bowl with a spoon. "Perhaps he wanted him removed so he could take his place as Duffield's apprentice."

"Maybe," Cyclops said. "But he's not the only one who didn't like Daniel. None of the servants thought much of him. He lorded it over them, they said, like he was someone special."

"He was," Matt said. "Is. He's a magician."

"Ain't no reason to think himself better than the rest of us," Duke said. "India ain't like that."

"Perhaps I would be if I were a nineteen year-old lad who knew how to wield his magic," I said. "Something he clearly did, if McArdle commissioned a map from him. Yet Daniel's family didn't teach him."

Cyclops finished his flummery and inspected the remainder on the platter. "According to one of the guild's footmen, Daniel didn't get along with anyone, including his own master. He used to tell Duffield he was a fool, and claimed he was a better mapmaker than him and all the rest of them."

"That wouldn't go down well," Duke said. "Not a wise move either, considering magicians are feared."

"It's likely he didn't understand the implications of his boasts," I said with a shake of my head. "If only his grandfather had explained about the dangers of being openly magical. Instead, someone like McArdle breaks the news to Daniel then uses him to create a magical map, without warning him about the consequences."

Cyclops shook his head as he tucked into his second helping of dessert. "Daniel's boasts came *before* he met McArdle. He was boastful from the beginning of his apprenticeship, but he only met McArdle a few weeks ago."

"So he's a little turd," Willie said on a sigh. "Do we really want to—" She clamped her mouth shut upon a glare from Matt.

"Did Hogarth say anything else of importance?" I asked.

"Not much," Cyclops said. "I asked him what he'll do when Daniel gets back. He reckons he'll wait and see. Maybe Daniel won't want to be Duffield's apprentice again, he said."

We finished dinner and withdrew to the sitting room, the smaller and cozier of the two reception rooms. Matt summoned Polly and asked after his aunt. Polly said she was sitting up in bed, too tired to join us but not yet asleep.

"I'll spend a few minutes with her." He retrieved two decks of cards from the drawer in the card table and tossed one to Duke and held onto the other.

After he left, I sat at the card table with Duke and Cyclops. Willie refused to join us and closed her eyes in the chair by the fire.

"You'd rather sleep than play?" Duke asked her, shuffling the deck.

"I ain't playing for matches," she shot back without opening her eyes. "I got my dignity."

Duke dealt, and I looked at my hand. I had two picture cards but nothing to make up a good poker hand. I threw in my cards.

"You giving in already?" Cyclops asked.

"I have a question," I said, eyeing the door. "What's a wag-tail?"

"A bird," Cyclops said.

"Does it have another meaning in America?"

Willie chuckled quietly in her chair. "Go on. Tell her."

Cyclops studied his hand hard. "I can't remember."

I looked at Duke, but he too took great interest in his cards.

"Willie?" I asked. "I know you'll tell me."

She opened her eyes and plucked her glass of brandy off the table beside her. "Why d'you want to know?"

"Sheriff Payne called me Matt's wag-tail."

Duke's face flamed but he didn't look up from his cards.

"You can't figure it out?" Willie asked, taking a sip.

I held her gaze. "Payne thinks I'm Matt's mistress, doesn't he?"

"That's the polite word. Telling you the un-polite ones would make a straight-laced Englishwoman like you blush."

"Impolite," Duke corrected.

"I am not straight-laced," I said, feeling my spine stiffen without intending it to.

Willie's smirk widened. "You're as slab-sided as a preacher's daughter."

"Speaking of Payne," Duke cut in before I could think of anything witty to throw back at her. "Willie, don't do anything about him."

Her face hardened and her brows crashed. She looked like she would throw her glass at him. "Meaning?"

"Matt has enough to worry about without you haring off after Payne."

"I'm aware of Matt's problems, so you can shut your big bazoo, Duke."

Matt strolled in and headed straight for the sideboard. "I leave for one moment and you start bickering." He tossed the deck of cards down and poured himself a brandy. "Aunt Letitia is asleep, and I'm not ready to retire. Who's up for a game of poker? Or would you two rather kiss and make up?"

Willie turned away and drained her glass. Duke held his cards low, almost under the table. The angle meant he had to press his chin to his chest so he could see them. Neither Willie nor Duke managed to hide their blushes.

***

Matt wanted me to join him at the Mapmakers' Guild hall to spy on Onslow and Hallam's meeting. I thought it odd, at first. Wouldn't I just be in the way? But he explained that two people acting a role was more believable, particularly when one was a woman.

"Gentlemen believe ladies," he said. "They don't expect them to lie to their faces. Some men are gullible when it comes to gently-bred women. They believe them all to be pure and innocent."

"Are you gullible with regard to gently-bred women?" I asked as I pulled on my gloves in the entrance hall.

"Very," he said with that lopsided smile I liked immensely. "It's my greatest weakness."

"I'd wager it's your greatest asset; as far as the ladies are concerned, I mean."

His smile turned devilish.

Bristow opened the front door just as a man approached along the pavement. He paused, one foot on the lowest step. He dressed like a gentleman, albeit without a hat, but sported an untrimmed beard and scraggly hair.

"Good morning, sir, madam," he said.

"Good morning," Matt said. "May I help you?"

"That depends." The man glanced to the road where Bryce waited with the brougham, then to Bristow standing behind us in the doorway. Finally, his gaze settled on me. Or, rather, my reticule. He smiled. I didn't trust it.

Matt drew me behind him. "State your name and business."

"I don't know whether you are Mr. Glass and Miss Steel or Mr. and Mrs. Prescott, and I don't really care. All I want is what's mine."

"I have nothing of yours."

"Yes, sir, you do. Mrs. Dawson told me she gave my button to Mr. and Mrs. Prescott, and Rosemont said two people by the name of Glass and Steele brought a button made from a Roman coin to him."

I gasped.

"McArdle." Matt sounded as stunned as I felt. "We've been looking for you."

CHAPTER 12

"My coin, please," McArdle said.

Matt stepped down the first step, but McArdle put up his hand to stay him. Behind him, the horse moved, rattling the bridle and rocking the carriage. Bryce watched on, curious.

"Come no further." McArdle pointed at me. "I want her to hand it over to me. Slowly."

"You have nothing to fear from us," Matt said. "We'll give you back your coin, but we need some answers first."

I stepped forward and opened the drawstring of my reticule but didn't remove the coin. Now that I was closer, I could see the creases in McArdle's clothing and smell his unwashed scent. His greasy blond hair hung in clumps and grime rimmed his limp collar. He'd been sleeping rough, perhaps, but why?

"I'm not answering your questions," he said.

"Why not?" Matt asked with genuine affront. "We're simply looking for Daniel Gibbons."

McArdle showed no surprise. "What do you want with him?"

"His family asked me to find him. They're extremely worried about him. You don't know where he is?"

"No."

Matt inched forward, but McArdle put up his hand again. "No further. Just her."

Matt drew in a frustrated breath. "If we work together, we can find him. I know we can. Tell us about the map Daniel made for you."

"It's just a map," McArdle said, watching Matt carefully. "I paid for it, and it's mine. Do you know where it is?"

"No," Matt lied. He glanced over his shoulder. "That will be all, Bristow."

"Very good, sir." The butler retreated inside along with the footman and closed the door.

"Hand over my bloody coin," McArdle snarled. "Don't test me. It's been a trying few days looking for you two, and my patience is stretched thin. If I hadn't given up and decided to spend some time in the Roman room at the museum, I wouldn't have spoken to Rosemont and learned that I should be looking for an American named Glass and not an American named Prescott."

"I understand your frustration." Matt's own frustration seemed to have vanished, replaced with a calmly soothing tone that I'd heard Cyclops use with the horses. "And we're sorry for any problems we've caused you, but I must insist that we speak to you about Daniel before we hand the coin over. He's just nineteen. We have to find him."

"Don't have any sympathy for the little blighter. He might be only nineteen, but he's as crooked as a swindler twice his age. He made me a map then wouldn't give it to me. I spent years looking for someone who could produce that map. Years! And when I finally do find him, he refuses to give it to me then disappears. When I find him, I'll kill him." Two spots of color appeared on his cheeks and his eyes flashed.

"You want to find him just as much as we do," Matt said. "If we work together—"

"I work alone."

"We don't want your coin hoard, Mr. McArdle," I said.

He blinked at me. Was he surprised that we knew that much?

"We just want to find Daniel."

"So do I," he growled. "But I'll find him on my own. I'm not sharing with anyone. Now, give me the coin or I'll take it."

Matt put up his hands in surrender. "We know it's a magical map," he said taking a slow step down.

McArdle's gaze darted to the five steps between them. He licked his top lip. "I don't know what you mean," he said, not sounding in the least convincing.

"Does it show the location of the magical coin hoard?"

McArdle's nostrils flared.

Matt took another slow step forward. He'd better be prepared to fight because McArdle didn't back away. He looked determined to get his coin. "We know Daniel is a magical mapmaker," Matt went on when he didn't get an answer, "just like we know you're a goldsmith magician—"

McArdle flipped back his jacket and drew a small pistol from his trouser waistband. "I warned you. Give me my coin. *Now!*" He used his jacket to shield the pistol, which he pointed at me.

"Don't shoot." Matt put up a hand to halt Bryce as much as McArdle. The coachman had risen from his perch. "India will give it to you."

I reached into the reticule and fished for the coin. I held it out to McArdle but he had to come closer to take it.

"Bring it to me, Miss Steele," he said.

"No." Matt put out his hand. "I'll take it to you."

"She will."

The muscles in Matt's jaw pulsed. I stepped past him and handed McArdle the coin. He backed down to the bottom step.

I rejoined Matt. His hand closed around mine, anchoring me to his side and a little behind him. "Damn it, man," he growled at the retreating figure. "We can find Daniel together if you tell me what you know."

"I don't know anything, that's the whole bloody problem. And nor, I wager, do you." He held up the coin. The gold glinted in the sunshine. "At least I can begin again now." He pocketed the coin and slipped the gun back down his trouser band. He turned and ran.

A moment later, he rounded the corner and disappeared from sight. Matt stalked down the steps, shook his head, then returned to me.

"Are you all right, India?"

I felt remarkably calm, considering I'd just had a gun pointed at me. Perhaps that was because I didn't think McArdle was a killer. Avaricious, yes, but not a murderer.

Matt, however, looked furious. It must gall him that he'd not been able to stop McArdle from drawing his weapon. Or perhaps he hated losing the coin.

"I'm fine, Matt. Really. There's no need to worry."

He let me go and indicated the front door with a nod. "Would you like to go back inside?"

"Certainly not. I'm hardly going to wilt after a little danger."

"I wouldn't call it little. But if you insist."

"I do."

"Then we'll continue to the guild, right after I tell Bristow not to allow McArdle into the house."

"Our list of banned people is growing at a rapid rate."

He rejoined me in the carriage a moment later, looking like he regretted not punching McArdle when he had the chance. "At least we still have the map," I said, trying to reassure him.

"It may not have been the right thing to keep it from him. We can't use it, but he possibly can."

"But will he use it to find Daniel? It's more likely he would have run off with it, like he did the coin, leaving us with nothing."

His face lifted a little. "You always know the right thing to say."

"Not always. For example, telling you that McArdle doesn't seem to know where Daniel is won't make you feel any better."

"It doesn't make me feel worse." He sighed. "If McArdle doesn't know, that puts us back where we began, less one suspect, of course."

"Speaking of beginnings, what do you think McArdle meant when he said he can begin again now?"

He shrugged. "He can get another map made, perhaps."

"Using the coin?"

"Quite possibly. It would explain why he wanted it so badly. The coin itself may have some value if he could remove the shank, but if it led him to the rest of the hoard, it would be priceless."

***

The guild's footman informed us that Mr. Onslow was in a meeting, as we knew he would. What we didn't expect was the presence of Mr. Duffield and Ronald Hogarth, his apprentice.

"Mr. Prescott," Mr. Duffield said, shaking hands with Matt. "And Mrs. Prescott, too. How intriguing to find you both here."

Matt didn't so much as hesitate in his greeting, nor did he let on in any way that Duffield's presence had scuttled his plans. Yet I knew everything needed to change now. There would be no sneaking about while Duffield remained.

"How pleasant to see you here," Matt said. "And quite unexpected. Are you on your way out?"

"Soon. This is my new apprentice, Hogarth."

The youth stepped forward. "We've met. Nice to see you again, sir, ma'am. Is it Mr. Onslow you're here for?"

"Yes, but apparently he's in a meeting."

"Is there something I can help you with?" Mr. Duffield asked. "Is it something to do with the guild, or maps?"

"Mr. Duffield's an excellent mapmaker," Hogarth said, swelling his chest. "Much better than Mr. Onslow."

"Thank you, Ronald," Mr. Duffield said tightly. "Perhaps if you could go ahead of me back to the shop. I'll speak with Mr. Prescott and return soon."

"It's quite all right if you need to go," Matt said. "I'll admire your excellent globe as I wait for Onslow." He indicated the impressive bronze globe held up by the statue of the old man.

"Perhaps you'll be more comfortable in the sitting room. I'll join you until Mr. Onslow is free."

"It's quite all right."

"I insist. Ronald, ask someone to bring in tea on your way out."

The apprentice looked as if he'd protest, but must have thought better of it. He gave a curt nod to us and left.

Duffield blew out a breath and indicated the door leading to the sitting room. "This way. Refreshments will be served shortly."

Clearly he didn't want us waiting alone. Surely he didn't suspect our true reason for being there? As far as he knew, we were Mr. and Mrs. Prescott, adventurers on our way to India. I hoped.

"Now, tell me," he said, as we sat. "Is it another map you're after? From Onslow?"

Matt nodded. "We didn't know the location of his shop, so we came here instead."

"Well." Duffield glanced at the door then leaned in toward us. "I don't wish to speak ill of my colleague, but *my* maps have won awards." He indicated the walls where framed maps of all sizes and colors filled the spaces. "Many of these are mine. Few are his."

"I'm familiar with your work," Matt said with an agreeable smile. "I was simply curious to see that of another. Do you know how long Mr. Onslow will be?"

"It could be an age."

"Why? Is he meeting with the queen's agent?" Matt laughed.

Duffield laughed too. "No one like that, I'm sure. I would recognize anyone important."

So he didn't know who Onslow was meeting, and nor did it look like he was going anywhere. I tried to catch Matt's attention but he wasn't looking at me.

"Mr. Duffield," I said, "can you point me in the direction of the ladies' cloak room?"

Matt turned slowly to me. He glared at me through narrowed eyes. He'd guessed what I was about to do and didn't like it.

"Er, uh, yes, of course. It's up one flight and to the right."

I hurried out of the sitting room before I changed my mind, or Matt could suggest we leave. I didn't want to leave. I wanted answers and to have something to show for our visit. As Matt said, gentlemen believed ladies, mostly. If someone stumbled upon me, I'd pretend to be lost.

I traversed the corridor on the first floor, listening at closed doors for voices. Greeted with silence, I returned to the staircase. Footsteps approached, like someone taking two steps at a time. I held my breath, smoothed down my skirts and prepared my excuse.

I let out my breath upon seeing Cyclops, dressed in his footman's livery.

"There you are," he whispered, sounding as relieved as I felt. "I delivered tea and saw you weren't with Matt. He indicated I should help you."

"How did he do that?"

"He twitched an eyebrow. Come with me. I know where Onslow is."

We headed up to the next level and crept quietly to a closed door. He pressed his ear to it, so I did too. I could make out male voices, but not what they said. I needed to get closer.

I grasped the doorknob, but Cyclops caught my hand. He shook his head. I nodded and plucked his hand off mine. He flattened his lips and stepped away.

I opened the door as quietly as possible and caught Onslow saying, "I can get more."

"How?" asked the other man who must be Hallam. "Do you know the maker?"

Onslow didn't answer. "Is someone there?

I opened the door fully and gasped. "Oh, I am sorry. Please forgive me, gentlemen, I was looking for..." I touched my cheek, wishing I could blush on cue. "I'll be on my way."

"Mrs. Prescott, isn't it?" Onslow came around the desk, staring at me as if he couldn't believe his eyes. "I remember you. What are you doing here?"

"My husband and I came to see you, but Mr. Duffield said you were in a meeting. I felt a little faint and came looking for the cloak room. It would seem I haven't found it."

"It's down a level."

"Thank you. I am very sorry to interrupt." I touched my temple and winced.

"Are you all right?"

"I think I need to sit down. But I don't want to intrude."

Hallam stood and buttoned up his jacket. "I was just leaving anyway. Our business is concluded." The slender, bespectacled man gave Onslow a nod.

Onslow nodded back then took my arm and steered me to the chair Hallam had vacated. The blue ledger that he usually held close to his chest lay open on the desk. "Water, Mrs. Prescott?"

"Yes, thank you."

He poured me a glass from the jug on the bookshelf. I took it but my shaking hand caused some water to spill. It wasn't all an act. I felt quite nervous, alone with a suspect. Cyclops had disappeared.

"Did you say Duffield is with your husband?" Onslow asked.

"Yes," I said, faintly. "They're in the sitting room. Mr. Duffield is trying to convince Mr. Prescott that he's the better mapmaker."

The inner corner of Onslow's drooping eyelid twitched. "I'll fetch your husband for you, madam. In the meantime, rest here." He looked to the ledger on the other side of the desk.

I whimpered loudly and drooped into the chair, doing my best impression of an attack of the vapors.

"Mrs. Prescott!" He took my hand and patted it. "Are you all right?"

"Hurry," I whispered.

He ran out of the office. As soon as he was gone, I rounded the desk and scanned the ledger page. It was an account book, filled with figures that meant nothing to me. Damn. Surely there had to be something useful somewhere in it. I flipped through the pages, but it seemed to be only a list of expenses and receipts. None of the expenses seemed unusual for a guild, and all the receipts appeared to be listed as DUES with a member's name beside them.

"Found anything?"

I almost jumped out of my skin, even though I recognized Cyclops's voice. He popped his head around the door, his one good eye gleaming. He was enjoying this adventure.

"Not yet."

"I'll tap on the wall when someone approaches." He disappeared again.

I tracked my finger down the list of names in the Receipts column, smudging the final one. The ink was fresh. Lord Coyle, the name read, not Mr. Hallam. The amount of fifteen pounds written against the name was also fresh. I scanned the other entries, going backward through the ledger. There were two others against Lord Coyle's name, one for twenty pounds, the other for another payment of fifteen. Could Hallam be the man of business for Lord Coyle?

I returned the ledger to the precise position on the desk as I'd found it, and quickly looked through the pile of papers. Nothing. I opened the first drawer and smiled. A wad of bank notes sat on the top, tied together with string. I counted out fifteen pounds.

Onslow hadn't had a chance to put them in a safer place yet.

I returned the money to the drawer just as Cyclops tapped the wall. I had ample time to return to my chair and resume the role of fainting female.

"My dear," Matt said upon entering. "Are you all right? Mr. Onslow said you had a turn." He crouched by my chair and took my hands in his. His gaze was completely without guile and filled with deep concern.

"I...I felt quite overcome," I said weakly.

"I've sent the footman to fetch a cool cloth," said Mr. Duffield, standing behind Matt.

Mr. Onslow slipped past them both and opened his top drawer. He reached in and a moment later, closed the drawer again. Relief made him smile. He must have regretted his hasty exit, leaving me with his money.

"Thank you," I said, "but I feel a little better. Mr. Prescott, is it all right if we leave now?"

"Of course, my dear. Our business can wait."

"Oh," Mr. Duffield and Mr. Onslow both sounded disappointed.

"It wasn't urgent," Matt told them. "I'll come back another time."

"To see me," Mr. Onslow said.

Mr. Duffield moved between Matt and Mr. Onslow. "Or me." He held out his hand, and Matt shook it. He shot Onslow a triumphant look.

With a flattening of his lips, Onslow approached me. He assisted me to my feet. "Dear Mrs. Prescott, I do hope you'll feel better soon. You gave me quite a scare."

"Yes," Matt growled. "You did." He took my elbow and with his other hand on my lower back, steered me out and down the stairs.

He didn't let me go until I was inside the brougham, nor did his scowl ease. "Do not go against our plans again."

I waved off his concern. "They weren't set in stone."

"Even so—"

"Even so, I had some success, therefore you can't admonish me."

His scowl deepened.

I cleared my throat. "I'll tell you what I found, shall I?" When he didn't respond, I pushed on. "I think Hallam works for Lord Coyle."

"Who's he?"

"I don't know. There were three entries against his name in Onslow's ledger." I told him about the payment amounts and finding fifteen pounds in bank notes in the drawer. "Hallam had just paid Onslow on behalf of Coyle."

"For what?"

"The entry was simply listed as dues, but the amount paid was far more than every other dues payment. I overheard Onslow telling Hallam he could get more. More maps, perhaps. Then Hallam asked how. He specifically said, 'Do you know the maker?' Those were his *exact* words, Matt. I think it means mapmaker, and I wondered if he could be referring to magical maps and a magician mapmaker. If so, then Onslow must have kidnapped Daniel. He's using him to create magic maps on demand then selling the maps to exclusive customers."

Matt's brow remained furrowed. He didn't seem to be considering my theory at all. Did he not trust that I'd heard what I'd heard? Did he only believe what he saw and heard himself?

"Aren't you going to congratulate me?" I asked, my tone clipped. "Thank me?"

"You'll be lucky if I take you out with me again."

Good lord, he was still concerned that I could have got myself into trouble. "I did a marvelous job, and you know it. You're just jealous that I had all the fun while you were left with the dull part of the plan."

"None of that was part of my plan," he growled. "And you consider that fun?"

"No, not really." I showed him my gloved hands. They still shook. "My nerves were quite shredded there, for a while. They're still a little taut, but now that it's over, I feel invigorated."

He rolled his eyes to the cabin ceiling. "What have I created?"

I smiled. "Don't worry, I won't make a habit of it."

"See that you don't."

"Unless it's necessary."

He sighed.

"The problem is, Cyclops didn't find Onslow's movements suspicious, nor did he find a hidden room where Daniel could be kept," I said. "Our theory still contains some holes."

"It does. Cyclops will continue to follow him, but perhaps we should check if Onslow is indeed selling magical maps or if it is something else entirely."

"We could investigate the connection to Lord Coyle. Perhaps he'll be willing to tell us what he purchased from Onslow. I wonder if your aunt knows him."

***

Miss Glass did indeed know of him, although she'd never met him. "Oh yes," she said, accepting the cup of tea I handed to her after lunch. Matt went to his room to rest upon our return, so I'd waited until he joined us in the sitting room before asking about Coyle. "Intriguing fellow, by all accounts," she told me.

"Where does he live?" Matt asked.

"His estate is in Oxfordshire. Why?"

"I have some business to conduct with him."

She paused, the teacup at her lips. "Nothing underhanded, I hope?"

Matt and I both frowned. "Why would you think that?" he asked. "My affairs are all above board."

"I know *yours* are, Matthew. Lord Coyle, however..." She set the teacup down in the saucer without drinking. "I thought you might have been caught up in something with him that you couldn't get out of. I'm glad I'm wrong."

"What sort of thing is Coyle involved in?"

"It's all gossip, and I don't like to spread it about. Nasty stuff." She picked up her cup once again and sipped.

"Aunt," he said through a clenched jaw.

"You wouldn't want Matt to trust this Lord Coyle when you could have prevented him from making a mistake, would you?" I asked.

"When you put it like that." Miss Glass handed her teacup and saucer to me, and I placed them on the table. "I've never met him. He's not part of my set, or your Uncle Richard's. He's only a little younger than me, rich as Croesus, and is an earl, no less. Yet he's unwed."

Matt and I glanced at one another. "Is that his crime?" Matt asked.

"Good lord, no. It may be odd, but it's not illegal, more's the pity. I was just telling you a little about him so you know what sort of man you'll be dealing with. One must understand thy enemy to beat him."

"He's not my enemy, and I don't plan on beating him at anything."

"But we appreciate the extra information," I added with an encouraging smile.

Matt tapped his fingers on his knee. "Yes, we do. Go on, Aunt."

"Lord Coyle is a collector, and it's rumored that some of the objects in his collection are stolen," she said.

"Stolen!" I gasped. "From whom?"

"From the original owners, I suppose. He has a vast collection, so I heard, but he keeps it hidden."

"Then what's the point of collecting things if no one sees them?"

"Apparently he allows certain important people to see them."

"What sort of things does he collect?" Matt asked.

"I'm not sure. Some say artwork, others think rare books, and yet others say he collects anything that captures his interest."

Magical objects, perhaps.

Matt sat back in the armchair and stretched out his legs, crossing them at the ankles. It was a pose he struck when he was lost in thought; he wasn't aware of it at all. "Thank you, Aunt. But are you sure he steals them and doesn't buy them?"

She clasped her hands in her lap and lifted her chin. "I can't be absolutely certain, no. As I said, it's gossip, and gossip cannot be trusted fully. Even so, I'm glad I warned you." She indicated I should slice the sponge cake. "Now you can avoid Lord Coyle."

Matt shook his head. "I still want to speak with him. How far is it to Oxfordshire?"

"Quite a considerable way. Why not try his London residence first to see if he's in town?"

"He has a London residence?"

"My dear boy, all the best families do."

I passed Matt a slice of cake. "If he's got business in the city now, he might find it easier to be here for it."

He nodded slowly as he accepted the plate. "He might indeed. Aunt, do you know his London address?"

She bristled. "Of course not."

"Would Richard or Beatrice?"

"I doubt it. Why not try your lawyer? If he doesn't already know it, he can find it for you. Write to him today and you'll have an answer by tomorrow."

Matt smiled. "An excellent idea."

Miss Glass set down her plate, the cake hardly touched. She ate like a bird, and was as frail as one, too. I must urge her to eat more. Perhaps Polly could have Mrs. Potter prepare some of Miss Glass's favorite dishes.

"I'm glad you're home," she said to Matt. "We have callers this afternoon. Mrs Mortimer and her daughter."

Matt's chewing slowed. "I have to go out again."

I narrowed my gaze at him. That was unkind.

"Are you busy tonight?" his aunt asked, unfazed.

"Do we have guests for dinner?"

"No."

"We'll be here," he said. "It'll be nice to spend some time with you. I feel as though I've neglected you, of late."

"You have, but tonight will make up for it. We're going to the opera."

I pressed my lips together but couldn't suppress my smile. Matt was rarely at a loss for words, but his mouth opened and shut and nothing came out.

"Won't that be marvelous," I said.

"I don't like opera," he muttered.

His aunt waved her hand. "One doesn't go to the opera to watch the performance. One goes to the opera to be *seen*, and to meet friends. I've made some inquiries and some interesting people are going tonight. I'll introduce you."

"I'd wager they have eligible daughters," he said.

"Of course. It wouldn't be worth going if there weren't a few girls for you to meet. It'll be a great lark, and you'll enjoy yourself if you allow it. India, you'll come too, as my companion."

"That would be lovely," I said. "Thank you, Miss Glass. I've never been to the opera."

"If you don't have to go out with Matthew this afternoon, you ought to stay and meet my guests."

"Oh," I said. "Er, thank you, but I'm sure Matt needs me." I wasn't sure what he planned to do, or where he wanted to go, but even driving around the city would be better than making polite conversation with strangers and listening to Miss Glass list his attributes.

"Do reconsider, India. They're somewhat beneath we Glasses, but they're a nice family and I would enjoy your company."

"Beneath us?" Matt set his plate on the table with a frown, turned to his aunt, and said, "You never intended me to meet the Mortimers, did you?"

She reached for her plate and dug her fork into the cake. "I do love Mrs. Potter's sponge."

A small snort of laughter escaped my nose. Matt turned a withering glare onto me. "Fortunately for India, I don't need her assistance this afternoon, so she'll be available to meet your guests." He gave me a triumphant smile.

Cruel man.

***

Mrs. Mortimer and her daughter were indeed lovely people, and I was glad I stayed. They were educated, interesting, and didn't care for gossip. Nor did they pander to Miss Glass, their social superior. In fact, she seemed to enjoy their company just as much as I did, if her unselfconscious laughter was anything to go by.

I saw them off from the top of the front steps, when it was time for them to go, and watched them walk up the street. Admittedly, I was also looking for Matt's carriage. There was no sign of it, and I was about to return inside when I caught sight of a man leaning against the iron fence four houses away. His head was bowed, so I couldn't see his face, but the distinctive tall, slender frame gave away his identity.

Sheriff Payne.

I had a mind to march up to him and order him to leave, but held myself in check. It would achieve nothing. Besides, it would only make him realize that he'd rattled me. I would, however, warn Matt as soon as he arrived home.

"Let me know when Mr. Glass returns," I said to Bristow. "Before he alights from his carriage, if possible."

"Of course, madam."

I couldn't settle, however. I looked out the window every few minutes, only to see Payne still there. He glanced at every passing carriage, as did I, but none of them delivered Matt home.

It grew late. The sunshine dimmed as dusk moved in and the lamplighter lifted his pole to the first lamp at the end of the street. Matt had only gone to the Goldsmiths' Guild hall to ask about McArdle, so why hadn't he returned yet? He would need to rest and use his watch. He had it with him, but still, he usually waited until he was home to use it.

Finally, the rumble of wheels stopped outside the house. Bristow entered the sitting room where I sat to announce Matt's return, but I swept passed him and opened the front door before he could speak. The carriage door opened before I reached it. Willie emerged, followed by Duke. Matt must have gone to Worthey's factory and picked them up. They greeted me and I responded breathily, relieved beyond measure that Payne had kept his distance.

Behind them, the inside of the cabin glowed softly purple. Matt sat with his eyes closed, the watch clasped in his fist, his veins alight. It was an ethereally beautiful sight in the poor light and quite took my breath away.

Out of the corner of my eye, I saw something move. Payne!

"Matt!" I cried. "Stop!"

His eyes opened and he dropped the watch. It clattered to the floor and the light went out. "What is it?"

"Payne's here." I glanced up the street. The figure turned and ran off.

"Did he see me with the watch?"

From the angle he'd been standing at? "It's difficult to tell."

"We drove right past him with the curtains open," Matt said, picking up the watch. "He saw."

CHAPTER 13

There wasn't a single thing we could do about Payne. It was likely he'd seen the purple glow in the carriage, and perhaps even on Matt's skin, but unlikely that he knew what it meant. Hopefully he'd shrug it off as a trick of the fading light.

"Are you all right?" I asked him as he climbed out of the carriage.

"Fine," he growled. "I'm always fine, India, no matter how many times you ask."

I clasped my hands in front of me and twisted my fingers together. "It's just that you were gone so long..."

He bowed his head and his shoulders slumped. "I'm sorry." He touched my hands until I unclasped them, then he took my fingers in his. Neither of us wore gloves and the intimacy of skin touching skin set my pulse racing. "I shouldn't have snapped. Forgive me?"

How could I not when he blinked his long, thick lashes at me and gave me that tentative smile, as if he worried that I *wouldn't* forgive him? "There's nothing to forgive. Having everybody continually ask after your health must be trying. I'll do my best to refrain, in future."

"I don't mind you worrying about me sometimes." The smile grew more confident, but no less crooked. Then, as if he remembered where we were and what had just happened, he let me go and glanced up the street. "Did Payne bother you?"

"No. He's been standing out here for some time. I thought he would accost you, and I wanted to warn you."

"Seems he had another plan in mind."

"Yes, but what? Why just stand there and wait for you yet not approach?"

"Learning my movements, perhaps." He indicated I should climb the steps before him.

I lifted my skirts an inch to clear them from my shoes. "Did you learn anything at the Goldsmiths' Guild?"

"The footman told me where to find the guild master's shop, so I visited him there. From him I learned that McArdle is no longer a member. He stopped paying his dues when he closed his shop a few years ago and disappeared overseas. The guild master said he'd heard McArdle was obsessed with hunting for ancient treasures."

"That fits with what we know of him."

"The master didn't know McArdle had returned to London and looked a little worried when I mentioned it. When I asked what the matter was, he shrugged off my question and told me that McArdle is a madman, not to be believed."

I paused at the top step and waited for Matt to join me. "Do you think he was referring to McArdle's claims of magic?" I whispered, since Bristow hovering nearby.

"Perhaps."

"Did you ask him directly about magic?"

"No!"

"Why are you so horrified? His reaction could have been quite telling."

"I'm horrified at you for suggesting we attract attention to ourselves—to *you*—by mentioning magic to complete strangers. A guild master, no less." He took my arm and steered me inside, where Bristow's presence put an end to talk of magic.

"These came for you this afternoon, sir." The butler handed Matt two thin letters.

"Thank you, Bristow. How long until dinner?"

"About thirty minutes, sir. It's early tonight, and informal, due to the opera."

I glanced at the ebony and brass clock on the hall table. "Mrs. Bristow said Mrs. Potter will have dinner ready at six-thirty, which is only twenty-four minutes away." Upon Matt's smirk, I added, "Or thereabouts."

"If anyone needs me, I'll be in my study until then," he said. "India, will you join me after I speak with my aunt?" He waved the letters. "We have work to do."

He greeted his aunt in the drawing room and dutifully listened to her chatter about her afternoon with the Mortimers. "Were they really that nice?" he asked me as we entered his study nine minutes later.

"They were. I enjoyed their company."

"Good." He indicated I should sit and handed me a notepad and pencil. "I'm glad living here isn't all dull work."

"There's nothing dull about living here. Quite the contrary. Do you want me to open the letters? Is that what an assistant does?"

"I don't know. I've never had one before." He passed me one of the letters. "That's from Munro."

"And the other?"

He flipped the letter over. It was blank. "I don't know." He opened it while I opened the one from Munro and read.

"He wants us to work faster," I said, without looking up. "He says that while he understands investigations can be slow, Daniel's family do not. Daniel's grandfather, Mr. Gibbons, is demanding answers." I folded up the paper. "What does that one say?"

Matt had gone quite pale. I was about to ask him if he felt all right, but bit my tongue. When he didn't speak, I went to stand behind him and read over his shoulder.

> I have the watchmaker
> you seek. Come to
> Lemon Court in Bethnal
> Green with one
> thousand pounds at six
> in the morning.

I gasped. "Matt..."

"I know." He stroked his lower lip in thought.

My knees felt weak and I had to sit down again. I pressed a hand to my rapidly beating heart. "This is..."

"I know."

"Marvelous!"

He glanced up sharply. "You believe it's sincere?"

My spine weakened. I felt as if my entire body had caved in. "You don't?"

"It's a trap."

"Set up by Payne?"

"Perhaps. A court is a dead-end street, isn't it?"

"Usually."

"And Bethnal Green is a dangerous place?"

I wrinkled my nose. "Bethnal Green has a terrible reputation. The Ripper crimes occurred on its doorstep two years ago. According to the newspapers, it's going to be razed and rebuilt, but I doubt anything could erase the memories of the violence committed there. If you go, you must ask Munro for a police escort."

"That wouldn't be wise. The blackmailer won't keep his side of the bargain if he sees any sign of the police. The point is moot, however," he added. "I won't be going."

"Oh. Matt, if it's money you need, take the four hundred pounds I won for capturing the Dark Rider."

He smiled without humor. "Thank you, but it's not money that's keeping me from going. It's a trap, India. It would be madness to go."

"But what if it's not a trap?"

"It is."

"You don't know that."

The door opened and Willie and Duke entered. "What are you two arguing about?" Duke asked.

"We're not arguing, we're having a discussion," Matt said.

"About what?" Willie asked.

"Nothing."

"This." I plucked the letter out of Matt's hands and passed it to her. He scowled at me. I crossed my arms and scowled back. I wanted another opinion.

Duke read the note over Willie's shoulder. As the nearest person to her, he received the full force of her hug and almost deafened by her *whoop*.

"God be praised!" she cried. "It's a miracle."

"Sure is," Duke said, hugging her back, one hand buried in her hair.

Matt snatched the letter off her, tore it up and let the pieces scatter on his desk. "Enough! All of you. I smell a trap."

Willie pushed Duke away with a violent shove. He stumbled back into the armchair but didn't protest. He merely rejoined us as if it were an everyday occurrence.

"Are you telling us you're not going?" Willie asked. "Are you thick headed? Have you got wool between your ears?"

"Willie," Duke chided. "Maybe Matt's right. Maybe it is a trap."

"So? Go, but be prepared for an ambush."

"I agree," I said.

Matt drummed his fingers on the desk and pressed his lips together. "If the writer of this letter genuinely knew where Chronos was, he would come to me. Why withhold his identity? He's done nothing wrong. The only reason to meet me in a dead-end slum street is to attack me. If you all stopped to think about it, you'd see that I'm right."

Duke sat on the edge of the desk, head bowed. "It probably is a trap."

Matt did have a point. Somewhat reluctantly, I agreed.

"Willie?" Matt asked his cousin.

She lifted one shoulder. "Seems I'm outnumbered," she muttered.

The dinner gong sounded. Before I left the study, I glanced at the torn pieces of paper on the desk. Matt stared at them too. No matter what he said, he must feel at least a little compelled to go to Lemon Court to see who'd sent the letter. I certainly did.

***

The opera at Covent Garden wasn't what I expected. For one thing, I appeared to be the only one concentrating on the stage. Most of the audience whispered to one another behind fans—although not all were as discreet—or surveyed the other members of the audience as if deciding what to eat at a banquet. It was quite disconcerting, since most gazes eventually settled on us.

No less than four parties visited us in our third tier box. All visitors greeted Lady Rycroft, her daughters, and Miss Glass effusively, then turned their full attention to Matt as he was introduced. Either he or Miss Glass introduced me, too, but I was only given cursory nods before being ignored. Miss Glass's brother, the Baron of Rycroft, had rented the box for the season. Securing its use for one evening meant enduring the company of his wife and three daughters, but not Rycroft himself. Matt was the only man, surrounded by females. Even the visitors were all women.

Watching him hold court, laughing and chatting easily, it was obvious why they all clamored to throw invitations at him. By the end of the evening, he had a pocket stuffed with cards smelling of rose, lavender, and a dozen other scents that mingled together and made me sneeze whenever I got too close.

"He's quite charming," Hope Glass whispered in my ear as she watched Matt smiling at something the girl next to him said. "And extraordinarily handsome."

I turned away. "He is."

"We ought to be put out that he's ignoring us." She sighed theatrically. "But it is so hard to be cross with him. Don't you think?"

"I'm often cross with him. This is not one of those times, however." I tried to concentrate on the soprano on stage as she hit a particularly high note, but not even that could distract me from either Hope or Matt.

"You're very fortunate." The cool smoothness of her voice set me on edge. Everything about Hope Glass set me on edge, from her perfectly arranged curls to her pouting pink lips and shrewd eyes.

"Why?" I expected her to say that I was fortunate to gaze upon Matt's handsomeness every day, but her answer surprised me.

"To be taken in by Aunt Letitia and have her buy you such lovely dresses." She plucked at my ivory and sage silk gown. "She has remarkable taste for someone her age."

"Oh. She didn't buy it. I purchased it myself." Her face fell, and I admit I enjoyed seeing her eyes spark with shock instead of wickedness. "I chose the fabric but Madam Lisle created it." It had arrived early in the afternoon, and I'd paid the amount owing. The exorbitant price had given me pause—it cost as much as the silvered dial mahogany long case clock in my father's shop—but Miss Glass convinced me that I wouldn't regret spending the money. Besides, it had been too late to change my mind, and I had the reward money at my disposal anyway. Basking in Hope's shock, I didn't regret the expense even a little bit.

Hope didn't speak to me for the rest of the evening, and I managed to enjoy what was left of the opera after I noticed Matt's gaze stray to my décolletage, barely covered by the thin chiffon attached to my gown's bodice. The gown had certainly proved to be an excellent purchase. I felt quite elegant in it. Only those who knew me would know I was a mere watchmaker's daughter—and the people they told. I suspected Lady Rycroft and her daughters informed quite a few of their friends who entered our box.

After the performance, Miss Glass and I collected our cloaks and rejoined Matt in the foyer beneath the glittering central chandelier. We'd already said our goodbyes to Lady Rycroft and the Misses Glass, and I was eager to get away before bumping into another acquaintance. We'd already stopped to talk to no less than three parties in the foyer.

Matt offered me one arm and his aunt the other, and we sought out our carriage among the river of vehicles flowing slowly past the theater entrance.

"Did you enjoy yourself?" Matt asked me as his aunt fell into conversation with yet another acquaintance, a woman of advanced years wearing a tiara. Before this evening I thought only queens and princesses wore tiaras, but it would seem half the ladies attending the opera saw fit to sport them. They made the string of pearlescent beads threaded through my hair seem rather simple by comparison. Not that I minded; I had a lovely gown.

"I did," I said, surprising myself. "Yes, I did. I see you had an enjoyable time, too." Although for different reasons. He'd hardly even glanced at the stage.

He laughed softly. "Not particularly."

"Nonsense. You loved every moment of the attention."

"What attention?"

I rolled my eyes. "Don't pretend with me, Matt. I can see right through your act."

"I don't act when I'm with you, India." He leaned his head closer to mine. I sneezed. "Bless you. I didn't think I needed to."

"Oh? So all that simpering laughter and eyelash fluttering was an act?"

He handed me his handkerchief, but it reeked of all the perfumes used on the calling cards and I sneezed again. "Bless you. I do not simper, nor do I flutter my eyelashes. I was, however, putting on an act for my aunt's sake. She wants me to be polite to her friends, so I'll be polite." He half-turned his head to his aunt and greeted her friend. The woman smiled and dipped her head, as if to hide a blush. If she did blush, it was too dark to tell, despite the streetlights nearby. "I think it's working," Matt continued to whisper to me. "Her friends have all come out tonight. Even Beatrice seemed jealous of the friends greeting Aunt Letitia first."

I felt silly for thinking he'd wallowed in the attention now. He'd been agreeable for his aunt's sake, not because he enjoyed being the object of stares, whispers and simpering smiles. By the time we arrived home, I felt even worse for thinking so poorly of him. The tiny lines at the corners of his eyes had multiplied with the sudden onset of exhaustion. Being out so late didn't agree with him.

We reached the house, and he touched his chest where he kept his watch in his inside pocket. He caught me watching and dropped his hand.

Bristow greeted us and informed Miss Glass that Polly was waiting in her rooms to assist her. "Mr. Duke, Mr. Cyclops and Miss Johnson have all gone out for the evening, sir."

Matt paused. "Did they say where?"

"No, sir."

Matt must be worried that Willie was gambling again. I wanted to reassure him that the other two would keep her in line but refrained in the presence of Bristow.

"I'll see you to your rooms, Aunt," Matt said, accepting a candelabra from Bristow.

"Thank you, Matthew." Miss Glass clutched his arm. "Goodness, I am tired."

Bristow handed me another candlestick. "Mrs. Bristow has offered her services as ladies' maid, Miss Steele."

"That's kind of her, but I can manage. I do hope she and the others have already retired." I glanced at the clock. "It's almost midnight."

"They retired some time ago, but Mrs. Bristow was keen to offer her assistance."

"Please thank her for me."

He bowed his head. "I'll lock up, sir. Mr. Cyclops took a key to the servants' door in anticipation of a late evening."

Matt led his aunt upstairs, and I followed with my candle until they peeled away to Miss Glass's rooms and I to mine.

I opened my bedchamber door and stopped dead. Gasped. Someone rummaged through my dresser drawers. He whipped around, but the hood of his cloak covered the upper half of his face.

I opened my mouth to scream, but he was too fast. He slapped his hand over my mouth so hard that I staggered beneath the force. The leather scent of his glove filled my nostrils. I pushed back against him, but he was too solid.

"Where is it, Miss Steele?" I recognized the voice, but it was much harsher, more desperate. Desperate men sometimes did desperate things to get what they wanted. Dangerous things. "Where's the map?"

CHAPTER 14

I shoved again, but Mr. Gibbons didn't move. I felt weak, pathetic. Vulnerable.

"If I release you," Daniel's grandfather said, "will you scream?"

My watch chimed. It wasn't designed to, but the magic in it must recognize danger. My magic. I tried to reach my reticule, hanging from my wrist by a ribbon, but Mr. Gibbons was too close to me, and I couldn't maneuver my hands. My watch chimed again, louder.

I shook my head as best as I could.

Slowly, slowly, Mr. Gibbons released me. "I won't harm you," he said. "Not if you tell me where Daniel's map is."

"What map?"

"Don't play games, Miss Steele. Munro told me he gave it to your employer. I've searched Glass's rooms and it's not in there."

"I don't have it." It was true. Matt held it. Usually he kept it in his inside jacket pocket, along with his watch, but I wasn't sure if he'd taken it to the opera tonight.

"You must know where it is."

"If you want to see the map, you only had to ask Mr. Glass. There was no need to sneak about and frighten me witless. How did you get in past the servants, anyway?"

He sank onto the bed and tipped his hood back, all the fight drained out of him. He looked like a harmless old man. "The servants' entrance was open, and there was only a woman in the kitchen, her back to the passageway. She didn't see me."

"And Bristow was elsewhere, I suppose." I plucked the fingertips of my long glove and slipped it off. My hands shook a little, but not too much. I placed my gloves on the dresser and blushed as I realized Mr. Gibbons had been rifling through my unmentionables.

"My apologies," he mumbled, not sounding sorry at all. "I haven't taken anything."

"Even so."

"Yes. Even so." He cleared this throat. "It appears we are at an impasse, Miss Steele. I want the map and you seem not to have it."

"Why do you want it?"

The door crashed back on its hinges, causing my nerves to shatter all over again. Matt barreled into the room. "India!" He stopped short upon seeing me at the dresser. His gaze flicked from me to Mr. Gibbons. The worry in his eyes turned to fury. "What are you doing here?"

Mr. Gibbons got to his feet, but Matt squared up to him and forced him to sit again. While Mr. Gibbons wasn't a small man, Matt was taller, broader and younger. All signs of exhaustion on his face had vanished, or perhaps the light from Mr. Gibbons's lantern wasn't strong enough to reveal them. The older man swallowed heavily. I felt sorry for him. Almost. He had, after all, frightened the stuffing out of me moments earlier.

"I-I only want my grandson's map," Mr. Gibbons stammered. "Munro said he gave it to you."

"You broke into my house—into my friend's room, no less—for a map! I should thrash you."

Mr. Gibbons's eyes widened, and he leaned back, although Matt did not raise his hand. He folded his arms, gripping them so hard that his knuckles turned white. Holding himself back, perhaps?

"Mr. Gibbons didn't harm me," I said to dampen the crackling tension in the room.

"That is beside the point." Matt lowered his arms and came to my side. "Are you sure you're all right, India?"

"I am now. It was something of a shock finding a man in my room, however."

Matt shot Mr. Gibbons a flinty glare. "I imagine so. I just came from my study where some of the papers on my desk had been moved. Bristow knows not to touch anything in there. I worried that the intruder might still be inside so came here directly..." He sucked in a breath and let it out slowly.

"I wouldn't have hurt anyone," Mr. Gibbons grumbled.

"Don't try to diminish the severity of the crime you have committed," Matt growled.

"Mr. Gibbons was about to tell me why he wanted the map so much," I said quickly. "Go on, Mr. Gibbons." Matt and I leaned back against the dresser to hear the tale.

"I hoped it would lead me to Daniel," Mr. Gibbons said.

"How?" Matt asked.

"Through magic?" I suggested.

Mr. Gibbons wiped the back of his hand over his mouth and jaw. "I have a theory that Daniel is hiding within the vicinity of the map's area."

"Hiding?" Matt asked, the anger replaced by curiosity. "Not kidnapped?"

"Hiding, afraid to show himself. After revealing his magic, he must have come to realize that he's in danger, so he hid. He kept within the map's limits as a clue."

"I don't follow," I said, looking to Matt. He shook his head.

"Daniel suspected something that I have also come to suspect," Mr. Gibbons said. "That another map magician can use Daniel's map to seek out his location. The magic would reveal where he is."

"It's only a theory?" Matt pressed.

Mr. Gibbons shrugged. "I haven't used my magic much over the years. I've never experimented with it like this."

It sounded like a wild theory to me, one thought up by a desperately worried grandfather. "If he wanted you to protect him," I said, "why not come to you in the first place? Why hide from you and his mother?"

Mr. Gibbons shook his head sadly. I sat beside him and rested a hand on his shoulder.

"There's another flaw in your theory," Matt said. "Daniel gave the map to his father, Munro, for safekeeping. Munro is not magical. He couldn't use the map to find Daniel."

Mr. Gibbons suddenly stood. "I have to try."

"Do you have it?" I asked Matt.

Matt looked as if he would protest, then reached into his inside jacket pocket. He handed the folded map to Gibbons, who spread it out on the bed. Matt brought the lantern closer.

"If you haven't used magic much," I said, "how do you know what to do?"

Mr. Gibbons removed his gloves and smoothed his hands over the map. "I can feel its heat, its magic. Perhaps something will be revealed to me."

I still sat on the bed, near the map. I watched as Mr. Gibbons skimmed his hands from one corner to the other. He traced streets with his fingers, and touched the raised buildings and street names. He murmured words that I'd never heard before. I looked to Matt to see if he recognized the language, but his attention was focused on the map.

And then I felt it too. Warmth. Not searing heat, but certainly something. It was like a lantern with the gas turned higher. It emanated from the map, warming my right side.

Then it throbbed.

Mr. Gibbons withdrew his hands and stumbled back. I leaned away. Matt picked up the map and inspected it.

"Nothing," he said after a moment. "Can you see anything Gibbons? India?" He returned it to the bed and I inspected it.

"No," I said. "It looks the same to me. Mr. Gibbons?"

But Daniel's grandfather didn't look at the map. His wide eyes stared at me. "You...you're...magic."

"No," Matt said, quickly. "She's not. You're mistaken." He snatched up the map and folded it. "It's time for you to leave."

"Miss Steele? I felt another magic combine with mine. Strong magic." His breathing quickened, his eyes lit up. "It *must* be strong... You didn't say any words. You didn't need to. My magic simply...fed off your presence. Perhaps. I don't know...but—"

"I told you, she's not magical." Matt grabbed Gibbons's arm and marched him to the door.

I sprang to my feet. "Matt, stop. Let him go." I needed to talk to Gibbons, needed answers to the questions dancing through my head.

"No, India," Matt warned.

I ignored him. I knew he was worried, but I couldn't waylay his fears. The excitement of finally learning more about myself invigorated me. Answers were so close, I couldn't waste a single moment on anything else. "What do you mean you *felt* my magic?"

Mr. Gibbons shook his arm free, or Matt simply let him go. "Just that. It was like a pulse emanating from you. An invisible wave, if you like, rising as quickly as it fell. It strengthened my own magic, or..." He searched my face as if he could find the right word in it. "Or meshed with mine." He spread the fingers of both hands then linked them together. "How did you do that without speaking any words?"

"I don't know. I know nothing about my magic. It's all very new to me."

Matt dragged his hands through his hair, clumping some in his fist before letting it go.

"What sort of magician are you?" Mr. Gibbons asked.

"Time pieces."

"And no one explained your magic to you? Your family?"

"No. I don't think my parents were magical."

"Pity."

"Yes," Matt snapped. "One's relatives ought to explain about magic if and when they can. Otherwise, how will the young magician know the dangers of exposing herself? Or himself?"

Mr. Gibbons seemed to deflate beneath Matt's accusation. "I thought I was doing the right thing for Daniel. I know now that I was wrong, and I regret my silence."

"What can you tell me about my magic, Mr. Gibbons?" I asked. "Are the words you speak to infuse a map with magic the same for me and watches? Could I learn them from you? Could I fix another magician's watch, do you think, or does he need to fix it?"

He lifted one stooped shoulder. "I'm afraid I can't help you, Miss Steele. All magical disciplines developed separately, and as such, use different spells. The words are entirely different, I believe, although I've never heard any other kind of magic spoken."

Spells. It seemed so childish and ridiculous that I almost giggled. "Do you know of any watch or clock magicians?"

"I'm afraid not. I wish I could help you. I wish we could help each other." He glanced at the map in Matt's hand with such sorrow that I almost wanted to give it to him as a sentimental reminder of Daniel. "It seems we cannot."

"No," I said heavily.

"Come with me." Matt handed the lantern and gloves to Mr. Gibbons then tucked the map back into his jacket. "I'll keep this, for now. If you break in here again, you will have two options open to you. One, I will thrash you, or two, I'll hand you over to the police. Your connection to Munro might save you from arrest, or it might not."

"Matt," I chided, but I swallowed the rest of my sentence. I'd been about to tell him his threats were heavy-handed, but the look on his face stopped me. He was still worried and angry that someone had got into the house in the first place. Overriding both of those emotions was exhaustion, gripping him in its claws.

I removed the string of beads from my hair and unpinned the tresses while I waited for Matt to return. I knew he'd return, even though he'd not promised to. The soft knock came a mere three minutes later.

I opened the door to see him leaning against the wall opposite, his head tipped back and his eyes closed.

He'd removed his tailcoat and gloves. "You need to go to bed," I told him.

He opened his eyes. "I need to talk to you. May I?"

I checked up and down the corridor before allowing him in. It was utterly scandalous to have a gentleman in my bedroom, and I didn't want any of the servants seeing and gossiping. If they told servants from other households that Matt came into my bedroom during the night, our reputations would be ruined. At my age, my reputation was no longer important, but Matt didn't deserve to be known as a philanderer who preyed on the women in his household.

He closed the door behind him. "Are you all right?"

"Yes, thank you. Finding Gibbons in here gave me a fright, but he didn't harm me."

He indicated I should sit on the chair by the dressing table. I did and he looked around for another seat. Finding none, he sat on the bed. He sat awkwardly, as if he knew he was in the wrong place and really ought to leave, but wanted to say his piece.

I got in before him. "Don't speak for me, please."

He bristled. "I didn't want him knowing about your magic."

"I know why you did it, but I'm asking you not to do it again. I'm capable of thinking through the consequences of my answers and deciding how much to reveal about myself."

He scooted up the bed and rested against the pillows, his feet dangling off the edge. He lifted his chin and undid his tie. "I know you are, and I'm sorry. It was just that..." He sighed. "I have no justification for it. Forgive me?"

"Of course."

He placed the tie on the bedside table and undid the top button of his shirt. "If it had been anyone else, I'd think you answered him because you were mad at me and were doing the exact opposite of what I wanted. But you're not like that."

I turned away, because he looked so at home on my bed, and so desirable with his finger-combed hair and his evening clothes partially shed. My nerves hadn't yet recovered from the meeting with Mr. Gibbons, they didn't need the extra strain. "I'm glad you understand."

"Of course I understand. Indeed, I should have known better. If I'd answered for Willie, she'd have boxed my ears." His sentence faded into a yawn. "Fortunately, you're a kitten, where she's a bobcat."

I studied my reflection in the mirror, not sure I saw a kitten there, but certainly not a bobcat. "Poor Mr. Gibbons. He only wants to find Daniel."

"Hmmm."

"I liked his theory about using Daniel's map to find him. It's a shame it didn't work." I plucked pins out of my hair. "I wonder if that was because Mr. Gibbons didn't know the right magic words—spell—or whether Daniel isn't in the map's area." If Mr. Gibbons didn't know the right spell, who did? It begged the question— if magicians were afraid to reveal themselves and even talk about their magic with one another, would the spells die out? Would they be forgotten? And would magic itself be forgotten and become nothing more than tales parents told their children. "It's strange to use the word 'spell.' It makes it feel so much more...fantastical. Don't you think?" When he didn't answer me, I turned around.

He lay on the bed, his eyes closed, his chest rising and falling with his deep, even breaths. He was asleep.

I set the last pin down and approached the bed. I wanted to sit on the edge, and stroke the lines of exhaustion away, but remained standing and kept my hands to myself. A sensible woman would wake him and order him to return to his own room.

But I wasn't feeling sensible. Perhaps it was the lingering effects from the glamor of the opera, or the madness of finding Mr. Gibbons in my room, or of learning that I was a strong magician, but I didn't want Matt to be anywhere else except precisely where he was. I watched him a few minutes more, taking in the way his mouth curved in his sleep and marveling at how the worry lines completely disappeared. Spidery red veins webbed his eyelids, but a good rest should see them vanish too. I intended for him to have an excellent rest.

I folded the bedcover over him, holding my breath when he took the edge and wrapped it tighter around himself. But he didn't wake. I pulled a blanket out of the trunk by the window, settled into the chair, and blew out the candle.

***

The rustling bedcover woke me. I stretched my legs, toes, arms and fingers, but the knot in my neck remained. I'd stayed awake for hours, partly because the chair was uncomfortable, and partly because I couldn't stop thinking about what Mr. Gibbons had said. But mostly because I was very aware of the man sleeping on my bed.

"India?" Matt murmured. "What time is it?"

I glanced at the clock, but it was too dark. Pale light rimmed the curtains but it wasn't enough to see properly. "I'm not sure. Dawn, I think."

"Christ." I could just make out his silhouette flinging the bedcover off and standing.

"What's wrong?"

"What's wrong?" He sounded cross. "The servants will be up soon, if they aren't already. If they see me in here your reputation will be ruined. I cannot believe I was so weak as to fall asleep. On your bed, no less."

I couldn't help but laugh, somewhat in relief that he was cross with himself, not me. "It's all right, Matt. My reputation isn't worth worrying about."

He paused. "Don't say that."

"It's true." Not only was I past the age where rumors of my dalliances would stop a man from courting me, there was no man interested in courting me to begin with. "But I appreciate your gentlemanly concern."

"Hardly gentlemanly. A gentleman doesn't lose his tie on his assistant's bed, and he certainly shouldn't have slept in it."

"Your tie is on the table."

He turned his attention to the table, only to knock the photograph of my parents on their wedding day. He swore under his breath, but caught it before it fell.

Why was he so rattled? The usually unflappable Matthew Glass seemed wound up tighter than a mainspring. Perhaps he was worried about his own reputation. That made more sense; I worried too. "Matt? Is something wrong?"

"I must go."

"Did you find your tie?"

His silhouette held up a scrap of fabric. "I think so."

"I'll have another look in daylight, just in case," I said.

"Before the maid comes in. God, imagine if she found it and told the other servants, and they told servants from other households... I'd never forgive myself if your new friends thought you were...you know."

He truly was worried about my reputation, not his own. "Before the maid comes in," I repeated, unable to stop smiling.

He must have heard it in my voice, because he said, "It's not funny, India."

It was a little bit, but he clearly wasn't in the mood to see the humor. "Goodnight, Matt." I held open the door. "Or is it good morning?"

"There is very little that is good about this situation at all. If anyone sees me leave, they'll think I've taken advantage of you."

"Or that I've taken advantage of you."

"Again, not amusing, India."

He peeked out the door, glanced left then right, and tiptoed away. I watched him all the way to his own door where he paused, turned, and lifted a hand to wave. At least, I thought it was a wave. It could have been a shooing motion.

***

Breakfast was an unusually quiet affair. Willie and Duke slept in and missed it, Cyclops had already left to spy on Onslow, and Miss Glass had a tray sent to her room. It was just the two of us, and Matt was unusually contemplative.

"Are you thinking about last night?" I asked, since we were alone. Bristow had left to refill the teapot.

"The opera, yes," he said with a hard edge and a glance at the door. "And this afternoon."

"Of course. The bank." Today was the day that Mirth drew money from his bank account. Today, we'd discover if Mirth was Chronos. "Do you want me to come with you?"

"There's no need, but I'd welcome your company. If you'd rather stay home with Aunt Letitia..."

"I'll come."

Bristow re-entered carrying the teapot.

"Any letters yet?" Matt asked him.

"Nothing, sir."

"Damn," Matt muttered. "There's nothing to do this morning, India. I'd hoped to hear from my lawyer about Lord Coyle, but it would seem we have to wait."

Matt wasn't very good at waiting. He paced his study, the drawing room, the sitting room, the entrance hall, and that was all within the first hour after breakfast. I gave up trying to calm him and retreated to the sitting room with a book.

Duke joined me. With nothing better to do, he'd decided to watch Worthey's factory with Willie, although our hope that DuPont would reappear at his place of employment had almost entirely vanished. Willie, however, had not woken by ten, so he left without her. At eleven, I grew worried and knocked on her door. There was no answer.

According to Duke, Willie had drunk quite a few whiskeys at the tavern, so her sleep-in came as no surprise. But what if she was ill? I'd seen Willie down glass after glass of whiskey before, and aside from slurring her words, she endured no ill effects the following day, and she had certainly never slept this late.

I opened the door and knew immediately that the room was empty without having to wait for my eyes to adjust to the dim light. Even so, I checked the bed. It had been slept in but was cold.

"Willie?" It was silly to call her name since there was no dressing room off this bedroom. "Willie?" I called, louder.

No answer. I suddenly realized where she'd gone.

I ran out of the room and down the stairs, my slippered feet thumping loudly. There was no sign of Bristow or any of the other servants, and I didn't want to summon them with the bell. It would take too long. I ran to the back of the house then down the service stairs.

I met Mrs. Bristow coming out of the kitchen. She gasped upon seeing me, but whether I'd shocked her by appearing in the service area or with the wild gleam in my eye, I didn't know.

"Mrs. Bristow, have you seen Willie this morning?"

"She left early, madam, not long after I rose myself."

"Thank you," I tossed over my shoulder as I ran off again.

I retraced my steps, all the way to Matt's study. I banged on the door then barged in without waiting for him to open it.

He pushed up from the chair at his desk. "India? What—"

"Willie's gone," I gasped out between my heaving breaths. "She left very early. I think she went to meet the author of that blackmail note."

His face paled. "And she hasn't come back." It wasn't a question. He patted his waistcoat watch pocket and strode past me. "Bristow!" he shouted from the corridor. "Bristow, have the carriage brought around *now*!"

I pressed a hand to my thundering heart and followed him. "Is it wise to go after her? What if I'm wrong? What if she went to Worthey's ahead of Duke?"

"You're not wrong." He didn't run, yet his long, purposeful strides meant I had the devil of a time catching up to him, even though I trotted. "Bristow!" he shouted again. "The carriage."

"Yes, sir," the butler called up from somewhere down below.

Miss Glass emerged from her room as I passed. "Matthew? What's all this noise?"

"I have to go out," he told her without pausing. "India will keep you company until my return."

That seemed to satisfy her, and she retreated to her room.

"Matt," I said, trailing several steps behind. "What if it's a trap? What if—"

"I have to go," was all he said. "You know I do."

Damn Willie. Damn her impetuousness. "You also have to go to the bank soon. I can't go in your stead. I don't know what Chronos looks like."

"I'll go to Lemon Street then directly to the bank."

"And what if you're held up? What if you can't find her?"

He reached the bottom of the stairs and plucked his hat off the hat stand. "I'll cross that bridge when I come to it."

Or, more likely, miss Mirth altogether. We both knew he wouldn't leave Lemon Street until he found some clue as to Willie's whereabouts. I prayed she was still there, waiting, or had gone on to Worthey's if the blackmailer didn't reveal himself to her.

I waited an hour for word from Matt, but none came. All the clocks in the house tormented me, particularly the chiming ones. I swear I could hear every tick and tock of every clock, and number sixteen Park Street had more than a dozen. It was an excruciating hour. By midday, every part of me felt so tight with worry that I could no longer sit by and do nothing.

"I'm going out," I told Miss Glass, sitting in the sunlight by the window. "I have to go the bank." That should be enough of a clue for Matt if he returned.

But I didn't think he would return. If he'd found Willie, either at Lemon Street or Worthey's, he would have sent word to me before going on to the bank. He had not. Dread settled into my bones.

It was already midday. While I would dearly have liked to fetch Duke or Cyclops, since they'd seen Chronos and knew what he looked like, I didn't want to waste time finding them. I collected the ten pounds I kept in the house for emergencies and asked Bristow to find a hansom. While I waited, I clasped my watch in my fist. Its familiar shape and warmth helped settle my racing heart and gather my thoughts.

But one thought was clear above all else. What if Matt had fallen into the blackmailer's trap? What if going to the bank wasted valuable time that could be spent rescuing him?

And what if he could not be rescued at all?

CHAPTER 15

An overly cautious nature had led me to wear a wide-brimmed hat with a half-veil, and to ask the driver to stop in Princes Street, around the corner from the Bank of England. Even so, my heart still leapt into my throat when I saw Abercrombie standing by one of the columns at the entrance. My step faltered and I paused by the iron fence. If Abercrombie was here loitering, then it was likely he was also waiting for Mirth—perhaps even for Matt.

Abercrombie had told me that Mirth collected his allowance every week from the Bank of England. Had he realized too late that he'd given away a vital clue to help us find Mirth? Perhaps that was why he now waited like a predatory cat beneath the vast shadow cast by the bank.

He stood toward the center of the steps, and there was no way to avoid him completely. His gaze swept the vicinity, constantly moving, taking note of everyone who climbed the steps. My veil and hat would not be enough to hide me completely.

Should I let him see me? He couldn't stop me from entering, but he might stop me from bribing the bank clerk. I had to pass him without being noticed. What I needed was a distraction in the other direction, something to take his attention away from me.

And then I saw a gentleman crossing the road and got a better idea. "Excuse me, sir," I said to the enormous man heading toward the bank with an unhurried gait.

He paused, looked over his shoulder as if surprised that I would address him, then smiled at me. "Yes, ma'am? May I help you?" He wasn't particularly tall but his frame was so broad that the width of my skirt at the hem would be about the same as his middle.

"I'm feeling a little faint, but I'm determined to make it to the bank. Would you mind escorting me?"

Again, he glanced over his shoulder, as if surprised that I would address him. When he realized I was, his smile turned shy and his cheeks, already quite pink, flamed. "Of course. Can't have a lady fainting out here, now, can we?" He held out his right arm, which would put me on the side closest to Abercrombie.

I skirted him and with a nervous chuckle, he offered me his other arm. "Thank you, this is very kind."

"Not at all," he said as we walked steadily but slowly toward the bank steps and Abercrombie. "I do hope it's nothing serious."

"I just need to get out of the sun for a few minutes." I introduced myself and we chatted quietly. With the veil over my eyes, my face wasn't immediately recognizable, but Abercrombie would notice if he looked.

Yet he did not look. Not properly. He didn't recognize the man whose arm supported me, so he didn't check the woman behind the veil. My ruse had worked.

"I'm sure I can manage from here," I said once we were inside the bank.

"Would you like to sit? Do you need water?"

"You're very gallant, sir, but I'm already feeling better. Thank you for your assistance."

He touched the brim of his hat. "My pleasure."

None of the clerks were the fellow from last week, so I went up to the first available one, a young man with a kind face. "My name is Miss Jane Markham " I said, assuming the identity I'd used the week before. "I am the granddaughter of Mr. Oliver Warwick Mirth. He comes in every Wednesday afternoon to collect his allowance. Do you know if he's been in yet today?"

The young man gave me an apologetic smile. "I am sorry, Miss Markham, but that's confidential information."

I pulled out a sovereign from my reticule. "It's important that I find out. My grandfather is a little soft in the head, and it has come to our attention that we need to keep an eye on him."

The clerk pushed his glasses up his nose. They made his eyes appear even rounder. "I...er..." He glanced to the teller on his left, an older man with a sharp chin and nose.

I pulled out another sovereign and placed my hand over both coins to hide them. I revealed them only to the young clerk. He nodded quickly, and I slid the coins across the polished wooden counter.

"Wait here a moment." He wrote down some instructions on a piece of paper and passed it to another lad lingering behind. The lad exited through a door and reemerged moments later with a file.

"According to this," the clerk said, tapping his finger against the last page in the file, "your grandfather hasn't been in yet." He snapped the file closed and passed it back to the lad who once again disappeared into the filing room. The clerk glanced at the man beside him then jerked his head at me to leave.

I thanked him and sat on one of the chairs set out along the wall. Other ladies waited for their husbands to finish their business before leaving together. I kept my gaze on the entrance, unsure why I waited. I didn't know what Mirth or Chronos looked like, but I waited anyway in case Matt arrived.

An hour passed, and I was stifling a yawn when Abercrombie strode in. I touched the brim of my hat to cover my face, but Abercrombie didn't look my way. He focused on a stooped man with white hair and a limp who'd entered a moment before. The man limped up to a clerk while Abercrombie hung back. A few minutes later, the man tipped his new coins into his pocket and limped away. He passed Abercrombie without either man acknowledging the other. Indeed, Abercrombie turned his back momentarily. He did not want the fellow to see him.

It must be Mirth.

Mirth exited into the sunshine, and Abercrombie followed. I followed him. The clicks of my heels on the tiled floor might as well have announced my presence to the world, but Abercrombie didn't turn around. He must have decided that none of Matt's friends had passed him by as he waited outside, so one on the inside was an impossibility.

I hadn't a clue what to do next. I couldn't confront the elderly man without being noticed by Abercrombie. All I knew was that I had to bide my time; I had to do whatever I could to help Matt. So I simply followed them down the steps to the pavement. Mirth limped off to the right, his gait interminably slow, his head bowed as if he were inspecting the pavement for dropped coins.

A carriage rattled past, and Mirth looked up. Suddenly animated, he signaled to an omnibus approaching at a treacherous pace. The passenger riding the garden seat up the top clutched the iron rails with both hands as the omnibus swerved to the curb. The conductor assisted Mirth up the step and inside.

Damnation! I would lose him.

If I wanted to get on the omnibus too, I had to shout to alert the driver to wait for me as I caught up. My shout would also alert Abercrombie who remained on the pavement, watching.

The omnibus drove off, and my heart sank. At least I could give a good description of the man to Matt. Hopefully it would be enough.

Abercrombie hurried across the road, his attention no longer on the omnibus—the omnibus that had not quite disappeared from site yet.

A hansom cab passed me, its pace slowing. It pulled over behind me and deposited a gentleman at the bank's entrance. I picked up my skirts and ran. The gentleman noticed and asked the driver to wait.

I thanked him as he assisted me up to the seat and closed the door. "Do you see the omnibus turning the corner back there?" I asked the driver through the hatch in the roof. "Follow it. Quickly, man." I handed him what I hoped would be enough money for the journey. "When it stops, I'd like to get on it."

The driver somehow managed to turn his vehicle around amid the traffic, earning a few raised fists and angry shouts from other drivers. The horse sped along as fast as it could, passing around the slower moving coaches. The waist-height door protected my skirts from the worst of the dirt flicked up by the hooves, but some landed on my jacket. I didn't dare dust myself off; I didn't want to lose the omnibus ahead. We'd caught up to it, and as soon as it pulled to the curb to collect a passenger, my hansom stopped directly behind it.

"Wait for this lady," called my driver as I alighted.

The conductor held out his hand to me as I approached. "Good afternoon, miss."

"Thank you and good afternoon," I said, scanning the faces of the gentlemen in the omnibus. Mirth sat near the middle. "Excuse me, may I sit here?" I asked the fellow beside him. The omnibus lurched forward and he had to steady me as he slid down the seat to make room.

I plopped down next to Mirth, out of breath from the exercise and the airless confines of the omnibus cabin. From excited anticipation, too. I couldn't believe I was about to speak to the man who may be able to fix Matt's watch.

Mirth, however, didn't notice my excitement. He was dozing, his chin resting on his chest, his hands clasped over his stomach. I cleared my throat, and when that didn't work, nudged him sharply with my elbow.

He awoke and took in his surroundings with dreary eyes.

"Good afternoon, Mr. Mirth," I said.

He blinked at me. "Do I know you?"

"My name is India Steele. I'm the daughter of Elliot Steele, a watchmaker lately of St. Martin's Lane."

"Elliot Steele? I know him. Good fellow. I was sorry to hear of his passing." He touched the brim of his hat. "Pleased to meet you, Miss Steele. Remarkable that you would recognize me. Have we met?"

"We have now." I grinned. I couldn't help it. I felt so elated. "I'd heard you were in a hospice," I said. "Are you still living there?"

The wrinkles on his forehead arrowed toward the bridge of his nose in a frown. I'd had an hour in the bank to consider what to say if I spoke to Mirth, but hadn't thought how odd my questions would sound. "No," he said cautiously. "I moved. Why?"

What if he didn't want to answer me? What if he wanted to remain anonymous forever? It was a strong possibility yet I had to take a risk and tell him what I really needed to know. Time was not on my side, and evasive questions would only earn evasive answers.

The fellow beside me got off, leaving Mirth and I as the only passengers on the right side of the omnibus. Even so, I bent my head to his ear and thanked heaven he wasn't deaf. "Mr. Mirth, I have a friend who is in possession of a magical watch that was given to him by an elderly gentleman known as Chronos, five years ago, in America."

Mirth's lips parted in a soft gasp. He glanced at the other passengers and lifted a hand to catch the conductor's attention. "Stop," he said.

"We just stopped," the conductor grumbled as he thumped on the cabin wall.

"Mr. Mirth, *please*," I begged as the omnibus lurched. "I need your help."

"Shush, Miss Steele. We're going for a quiet walk."

Oh. Right. I assisted him down to the pavement. We were on Cheapside, not having got very far thanks to the stream of traffic that the omnibus now tried to dig its way through. I glanced back the way we'd come, half afraid to see Abercrombie. But he'd gone in the other direction. Besides, with so many people milling about, we ought to be safe.

Mr. Mirth set off, his limp making progress slow. I strolled alongside him. Anyone would think we were father and daughter, out shopping. He was a small man with a worn face and tired but clear eyes that now seemed even clearer as he kept vigilant.

"Are you looking for Abercrombie?" I asked.

"You saw him?"

I nodded. "He wanted to stop me speaking to you."

"Is that so? I think you need to start at the beginning."

I told him about Matt's watch, about it failing, and his need to find the watchmaker known as Chronos. The mention of magic didn't cause so much as an eyelash to flicker—until I spoke about combining the doctor and watchmaker's magic to keep Matt alive.

"And it worked?" he said in an awed whisper.

I nodded. "Since you were known to be overseas at the same time as Chronos, it was suggested that we seek you out. Well?" I pressed, unable to wait any longer. "Did you put a spell on Matt's watch along with Dr. Parsons?"

He shook his head and my heart fell through my stomach to my toes. Tears pricked my eyes. All this effort, all this waiting...for nothing.

"I've never been to America, Miss Steele. I'm not your employer's Chronos."

"Then why not just say so in the omnibus?" Frustration made my voice harsh, but I didn't apologize. I was too heart sore to feel guilty. "I've wasted my time."

"I may not be Chronos, but I might know who he is."

All the air left my lungs. "Go on."

"Before you get your hopes up, let me begin by saying I am not a magician. I'm just a simple watchmaker who has long known about magicians and admired their work. Do you know that magicians create unique and exquisite creations? That their work is the finest in the world, unsurpassed by those who lack magic?"

I nodded.

"Then you'll know they can be easy to spot if you know what to look for and the magician isn't very adept at hiding themselves. Some magicians aren't aware of their excellence until too late—until they create something so marvelous that the world has already sat up and taken notice. At least, the world of watches and clocks, in this case. There's a horologist, here in London, who creates wonderful pieces. I believe he must be a magician. He may be the man you're looking for."

"He lives here in London now?"

"He certainly was the last time I met him. I first saw his work many years ago, then again quite recently. No one but a magician could create something so beautiful, so *accurate*. That first time, I knew so little about magicians and never broached the subject with him. The second time, I managed to corner him in the showroom where he worked, but only for a few minutes before he got away. He was sprightly for his age, and this damn gammy leg is a hindrance," he added, tapping his thigh.

"Where can I find him? What's his name?"

"DuPont. He's hiding out in Clerkenwell, in a rather insignificant little factory."

I sighed heavily. "I already know about him. We haven't spoken to him because he ran off when he saw us. He doesn't want to speak to us."

"Oh. That's a shame."

We walked on, my gait matching his slow one. I felt as if all the stuffing had been knocked out of me. My insides were hollow, and my head numb. All this waiting and effort for nothing.

"That must be why Abercrombie wanted to stop you from speaking to me," Mr. Mirth said.

"Pardon?"

"Abercrombie didn't want me to meet you because I guessed that DuPont was a magician and he knew I could point you in his direction."

"I suppose."

"Miss Steele, you don't quite understand. I'm the *only* one who would have helped you. *That's* why he wanted me to leave the hospice and go somewhere more private," he added before I could press him. "He came to collect me one day and took me to new accommodation. Not a word of an explanation. It was very odd. No one has visited me since the move, and now I know why. Abercrombie kept my new location secret."

"Very odd, indeed. I suppose you're right." We passed a watch and clock shop, so I tugged on the veil to insure it was in place. "What do you mean you're the only one who would help me?"

"I'm not afraid of magicians like the rest of them," Mirth said. "I'm quite willing to discuss them and their work. As I said, I spoke to DuPont quite recently."

"Did you ask him if he was a magician?"

"I did, but he didn't admit it—for fear of recriminations, perhaps. But I knew." He huffed a soft laugh. "DuPont."

"Pardon?"

"I don't think that's his real name, and I don't think he's French at all."

I rounded on him. "What do you mean?" The main reason we hadn't fully believed that DuPont was Chronos was because Chronos was English, not French, and Worthey had said DuPont came from France.

"His accent isn't quite right. I've traveled to France, Miss Steele, and DuPont's vowels are too round, like an English gentleman's. Whatever nationality he is, it's not French."

"Could he be English?"

"It's possible."

Mirth fell silent, seemingly lost in his own thoughts. I, however, felt more aware of my surroundings than ever. I was discussing magic with a stranger, something that would worry Matt if he were here. I kept vigilant for Abercrombie, but saw no sign of him among the Cheapside shoppers and shopkeepers' apprentices shouting about their "fine" goods from doorways. I took Mirth's arm and steered him around a hawker whose cart blocked most of the pavement.

"It's not just that I'm the only one who could have told you that DuPont is a magician and not French, Miss Steele," he said, his excitement making his words tumble together. "It's that I'm the only one who *would* help. That's why Abercrombie has tried to stop us from meeting."

"Why are you so willing? No one else from the guild is."

"Of all the watchmakers left in this city who know about magic, I'd wager I'm the only one who has nothing to fear. I have nothing to fear because I have nothing to lose. I have no shop and no profession anymore. No family either." His gaze focused on the crowd ahead and he resumed his slow, limping pace. "I'm not afraid of magic because I see it as something wonderful, beautiful. I'm intrigued by magic, and a little in awe. Perhaps if I were like Abercrombie, with a shop and reputation to maintain, I'd be frightened of a magical watchmaker taking that away from me. Combining different types of magic...that isn't something I've contemplated until now, however. I didn't know it was possible."

"It seems as if few magicians are experimenting with it."

"And rightly so."

"What do you mean?"

He stopped at a flower seller crying, "All a-growing, all a-blooming!" She held out her basket for us to see her wares. "I got daisies, violets, pinks, all of 'em quality."

He bought a small bouquet of mixed flowers, paid the girl, and handed it to me. "Combining magic sounds dangerous, Miss Steele," he said, after the flower seller walked off. "Particularly when a man who ought to be dead is brought back to life. None of us have a right to undo God's will. Not even a magician."

"Shooting a living being is not God's will either, Mr. Mirth. It's a violent act committed by one who cares nothing for life. I have no qualms in bringing back a good man who doesn't deserve to die because he tried to make the world a better place. No qualms at all."

"I see I've upset you. I apologize. I do hope we can still be friends."

I tried to smile but it felt strained. "Of course. I'm glad we spoke, Mr. Mirth. Can I walk you to your new residence?"

"It's not far from here, and I have some marketing to do first." He touched the brim of his hat. "I wish your friend luck. But be careful, Miss Steele. Don't let your endeavor to save your friend's life endanger yours."

I watched him limp away until the crowd swallowed him up, then I caught a hansom back to Park Street. I asked the driver to wait for me as I checked with Bristow if Matt had returned. He hadn't, but Bryce had come back alone after Matt failed to reappear. I felt sick.

He'd walked into the blackmailer's trap. Both he and Willie.

Matt was clever, however, and aware of the dangers. He wouldn't have simply wandered into Lemon Street without a plan and possibly a weapon. Nor would Willie. Knowing that didn't make me feel any better.

Bryce drove me to Clerkenwell, and I found Duke lounging against a wall opposite Worthey's factory, his hat brim pulled low. When I apprised him of the situation, he was eager to abandon his post and come with me. We collected Cyclops from the guild hall, although the police almost wouldn't let him go. It seemed there'd been a break-in overnight, and the staff were being questioned.

"What did the thieves take?" I asked as we drove away.

"Nothing," he said.

"Then why are the police there at all?"

"Because the footman thinks there're strange goings-on. A window was broken. He reckons the thieves were disturbed and scarpered, but I disagree. The glass was on the outside of the window, in the courtyard."

"So?" Duke shrugged.

"So, if it were a break-in, the glass would fall *inside*."

"True enough."

"Are they sure nothing was taken?" I asked.

Cyclops lifted one shoulder. "Maybe they'll find something later."

We drove to Lemon Street in Bethnal Green in silence. The dread that had been with me all day now squeezed my heart; it must have been affecting the men too. The sight of the cumbersome four-wheeler in Bethnal Green drew suspicious stares from the hollow-eyed locals. Despite being marked for clearance, the area still teemed with residents with nowhere else to go. Scrawny, shoeless children dressed in patched-up clothes hid behind curtains of greasy hair, their eyes filled with a mixture of wariness and wonder. Hopelessness clung to the shadowy stoops where grim-faced women with bent backs dared us to leave the safety of our vehicle and enter their domain. I clutched my reticule tighter.

"Stay in here," Duke told me as Bryce pulled to a stop. "Is this Lemon Street?" he called out the window.

A child pointed to a red brick archway, too narrow for the carriage to drive through. Beyond, I could only see a stunted lane surrounded on three sides by crumbling tenements. Washing hung motionless from lines strung between the upper windows. No breeze or sunlight penetrated the street to dry even the thinnest linen.

"Ready?" Duke asked Cyclops.

Cyclops nodded. "Bring a weapon with you?"

Duke revealed a knife strapped to his forearm and another to his leg. "You?"

Cyclops made fists. "Let's go."

They passed beneath the archway, a small collection of children trailing behind before a woman barked at them to come back. I craned my neck but could no longer see Cyclops and Duke.

The horses shifted. "We shouldn't stay here long," Bryce called down to me.

I checked my watch. Two minutes passed. Three. The warm silver throbbed, or perhaps that was the blood pounding through my veins. It seemed an interminably long time for them to be absent, but another check of my watch proved that it had only been five minutes.

Finally, they emerged. Alone. My stomach plunged, even though I'd not truly expected to see Matt or Willie with them.

"Well?" I asked as they approached.

"Nothing," Duke bit off. "Everyone's closed up tighter than a vicar's—" He glanced at me. "They ain't talking."

"We should have brought money," Cyclops said.

"I have money." Why hadn't I thought of it before? I'd taken ten pounds to bribe the bank clerk, but only used two.

Cyclops held out his hand through the window, but I shook my head and opened the door. "I can't sit here and wait again."

The men exchanged glances. "Matt wouldn't like it," Duke said.

"He's not here," I reminded them. "If we're not back in ten minutes, fetch the police," I told Bryce.

I marched through to Lemon Street, flanked by Duke and Cyclops. Their presence was a comfort, until I noticed the group of five men lounging on the pile of crates and barrels near a door that had probably once been red but was now a faded, dirty pink. The men watched us from beneath heavy eyelids that lifted ever so slightly upon spying me. Ragged, filthy beards twitched with their smirks. The tongue of one darted out, lizard-like, to lick his lips.

I had two guards to their five. Despite my confidence in Duke and Cyclops, I wasn't entirely sure if those odds were in my favor. "They look like they know everything that goes on here," I said.

"They look like trouble," Duke said. "We already spoke to them. They said neither Willie nor Matt were here."

"We know that's false."

"Give me the money," Cyclops said. "Let's see what a few coins can get out of them."

I almost argued with him then thought better of it. There was no point me going with him. It might make matters worse. He put out both hands and I tipped everything I had onto them. That way the thugs could see there was nothing more to give.

Cyclops approached the men alone. Duke stuck to me like toffee to teeth, his hands lightly clasped in front of him. The position meant he could quickly grab the dagger up his sleeve if necessary. Cyclops spoke to the men and passed around the money. The coins disappeared into pockets so fast I never saw it happen. The man who'd licked his lips answered Cyclops then shook his head. They all shook their heads.

Cyclops lashed out and grabbed the man in front by his shirt, hauling him up so that his feet no longer touched the ground. "Tell me!"

The friends sprang to their feet. Duke moved and I glanced down to see the knife in his hand. "Be ready to run back to the carriage," he told me.

I picked up my skirts. "Cyclops!" I shouted. "Let the man go."

"He knows, India," he called back. "I know he does. They all do."

Yes, but clearly no one wanted to tell and we couldn't fight them all. "Come away, Cyclops."

"We need a gun," Duke muttered. To Cyclops, he said, "We'll come back later."

Cyclops dropped the man, giving him a shove for good measure so that his friends had to catch him before he tumbled back into the crates. Amid jeers and threats, Cyclops simply walked back to us, his face set like stone. I'd never seen him look so fearsome.

"They seen 'em, all right," he said, rejoining us without stopping. He continued toward the archway. I picked up my skirts and followed with Duke. "They said they saw some men capture them and take them away. First Willie, early this morning, then Matt, some time later."

"Capture them?" I echoed as we reached the carriage just in time. Bryce was about to whip one of the children sneaking up to the horses. "Without a fight?"

"There was a fight, all right." Cyclops opened the carriage door and Duke assisted me up. The men climbed in behind me after Cyclops gave Bryce instructions to return to Park Street.

"And?" I prompted. "What happened?"

"They were overpowered and taken away."

"By whom?"

"By how many?" Duke asked darkly.

"Five men," Cyclops said as the carriage rolled away.

"Five?" Duke grunted. "What a coincidence. There were five in Lemon Street just now."

Cyclops's jaw hardened. "I noticed."

"You think it was them?" I said. "You think those men overpowered Willie and Matt? And did what with them?"

"They were paid," Cyclops said with certainty. "Hired muscle to do a coward's work. They know where Willie and Matt are but won't say. It ain't worth it to them to blab to us."

"We'll report them to the police," I said. "That will get them to tell us—"

"No," both Duke and Cyclops said. "It won't."

"Then what?" My voice pitched high, hysterical. "We can't just walk away. We can't leave until we know where they are. Turn back." I lifted my arm to thump on the roof, but Cyclops caught my hand.

"There is another way." His one-eyed glare bored into me like a drill. The intensity of it on such a gentle man alarmed me. "We return with firearms."

I swallowed and sank into the corner. He let me go, but his grip had left a mark on my skin. I turned to the window but hardly saw anything through the blur of tears.

When would this end? How? With bloodshed and loss of life?

Surely there had to be another way. Surely, if we thought it through, we could work out who took them and why. Surely we could find them in a peaceful manner.

And then it struck me. I sat up straight and thumped on the cabin roof. "Open the window," I directed Duke, unable to keep the elation from my voice.

He and Cyclops frowned at me, but did as asked. "What do you want me to tell the driver?" Duke asked, holding onto his hat as the breeze streamed in. "Where do you want to go?"

CHAPTER 16

"Mr. Gibbons, please, we don't know where else to turn." I hated to beg, but this was an exceptional circumstance. Daniel's grandfather was the only person who might be able to help find Matt and Willie, although my wild theory may not work in practice. Indeed, the chance of failure was very high.

But I had to try.

"Don't be absurd." Mr. Gibbons's gruff reply dismissed us as clearly as his wave at the door. "Now, unless you have something to tell us about Daniel, please leave. You're upsetting my daughter."

Miss Gibbons, Daniel's mother, did indeed look upset, but that could have been because I'd just informed her that there was no news of Daniel and the man commissioned with finding him had also disappeared. She pressed her handkerchief to her nose and sniffed.

"You owe us this, after the fright you gave me last night," I said.

Miss Gibbons lowered her handkerchief. "Last night?" She frowned at her father. "You told me you were with friends last night."

Mr. Gibbons puffed out his chest and offered no explanation. His daughter didn't press him.

"I cannot find Daniel alone," I said, my voice thin. My nerves were stretched tight. We were being blocked at every turn, and this time by someone who was supposed to be on our side. "I need Matt."

"Explain why you think my father could help you find him," Miss Gibbons asked. "I'm not sure I understand."

"Last night, your father...came to our house in search of one of Daniel's maps."

"Which Munro, the bloody fool, gave them," Mr. Gibbons growled with an accusatory glare at his daughter.

She lowered her head and sat demurely with her hands clasped in her lap.

"He thought he might be able to use his magic and the map to find Daniel, since it's infused with his magic." At her hopeful gaze, I added, "It didn't work."

"Precisely," Mr. Gibbons said. "So why do you think it would work for you and your friend?" I opened my mouth to speak, when he indicated the door. "I'd like you to leave."

"*Listen* to her." Cyclops closed the gap between them and looked as if he'd pull Gibbons up by his shirt, as he'd done with the thug in Lemon Street. But he simply stood over Gibbons, a tower of muscle and fury.

Mr. Gibbons shrank into his armchair and swallowed. "I'm listening," he said without taking his wide gaze off Cyclops.

Cyclops rejoined Duke. Both stood by the door, arms crossed over their chests, looking every bit like warriors on guard.

"Thank you," I said. "What I'm proposing may not work, but I want to try anyway. I want to try combining my magic and yours to find Matt."

Miss Gibbons gasped. "You? You're...?"

I nodded. "I'm...raw. I don't know any spells, but every watch or clock I've worked on seems to respond to me. I've worked on Matt's watch, and I know he has it on him." I closed my eyes briefly, and drew in a fortifying breath. It had occurred to me—to all three of us—that Matt may have lost his watch in the scuffle, or that the five thugs had stolen it from him. He'd left home four and a half hours ago. Time was running out.

"And you want my father to use his magic to draw you a map of his location," Miss Gibbons finished. "Or that of his watch, at least."

I nodded.

"It didn't work last night," Mr. Gibbons said heavily. "And nor will this. It's foolish."

"Even so, you have to try," Duke growled.

"Why do you think it will work this time, Miss Steele?" Miss Gibbons asked. "Why should your magic be any different, particularly if you don't know any spells?"

"Because my magic is strong. Your father told me so. And I'm hoping that the magic watch in Matt's possession will be the key difference." And because I had a hunch. I couldn't explain it, but this *felt* right.

Father and daughter eyed one another. Miss Gibbons said, "You have to help, Papa."

He nodded. "Come with me to my workshop." Mr. Gibbons led the way down the dimly lit corridor to the back of the house and out into the small courtyard.

Behind the kitchen addition, a lean-to looked as if it would blow over in a strong wind. Mr. Gibbons unlocked the door and pulled aside the curtains. Light streamed into the workshop, which barely had enough space to contain all five of us as well as Mr. Gibbons's sloping desk and small chest of drawers. Unframed maps had been nailed to the walls, some of them quite beautiful. Magical maps? I touched the corner of one and my hand warmed.

Miss Gibbons watched me.

"Come stand here, Miss Steele." Mr. Gibbons pointed to the side of the desk where he spread out a large piece of paper. His daughter wordlessly picked out pencils and rulers from one of the drawers, and another map of greater London.

"The watch may not be in London," Mr. Gibbons said as his daughter spread the map on the desk.

"I know," I said, removing my gloves. "But we have to begin somewhere."

Mr. Gibbons leaned over the large blank page and began to sketch. His hands moved quickly, as did his lips as he chanted strange, lyrical words. If his words could be drawn, they'd feature swirls and loops and a flowing pattern. I recognized none of them.

He drew a copy of the map of London, but so much better. It filled with dense detail, street names, and identifiable landmarks. Roof tiles and brickwork emerged from the page as if they were real, only in black, white and gray, and to my amazement, even buildings under construction took shape, the scaffold a skeletal shell that seemed to reach up from the surface. His new map was the same scale as the original, even though Mr. Gibbons took no measurements.

"Beautiful," Duke breathed from behind me. "There's Park Street," he said, pointing.

Mr. Gibbons batted his hand away without breaking his chant. A moment later, he set down his pencil.

I placed my hand on the map's nearest corner. Heat surged through my fingers up my hand to my wrist where it petered away. I gasped and pulled back. Mr.

Gibbons and his daughter exchanged glances, and he resumed his chanting.

"India?" Cyclops whispered.

"I'm all right." I returned my hand to the map, this time ready for the heat. It burned fiercely but was bearable.

I felt somewhat foolish, simply standing there while Mr. Gibbons did all the work. I ought to be chanting too. His words flowed around me, and the warmth from the map swarmed past my wrist, up my arm to my shoulder. I closed my eyes to concentrate on it, to let it into my body, though I did not allow it to overpower me. I could almost hear Matt warning me to be careful, to not do anything that could endanger me. Yet this felt natural. It felt *real*, like I could draw on the magic and use it. Build on it.

The watch in my reticule throbbed. I didn't know if the others could feel or hear it, or even if I could. Perhaps I simply sensed it.

"*There!*" Duke cried.

The chanting stopped.

"That's here," Cyclops growled. "This house."

Mr. Gibbons continued his chant.

I cracked open my eyes and stared at the bright purple glow on the map. The sketch had been done in pencil, not with colors. That glow...that was me. My watch, to be precise. That's why it had throbbed. It had felt my magic.

I pressed both my palms down on the map. The heat no longer bothered me, even though it felt fiercer, stronger. It coursed through me, and I wondered if my veins lit up like Matt's did when he used his watch.

The map throbbed, just like my watch had. Mr. Gibbons must have felt it too, because he stopped chanting.

"Keep going," I urged. *Think about Matt's watch again*, a small voice told me.

I pictured the way it made his veins glow, the way it erased the lines of tiredness, the shadows of exhaustion. I pictured the watch's housing, and recalled each individual spring and cog that I'd carefully cleaned and replaced mere weeks ago.

"My God," Duke whispered, leaning over my shoulder. "Cyclops?"

"I see it," he intoned. "A curved street in the city. I can't make out the writing. It's a long name for a small street."

The chanting stopped. Miss Gibbons drew in a sharp breath. "It worked!"

"Bucklersbury Street," her father said.

"Bucklersbury!" I opened my eyes to see a glowing patch over the heart of the city. Over the exact position of the Roman mosaic excavation, if I wasn't mistaken. "I was there only recently."

I straightened and removed my hands from the map. The glow vanished. The map was a masterpiece that could grace an art gallery. But it was just a map now.

"India." Cyclops's voice commanded my attention. "We have to go."

"Thank you," I said to Mr. Gibbons. "Your help has been invaluable."

"Good luck," Miss Gibbons said with a tentative smile. "I hope this means Mr. Glass will resume the search for Daniel."

"As soon as he is able, I assure you." To Mr. Gibbons, I said, "We are trying our best."

He nodded but hardly seemed aware of me. He stared at the map, at my hands, and then at his own. "Remarkable," he murmured.

It was, but I didn't have time to ponder it, or my part in the exercise. Matt and Willie needed rescuing.

***

For once, I was glad Bryce liked to drive fast. He managed to maneuver the cumbersome coach through the traffic at speed and we made it to Bucklersbury Street in good time. He didn't stop outside the scaffold-clad building where we'd seen the mosaic floor, however, and I was about to call out to him when I heard him shout.

"Sir!"

I craned my neck out the window and my heart leaped into my throat. Matt! Beside him stood Willie. They were alive and free. *Thank God. Thank God.*

"Matt!" I shouted, opening the door and springing out of the carriage without a care for my skirts. They wrapped around my legs and flapped behind me as I ran.

Both Duke and Cyclops passed me and reached them first. Duke embraced Willie and looked as if he wanted to envelope Matt in a hug too. Cyclops slapped them both on the shoulder.

"Matt! Willie!" I was too happy to see them and *not* embrace each of them in turn. I held onto Matt the longest. His arms tightened before he released me and set me at arm's length.

He looked tired but not exhausted, and the bruises on his face and cut lip told part of the story of his capture. I lifted a hand to touch his cheek, but thought better of it. He wouldn't want my sympathy.

Duke, Cyclops and Willie spoke over the top of each other. Matt and I remained silent, our gazes locked. I knew mine held all the relief swirling through me. I couldn't contain my happiness at seeing them safe, and I suspected that was why he gave me a small smile despite looking thunderous.

"I'm half starved," Willie said. "There's a chop house around the corner. What's say we get us a steak and talk revenge there."

"We have to know who kidnapped us to get revenge," Matt growled. But he nodded. "We'll talk as we eat."

"Are you sure?" I asked. "Shouldn't you rest?"

"I've been resting all damned day. I've had enough resting."

He strode off. I eyed Willie and she gave me a flat smile. "It's been a long day," she said. "And Matt don't like getting tied up like a hog."

"How did you get away?" I glanced back at the building down the street. "And why is no one coming after you?"

"We'll tell you after we eat. I can't talk with an empty stomach."

Cyclops trotted back to the coach to inform Bryce of our plans, and we walked to the chop house. It was too early for dinner and too late for luncheon, so the place wasn't busy. We slipped onto the bench seats in the furthest corner, where the sunshine didn't reach and the lamplight barely did either. The portrait of a woman lounging against a bar stared down at us, an expectant glimmer in her eyes. I wondered if I looked like that as I waited for Matt and Willie to tell their tale.

A waiter wearing a white neck cloth took our orders. As soon as he disappeared, Duke leaned forward, elbows on the table, and said, "Well?"

Matt glanced at Willie. His eyes narrowed. She swallowed and studied her dirty fingernails. "Well," she began, "I made a mess of things."

When she didn't continue, Matt prompted her. "Go on. They deserve to know."

Willie cleared her throat. "I told you I'm sorry, Matt. I mean it."

He held up his hand. "No more," he said, gentler. "Tell them."

"I arrived in Lemon Street at six, but I was ambushed by five men. I didn't stand a chance. They hog-tied me, gagged me, and bundled me into a cart."

"Did they hurt you?" Duke growled.

She winced. "Only a few bruises."

"You went without your gun?"

"I didn't get a chance to use it." She touched her hip where her gun usually hung when she carried it. "They drove me here, to that building where the archaeologists are digging up the floor. It was empty. They took me down to the cellar and left me there, all trussed up."

Duke pushed up her cuff to reveal wrists rubbed raw from rope burn. He swore under his breath.

"Didn't anyone see?" Cyclops asked.

"They threw a coat around me and hustled me inside," Willie said. "But no one was around anyway."

"And then?"

"And then Matt arrived a few hours later, the same way. They left him with me in the cellar."

I glanced at Matt. He looked like he'd rather snap someone's head off than talk about what happened.

The waiter deposited five frothing ales on the table. Willie pounced on hers and drank half the contents in one gulp. Matt drank all of his.

"You were ambushed too?" I asked him when he set the pewter tankard down. "By the gang from Lemon Street?"

He inclined his head in a nod. "They were waiting for me, four inside the arch where I couldn't see them, and one dead ahead as bait. I didn't have time to draw."

But he must have fought them. The evidence of the struggle was all over his face. "Where are your weapons now?" I asked.

"Stolen," Willie spat.

"But not your watch?" I asked Matt.

He shook his head. "They inspected it, but the leader told the others that it was the watch they were ordered to leave with me."

I sat back in the chair, all the air knocked out of me.

"Someone knew how important it was to you," Cyclops said, rubbing his bristly jaw. "That means the one who paid them knows it's magic and you need it."

"It means they didn't want me dead," Matt said with an incline of his head.

"Just out of the way," I murmured. "Abercrombie is my guess, keeping you from meeting Mirth. That means he knows more than we thought—he knows two magics are combined in your watch."

"Or he simply knows it's important to me in some manner."

Willie thumped her elbows on the table and buried her hands in her hair. It had come loose and hung around her shoulders in wild tangles. "You missed meeting Mirth," she groaned.

"I met him," I told them.

Willie peeped through her fingers at me. "You did?"

"And?" Matt asked.

"He's not Chronos," I said. The shoulders of both slumped. "I'll explain more after you tell me how you escaped."

"Willie and I were locked in the cellar," Matt said, "tied up but not gagged. We shouted but no one came. Willie managed to untie my bonds and I freed her, but we couldn't get out of the cellar itself."

"We even tried digging," Willie said. "We found some of the archaeology tools, but it was hopeless in the dark."

"Where was Mr. Young?" I asked.

"Not working today, it would seem," Matt said. "He keeps his tools in the cellar, locked up and out of sight."

"So we waited." Willie glanced at Matt. "Rested. Then suddenly we heard the bolt slide back. We had to fumble our way to the door in the dark. By the time we got there and opened it, whoever unlocked it was gone. We searched the building, and up and down the street, but couldn't see no one."

"And then you three arrived," Matt said. "Did you see anyone you recognized leaving?"

We shook our heads. "We weren't really looking," I said.

"It don't make sense," Duke said with a shake of his head. "They just let you go?"

Matt nodded. "I've had all day to contemplate it, and I think India's right. Someone went to great lengths to keep me from the bank today. Someone who knew there was a cellar in that building and knew we wouldn't be stumbled upon. Someone who didn't want us to die but wanted me out of the way."

Duke swore softly. "It must be Abercrombie."

"But me, Willie and Duke know what Chronos looks like," Cyclops said. "You weren't the only one who could confirm if Mirth was Chronos."

"My kidnapper didn't know that," Matt said. "He thought it was all down to me."

"Which means it ain't Chronos himself," Willie said. "Unless he's forgotten meeting us back then."

"You ain't forgettable," Duke told her with a wry smile.

She lifted her tankard in salute. "So I been told."

"It does seem like Abercrombie is behind it," I said. "I don't know how he knew about your watch, or the cellar in that abandoned building, but he certainly wanted to keep you away from the bank today, Matt, and prevent anyone else seeing Mirth too."

I told them about Abercrombie lurking outside the bank's entrance, and how I'd gotten past him. The more I spoke, the more Matt's expression changed from darkly serious to hopeful, yet no less intense. With his battered face, he looked every bit the formidable Wild West outlaw I'd once believed him to be.

I paused as our food arrived and resumed when the waiter left. I told them how Mirth suspected DuPont was Chronos; how he didn't think DuPont was French, and how we both suspected that was why Abercrombie tried so hard to prevent us speaking to him.

"He doesn't know that we're already aware of DuPont," Matt said, cutting through a boiled potato.

Willie picked up her chop with her fingers and gnawed on the bone. "Willie!" Duke hissed. "You ain't in the cellar now. Use your knife and fork."

"No one can see," she said, wiping grease off her chin with the back of her hand.

"So if Abercrombie is behind your kidnappings," I said, "is he connected to the mosaic dig in Bucklersbury Street? If so, that means he's connected to the archaeologist, Mr. Young, and perhaps even McArdle himself."

"And Daniel's disappearance." Cyclops's words dropped into the silence like lead weights.

Willie held her hand up but her mouth was too full to speak.

Matt filled the pause. "I can't believe Abercrombie would be that foolish. It would be unwise to take us to a place that could connect him to Daniel's disappearance, particularly if he planned on releasing us."

Willie swallowed. "Those pigs were talking when they took me to the cellar. One of them told the others that he walks down Bucklersbury every day, and that he thought it would be a good place to hide out since construction's stopped and the diggers don't work every day."

"By diggers he must mean archaeologists," I said.

"Well ain't you the smart one," Willie said, plucking the bone off Duke's plate and gnawing it too.

"So we don't have a link between Abercrombie and Daniel's disappearance after all." I sighed. "We're no closer to finding him than we were before."

"Speaking of finding people, how did you find us?" Matt asked. "I don't believe in coincidences either. You couldn't possibly have been driving down Bucklersbury hoping we'd be there."

Duke grinned and pointed his knife at Matt. "Wait till you hear this. Go on, India. Tell 'em."

Matt and Willie gave me their full attention, although Matt's brow furrowed slightly. I leaned forward and lowered my voice. "I combined my magic with that of Mr. Gibbons."

"Well done, India." Willie gave me a nod, impressed.

"Not well done." Matt pushed his plate aside and leaned forward too. "What were you thinking using your—"

"I was thinking about finding you," I snapped. "You've had an ordeal, Matt, and you're tired and worried so I won't quarrel with you. What is done is done, and I'll do it again if I have to, without hesitation. Now, kindly refrain from lecturing me. I don't want to hear it."

His eyes flashed for the first time that afternoon, as if the tiredness had suddenly vanished. It would seem arguing with me made him more alert. Not that he liked me admonishing him. Far from it, if his severe frown was an indication.

Duke took a keen interest in his gravy, mopping it up with a slice of bread. Cyclops downed the rest of his ale. Willie, however, seemed unconcerned with Matt's dark mood and asked how the magic worked, so I told her what had transpired in Mr. Gibbons's workshop.

"Pity Daniel never bought a watch from your father," she said. "One you'd worked on. We could use your method to find him."

I glanced at Matt. He was still watching me, and I swear I felt his temper simmering in the space between us. I offered him a smile, but he didn't return it.

We finished our meals and exited the chop house. Willie sucked in a deep breath and let it out slowly. "Never thought I'd appreciate London's stinking air, but I sure do now. The air in that cellar was stale, damp, and reeked of rats."

"Do you want to confront Abercrombie?" Cyclops asked Matt.

"We don't know for certain it was him," Matt said. "Until we do, I don't want him to know that we're aware of what he's up to."

"I disagree," I said, but closed my mouth upon Matt's glare. Perhaps now wasn't the time. He must be tired and eager to get home.

At home, however, there was no opportunity to rest. Matt had to sit through a polite conversation with his aunt's visitors, and I remained with him as a show of support. After the awkward questions about his bruised face were answered—he told them he'd tripped over uneven pavement—he sat quietly and rarely contributed to the conversation.

Even after the visitors left, we couldn't talk alone. His aunt turned to him as soon as they were gone. "Now, tell me the truth. What happened to your handsome face?"

"I told you. I tripped."

"Nonsense. Nobody believes that."

"Aunt," he said on a sigh. "Not now."

She sat silently, her fingers knotting in her lap, for all of ten seconds. "How can I present you to my friends looking like that? They'll think you're a pugilist."

They wouldn't be entirely wrong. "We didn't want to alarm you," I said. "That's why he made up the story about tripping." Matt raised his brows, and a hint of a smile played at his lips. He seemed to be curious as to how I would talk my way out of this. "The truth is, he got into a fight."

Miss Glass pressed a hand to her throat. "Matthew!"

Matt glared at me, the smile gone.

"It wasn't his fault," I said quickly. "There was an obscene man who wouldn't leave Willie alone. Matt was simply defending her honor."

That seemed to appease her, somewhat. Instead of shocked, she looked appalled. "I wasn't aware she had any honor."

"Nor was I," Matt said with a hard edge.

"India, ask Bristow to fetch Picket." Miss Glass touched her forehead. "It's been a long day after a long night."

"Perhaps Matt can escort you to your room," I said. "He ought to be going that way himself."

"I'm not," he said, "but I'd be happy to take you, Aunt." He dutifully rose and assisted Miss Glass to her feet.

"Such a good brother." She touched Matt's blue-black cheek and clicked her tongue. "Poor dear. You oughtn't slay so many dragons."

I didn't expect to see Matt until dinnertime, or perhaps even the next day, but he returned a few minutes later. "Is she all right?" I asked.

"Still spouting about dragons."

"You're her white knight."

He poured himself a glass of brandy at the sideboard. "I'm no one's damned knight. I can't even save myself."

"Matt." I halted. This required more than sympathetic words. I rose and joined him at the sideboard. "Not even knights can fight off five men who take them by surprise."

"I should have been more prepared. I should have expected an ambush."

"You shouldn't have gone alone."

He turned to me and leaned his hip against the sideboard. It was a casual stance, yet there was nothing casual about the anger that rolled off him. I'd thought he'd been angry with me for using my magic, but I now knew that wasn't the only reason.

"Aren't you supposed to be making me feel better?" he asked.

"I thought I was."

"By telling me I wasn't prepared enough?"

"Oh. I hadn't thought of it like that."

He grunted what I suspected was a grudging laugh, as if he were reluctant to abandon his sour mood. He poured me a brandy, but didn't let go of the glass when he handed it to me. "India," he murmured, "I haven't thanked you for coming to our rescue."

"We didn't rescue you. Besides, I thought you didn't like my methods."

"I don't, but I understand why you did it. I would have done the same thing had our situations been reversed."

"Thank you, Matt. I appreciate you acknowledging that."

He let go of the glass, but not before his thumb caressed mine. "I also know a losing battle when I see one. You put me in my place today."

"Yes. Well." I sipped. The brandy warmed my throat and tingled my nose. "I'm not used to being told what to do. It's been some years since Father lectured me. There was little need, really, since I've always been dutiful."

"You're dutiful here, too, on the whole."

"Except when you say something I cannot agree with."

His mouth twisted in a grimace. "You've found your voice, India, and you're not afraid to wield it."

I wasn't sure if he was admonishing me or congratulating me. "I hope there'll be few occasions to do so. I don't like it when we quarrel."

"Nor do I," he said quietly, heavily. "Nor do I." His fingers brushed mine, a light touch that was gone before I could react. He stepped away and downed the rest of his brandy.

The air in the drawing room felt dense, close, making it hard to breathe. I drank the rest of my brandy in one gulp. Unused to the fiery aftertaste, I coughed.

Matt smiled. It was so good to see him happier that I smiled back. "It's been quite a day," I said.

"Is that your polite way of telling me to go to my room to rest?"

I held up my hands. "I wouldn't dare tell you what to do."

"Hmmm."

Bristow entered carrying a salver with an envelope on it. "A letter came for you, sir."

Matt sliced the envelope open and read. "It's from my lawyer. He found Lord Coyle." He folded the letter and dismissed Bristow. "It's not too late. I think I'll pay the earl a visit now. Care to join me, India?"

"You want me to come too?"

"How else will I know if the objects in his collection are magical or not?"

CHAPTER 17

Lord Coyle's Belgravia house was ablaze with light. It streamed from the windows on the first, second and third levels, and the two lanterns by the front door hissed in welcome. The butler was less welcoming. His unprofessional frown upon seeing us on the doorstep made me feel awkward. Matt, however, didn't seem to care.

"Mr. Glass and Miss Steele to see Lord Coyle," he said in his most officious voice. "Tell him it's about the latest addition to his collection."

The butler made us wait while he sent a footman to find Coyle. He checked his watch then adjusted the minute hand on the walnut longcase clock, only to move it back again. It ran perfectly on time, by my reckoning, but clearly the butler needed to appear as if he were doing something and not keeping an eye on us.

A heavyset man with a drooping white mustache that dripped off his chin clomped down the steps, relieving the butler of his duty. "Who're you?" the earl snapped at Matt. "My guests will be arriving shortly, and I don't have time for this."

"Our apologies, sir. We won't take up much of your time," Matt said. "My name is Matthew Glass and this is—"

"You related to Rycroft?" Coyle stepped up to Matt then squinted at his face. The lines at the corners of his eyes flattened out as he blinked. Was it the sight of the bruises that unsettled him?

"He's my uncle," Matt said.

Coyle's mustache lifted with his hint of a smile. "You're the American heir. Bit of a pugilist, eh?" He chuckled. "Wager Rycroft isn't happy."

"Since you have guests arriving soon, let's get to the point. I've heard about your collection—"

"What collection?" Coyle's nose, already quite ruddy, reddened, along with his cheeks.

"Don't play the fool, sir. I am in no mood for games."

Coyle spluttered a half-hearted protest, until Matt interrupted.

"A promising mapmaker is missing, and your man of business has been talking to Onslow, the Mapmakers' Guild's treasurer. The coincidence is highly suspicious."

His eyes widened even more. Surprised that we knew so much? "What's my business got to do with a missing man?"

"We have reason to believe that he made a...special map which Onslow sold to you for your collection."

"If he did, then it's Onslow you need to speak to, not me."

"So you don't deny purchasing the map?"

"I haven't purchased a map from anyone," Coyle said smugly.

"A globe, perhaps?" I suggested.

Coyle looked at me for the first time. "Who're you?"

"My assistant, Miss Steele," Matt said. "Answer her question."

"Don't tell me what to do in my house!"

The butler, hovering not far away, stepped out of the shadows. Matt tensed.

"My lord," I said quickly before we were thrown out, "is there somewhere we can discuss this in private? What we have to say isn't for the ears of others."

"I don't think I like your tone, miss."

"And I don't like your evasiveness," Matt growled. "Very well, if you don't mind others knowing your business, then I'll fetch Commissioner Munro and you can tell him all about your collection at the police station."

"Don't be a fool, Glass. This is England, where people like me are treated with respect. It's not the backwater you crawled out of. Munro can't touch me."

"He can—and he will—if he thinks you have anything to do with the disappearance of his son."

Coyle recoiled. He passed a broad, stubby hand over his face. "Come with me."

We followed him into a small room with books lining two of the walls. A single brown leather armchair angled toward the fireplace, and a landscape hung above the mantel, the vibrant green of the rolling hills offering the only color in the masculine room.

Matt shut the door behind us. "Tell us about your business with Onslow."

Coyle clasped his hands behind his back and stood by the unlit fireplace. "Your assistant is correct. Onslow sold me a globe. There is nothing untoward about the transaction, and it has nothing to do with your missing mapmaker."

"How can you be sure?" Matt asked.

Coyle's Adam's apple bobbed furiously. "Ask Onslow."

"We will."

"Who made the globe?" I asked.

"I don't know, and I don't care," Coyle said.

"May we see it?" Matt asked.

"Certainly not."

"Why not?"

Coyle's mouth flapped but nothing came out for several beats. "Because my collection is private."

Matt strode up to Coyle who shrank away from him, as if trying to flatten himself into the mantel. Matt's extra height coupled with the bruises on his face, and his fierce mood, were an alarming combination. "Show us the globe *now*, sir, or I'll give you a demonstration of how I accrued these bruises."

"Is that a threat?" Strong words spoken by a much weakened voice.

"Yes."

Coyle swallowed. "You're mad."

"It's a family trait."

Coyle glanced at me as if I could rescue him. I simply offered a shrug. "Very well, but you must promise not to reveal the artifacts in my collection to anyone."

"Why not?" Matt asked.

"Because that is part of its mystery. My collection is famous, in certain circles, because of its uniqueness, but also because of its exclusivity. The fewer people who know what it contains, the more intriguing it becomes."

Did he mean it wasn't interesting in itself?

"Just show us the damned collection," Matt snarled.

Coyle skimmed his hand along a row of books until he reached one with a dark red cover. He pulled on it and the entire panel of bookshelves slid open to reveal a hidden room beyond. I drew in a breath, catching the stale scent of cigars beneath wood smoke.

Coyle lit a lantern hanging just inside the doorway and held it aloft. "This way."

I glanced at Matt, and he nodded, clearly thinking as I did—that it could be a trap, and one of us should remain in the library. Since he was the stronger, I thought it best that it be him.

In the end, it didn't matter. The secret room was no bigger than a cupboard, and Matt could see the contents from the doorway. Or some of the contents. The room was crammed with objects. I spotted sculptures of varying sizes and materials, several books, paintings, china plates, stuffed animals, decorative boxes, pieces of furniture, jewelry and even a carved brass mantel clock with a finely etched silver face. The clock didn't hold my attention for long, however. Nor did the large bronze globe resting on the shoulders of a bent old man.

It was the warmth emanating from the room that took me by surprise. No, not the room—the objects themselves. Magical warmth. I knew the difference now.

"You bought the guild's *globe*?" Matt asked, staring at the bronze.

Coyle sniffed. "Onslow sold it to me. The transaction was above board."

"When did it come into your possession?" I asked.

"Last night."

I edged into the room, careful not to knock the bowl full of coins at my feet. The warmth swamped me, enveloped me like a shroud. I drew in a deep breath to steady my nerves. So much magic in such a confined space. It made my skin tingle and dampened unmentionable places. Unable to resist, I rested a hand on the clock. It pulsed. Was it responding to me, even though I'd never tinkered with it?

"Don't touch that," Coyle swatted my hand away. "You've seen enough. Go on, out. Both of you." He shooed us with his hands, but neither Matt nor I moved.

"Are those Roman?" Matt asked, nodding at the bowl of coins on the floor.

Coyle angled himself in front of the bowl. "What of it?"

"Where did you get them?"

"An archaeological dig in the north."

"Who sold them to you?"

"That is none of your affair."

"McArdle?"

Coyle's jaw worked but no words came out. I took it as confirmation.

Arms spread wide, he ushered us out of the room and closed the false door. Now that I knew it was there I could see the door's outline on the bookshelves and the small scrapes on the wooden floor.

"Satisfied?" Coyle asked with a thrust of his chin.

"I'll be speaking to Onslow," Matt said. "If he doesn't confirm your story—"

"He will." He said it with such assuredness that I knew Onslow would back up his story. Coyle wasn't lying.

"Why those objects?" I asked. "There appears to be nothing similar about them, nothing connecting them." Except magic.

"I liked them," he said.

"Some didn't even appear all that valuable," Matt said.

"I simply liked the look of them." He indicated the door, urging us to leave.

"But there must be something about them that makes your collection unique," I went on, determined to get him to admit that they were magical objects.

"If you don't mind, my dinner guests will be arriving soon."

Matt placed a hand under my elbow and steered me out of the room and out the front door. "Thank—"

Coyle slammed the door in our faces. Matt touched the brim of his hat. "I think he wants us to leave." He opened the carriage door for me and assisted me inside. "The Mapmakers' Guild hall in Ludgate Hill," he ordered Bryce.

I waited until we were rolling out of Belgravia before I told Matt what I'd felt. He didn't look at all surprised.

"I suspected as much," he said.

"How?"

"The lack of theme in his collection, and the lack of both rarity and value. Also your reaction when you touched the clock."

"I didn't give myself away to Coyle, did I?"

"I don't think he noticed."

I smoothed down my skirts, feeling a little deflated. What had Matt needed me for if he was able to guess without me?

"I wonder why he collects it all," Matt mused.

"Why does anyone collect anything? To possess something, or out of habit, perhaps. It seems to have earned him a reputation within certain circles, as he put it, so that in itself might be the driving force."

"I wonder if Daniel made that globe."

I'd assumed the globe had stood in the guild's hall for a long time, but I could be wrong. Now that I thought about it, I remembered feeling warmth coming off it the first time I'd visited the hall. I hadn't realized the warmth came from its magic.

Matt put a hand to his mouth to hide his yawn, but I saw it. I bit my tongue to stop myself asking if he needed a rest. We would speak to Onslow quickly then return to Park Street. It shouldn't take long.

Our arrival coincided with that of a half dozen guild members, including Duffield and Onslow. All except Onslow were accompanied by their apprentices, perhaps because he hadn't yet found a new one.

"Mr. Prescott!" Duffield exclaimed as the footman let us in. His lips stretched into a false smile. "What a surprise. And your lovely wife, too. How curious to see you both here at this hour."

"Are you feeling better, Mrs. Prescott?" Mr. Onslow asked, the ledger clasped to his chest beneath folded arms.

"Much, thank you," I said.

Matt inspected the globe in the center of the entrance hall, an exact replica of the one in Coyle's collection. He circled it and scuffed the toe of his shoe on the tiles, but I couldn't see any marks there.

Duffield looked at him as if he were an eccentric, albeit one he needed to court for his custom. Onslow, however, stared straight ahead, not looking at anyone or anything in particular.

"Is there something I can do for you, Mr. Prescott?" Duffield asked.

"We need to speak to you, Onslow," Matt said. "Immediately."

Onslow's droopy eyelid twitched. "Oh?"

"I am sorry," Duffield said. "But we're about to begin an extraordinary meeting. There was a break-in, you see, and we're trying to assess if anything was taken."

Onslow's fingers tightened around the ledger. He stared down at the floor.

I'd almost forgotten about the break-in, which most likely wasn't a break-in at all. The glass had been found outside, not inside.

I ambled up to Matt. The bronze globe looked heavy. It would take three or four men to move it. Men who probably had trouble carrying it and perhaps lost their balance and knocked out a window before leaving. I stroked my fingers across Europe. Warm, just like the one in Coyle's secret room.

"Mr. Onslow," Matt said to the treasurer. "I'd like to speak to you in your office before the meeting. It's regarding a commission for Lord Coyle."

Onslow's eyelid twitched madly. He didn't move, didn't acknowledge Matt at all.

"It's this way, isn't it?" Matt said, approaching the stairs.

"Coyle?" Duffield asked. "You know his lordship?"

"We're acquaintances. Mr. Onslow? Now, if you please."

Onslow hurried after him, his footsteps light and quick, his gaze downcast.

"Onslow?" Duffield called after him. "The meeting."

"I won't be long." Onslow blinked hopefully at Matt.

The three of us headed up the stairs to Onslow's office. Even inside with the door closed, Onslow didn't release his grip on the ledger. He clutched it tighter to his chest.

"What do you want?" he asked.

Matt held out a chair for me to sit on. When I did, he remained standing, as did Onslow. "We want you to tell us how you made the globe you sold to Lord Coyle," Matt said.

Onslow plopped down on the chair behind the desk. "I don't know what you mean."

"Then allow me to tell you what we know. I'm sure that will help you think. We know that you secretly sold the bronze globe that used to be downstairs to Lord Coyle."

"You're mistaken." Onslow laughed, a nervous giggle. "You just saw it. It's still there."

"That's a copy you had made. The exchange happened last night. There was no break-in. The broken glass was probably caused by Coyle's men removing the globe." So he'd worked it out too.

Onslow's smile faded. "Are you accusing Lord Coyle of theft?"

"I'm accusing *you* of theft. You sold it to Coyle without the guild's permission and kept the proceeds for yourself."

"I did not!"

"Not for yourself," I said, realizing our mistake. "You're giving the money to the guild."

Matt turned to me, a small dent between his brows.

"The entries in the ledger." I nodded at the book. "The amounts next to Coyle's name were high. Mr. Onslow wouldn't enter them in the book at all if he was keeping the money himself."

"Very clever." Matt sounded more than a little impressed, but I wasn't sure if he was referring to Onslow's scheme or my discovery of it.

"We don't care if you stole the globe for your own gain, or the guild's, or simply to appease Lord Coyle," I said. "We care about finding Daniel."

"The apprentice?" Onslow frowned. "What has this got to do with him?"

"Who made the globe, Mr. Onslow?" Matt asked.

"I did."

"No," I said. "Be honest."

"I am! That globe is my work. Ask anyone. I made the original and the copy you saw downstairs." He lifted his chin and squared his shoulders. "So it was mine to sell. In a way."

Matt swore under his breath. I understood his frustration. If Onslow wanted to dupe us, we'd have to tell him the truth.

"The mapmaker who made that globe is a magician," I said.

"India," Matt warned.

I shook my head at him and he snapped his mouth closed, although I knew he wasn't happy about me speaking out of turn.

Onslow stared at me. "How...how do you know about magic?'

"That is none of your concern," Matt said. "We know that globe was magical, so you cannot possibly have made it unless you're a magician."

Onslow neither nodded nor shook his head. He sat perfectly still, as lifeless as the bronze statue holding up the globe.

Matt rubbed his hand over his jaw. "Ah."

"Don't tell anyone," Onslow blurted out. He pulled the ledger to his chin, as if he wanted to hide behind it. "Don't tell a soul. No one here knows and that's how it must remain. Do you understand?"

"We'll keep your secret," I assured him. "I am one too."

His eyes widened. He blinked back at me, searching my face. "Maps?"

"Timepieces."

Matt sighed. At least he'd given up trying to stop me.

"You can be assured of our silence," I told him again. "Utterly."

Onslow nodded quickly, but the haunted look in his eyes didn't disappear.

"Did you know that Daniel Gibbons was magical too?" Matt asked.

"I hardly knew the lad." He looked as if he would lie then thought better of it. "He told me, the fool. He'd only recently learned about his magic. Apparently someone recognized it in him and told him how to identify magic in objects. Daniel realized my globe had magical properties. He asked Duffield who'd made it and Duffield informed him that it was my creation, made years ago. Daniel came to me and demanded I teach him spells. If I didn't, he'd tell Duffield—everyone—about my magic."

"He blackmailed you," Matt said.

That explained how Daniel learned the spells to make his magical maps. It must have been McArdle that informed him he was a magical, after seeking out the gifted mapmaker selling beautiful and unusual maps from his cart on Oxford Street.

"I tried to warn Daniel," Onslow went on. "I begged him to hide his magical ability, to draw simpler maps, but he wouldn't listen. He was a precocious braggart. He thought he was the best, and he wanted the world to know it."

A knock on the door startled Onslow and set his droopy eye twitching again.

"Coming!" he called, his voice high. "I have to go, and so do you both. Your being here is highly suspicious."

He strode to the door, but Matt got there first, blocking the exit. "What I don't understand is why you made that globe in the first place when you're so reluctant to admit to us that you're a magician."

"I made it before I was fully aware of the dangers of exposure. My father warned me too late—the globe had already been entered into the guild's Best Globe Award that year. My father had to tell the officials that I'd found the globe, not made it, in case anyone suspected it was magical. Nobody did, thank God, but the experience frightened me. I kept quiet about my magic after that. Until Coyle came along and wanted to buy the globe. I never wanted it displayed in the entrance here, where everyone could see it. I should have fought harder for it to be removed."

"How did Lord Coyle know it was magical?" I asked.

Onslow shrugged. "He didn't say. When I told him that it wasn't for sale, he said he'd expose me. I couldn't risk it. After hearing the tales of what was done to magicians in times past..." He shuddered. "Keep your identity secret, Mrs. Prescott. Be sure your wife does, sir."

"Yes," Matt said darkly. "I'm trying."

"What about Daniel?" I asked. "Do you think anyone else from the guild knew he was a magician?"

"I haven't the foggiest. I don't know where he is or what happened to him." He peered around Matt to the door. "I must go."

"One more question," I said as Matt stepped aside. "What does your globe *do*? It's beautiful, of course, but does its magic do anything?"

"It was designed to show the location of the guild hall. A tiny golden light used to appear on it in the precise longitude and latitude of this spot. In my youthful naivety I thought that would be a nice touch to appeal to the award judges." He huffed out a humorless little laugh.

"Used to?"

"The magic lasted only a few weeks. You know how it is." At my blank look, he added, "The magic is temporary. It always fades, sometimes after a few hours or days, sometimes weeks. You must have noticed that with your magic too."

"I'd forgotten," I lied. Onslow mustn't know about combining horology magic with other types to extend their usefulness. It seemed few did.

McArdle must. That's why he was so desperate to get his hands on the map Daniel created for him. The magic could expire any day and he'd be left with a lovely but useless map.

Another rapid knock thumped on the door. "Mr. Onslow!" came a youth's voice. "They want to start. I've been sent to fetch you immediately."

Matt stepped aside and Onslow muttered his thanks. He didn't leave until we walked out first, then wedged the ledger under his arm and locked the door behind us.

Once we reached the entrance foyer again, he hurried to the meeting room where Duffield stood by the door, tapping his foot on the tiles. He nodded at us as Onslow slipped past him. Cyclops emerged, carrying an empty silver tray, his expression bland. He didn't acknowledge us as he turned toward the service area.

The elderly footman saw us out. "Well," I said, blinking as my eyes adjusted to the darkness. "That was enlightening."

Matt's hand pressed into the small of my back. "Do you think he's telling— Who's there?" he snapped at the shadows behind the carriage. "Show yourself!"

I'd heard the footsteps too but assumed it was merely a passerby. I was about to tell Matt as much when a man stepped in front of us.

I gasped. "McArdle!"

CHAPTER 18

Matt shoved me behind him as he drew a revolver from the waistband of his trousers. He'd been carrying a gun all this time!

McArdle put up his hands. "Don't shoot! I want to talk."

"Get in the carriage," Matt ordered.

"No. We'll talk out here where we're on equal footing. Put the bloody weapon away."

Matt adjusted his grip on the gun handle. More footsteps sounded on the pavement, but no one appeared through the dark veil of night. Matt tucked the revolver back into his waistband and jerked his head toward the carriage. "Other side, out of sight." He grabbed McArdle's arm and marched him around the carriage. I followed, trotting to keep up. "India, get in."

I was about to protest when I realized I could hear them quite well from the carriage with the window down. I climbed in and lowered the window in time to hear Matt order Bryce to cover the carriage lamp. A moment later, we were plunged into deeper darkness.

Lamps brightened the gloom further down the street, but very little light reached us.

"I don't know why you're being so suspicious," McArdle said to Matt. "You need me as much as I need you."

"If you know you need us, why did you run away last time?" Matt asked.

"I still thought I could find Daniel and my map on my own."

"And you didn't want to share your treasure with us."

"We don't want your coin hoard," I told him. "We only want Daniel."

The silhouette of McArdle nodded. "Then you have a partner in the search. Time is running out. We *must* find him."

He probably meant the magic in the map was running out, but I felt as if time was running out for Daniel too. He'd been missing for a week now.

"How did you know we'd be here?" Matt asked.

"I didn't. I went to your house, but you weren't there. I decided to come here and force them to give me Daniel's map. It's *mine*," he snarled. "I paid for it."

"Force who?"

"The other cartographers in the guild, and that man Duffield, in particular. He *must* know where my map is. He was Daniel's employer."

"If he had it, wouldn't he just give it to you?"

"Not if he knew it was magic. Him, and the artless like him, want to bury magic, keep it a secret to make their artless businesses more profitable."

"Artless?" I echoed.

"It's a word my father used to describe those without magic. It fits men like Duffield perfectly. The prick won't admit he has my map. If he destroyed it—"

"He doesn't have it," Matt said. "I do."

"What!" McArdle blurted out. "Why didn't you tell me before now?"

"You ran off last time before I had the chance." Matt's lie rolled off his tongue easily. We'd deliberately kept the information from McArdle when last we met, simply because we weren't sure if we could trust him.

We still didn't know, but if there was a chance that the map might lead us to Daniel, we had to take it. Mr. Gibbons's magic hadn't been able to connect with the map to find him, but the map hadn't been infused with his magic, nor had it been made for him. It had been made for McArdle. Perhaps it would respond to McArdle, as it was apparently intended to do.

I explained all this to him. "I know you're not a map magician," I told him, "but you are a magician, and this map belongs to you, in essence. It will reveal the location of the hoard only for you or Daniel."

"Unless the magic has run out," McArdle grumbled. "And anyway, how will revealing the location of the hoard lead you to him?"

"It might not, but I've been thinking." I looked to Matt. His eyes glittered back at me through the darkness, but his expression was impossible to see. He might stop me from speaking once he realized what I was about to say. "We recently discovered a way of combining my magic with map magic."

"You?" McArdle grunted a laugh. "Well, well."

"The combination led us to find Mr. Glass when he went missing."

"Is that so? Come on then, let's try. Where's the map now?"

"India, I don't think it will work," Matt said. "The situation is entirely different. I possess a watch you've worked on. Your magic responded to *that*."

"Just bloody try it," McArdle snapped.

"I know, Matt," I said. "But we don't have any other options left to us. Since McArdle is here, and we have the map, it's worth a try."

"You have the map *here*?" McArdle thumped Matt's arm. "Then what are you waiting for, man? Get it."

I may not have been able to see Matt's expression, but I knew he was holding himself back from thumping McArdle. He reached into his inside jacket pocket and pulled out the map.

McArdle released a heavy sigh of relief. Matt pressed the map up against the closed carriage door beneath the window and McArdle laid both hands on it. I removed my gloves, reached through the window and touched it too.

The parchment warmed my fingers, but the heat didn't escalate beyond a mild tingling sensation. It felt nothing like the magic in Gibbons's workshop. Had the magic in this map faded already, or did it simply not respond because neither I nor McArdle created it?

"Anything?" Matt asked.

"No," I said.

McArdle removed one of his hands, and with the other still pinning the map to the carriage door, reached into his pocket.

Matt grabbed his arm. "What are you doing?"

"Getting this." McArdle held up something small and round between his thumb and forefinger. "It's the coin—from my hoard—that you stole from me. It grew warmer just now. It responded to the magic from the map." He placed the coin flat on his palm and looked down at it, as if waiting for it to leap off.

"How curious," I said. "Is it from the same hoard that this map is supposed to reveal?" I studied the map upside down, but it didn't show any signs of a location, either with light or any other type of signal.

"I'm trying to concentrate," McArdle growled.

"Answer her," Matt growled back.

McArdle sighed. "I bought them off a rag man many years ago. They were in his collection of buttons. They responded to me, growing warm upon my touch, so I knew they were magic."

"But magic shouldn't last long," I said. "Only weeks or days, not years. This coin is ancient."

"The magic itself doesn't last, but the residue lingers for centuries, perhaps forever. That's the warmth we feel."

"What does gold magic do?" Matt asked.

"Magic does the one thing that people want most from that object. With maps, it's to direct you to a location. In the case of gold, what does everyone want?"

"More," I said on a breath.

"Precisely."

"But if you can make gold multiply, you ought to be a very wealthy man, Mr. McArdle. I mean no offence, but I don't see evidence of that."

He sighed. "The spells to multiply gold disappeared long ago. As far as I am aware, there are no other gold magicians left in the world, except me. I can't make more, I don't know the spell. I can only feel the residue of the magic infused into golden objects by my ancestors who did know the spell." He picked up the coin again. "The last gold magicians died out in ancient times."

"Hence the hoards," I whispered. "How extraordinary."

"How frustrating. I have the ability, but I don't know how to use it."

I understood his frustration. "So you now earn a living selling magical gold objects to wealthy collectors. Objects that you find through archaeology with a little help from your magical sensitivity."

"It's not illegal," McArdle whined. "I have a right to earn a living." He studied the coin again.

"You said 'they' and 'them' just now when referring to the coin," Matt said. "Did you buy more than one off the rag man?"

"There were two matching ones, both with a shank attached. I gave the other to Daniel to help him draw the map."

Matt glanced at me at the same moment I looked to him. "Mr. McArdle," I said, "is it possible that Daniel had that coin on him when he disappeared?"

"I wouldn't know. Why?"

"Earlier today I was able to find Matt by combining my watch magic with that of a map magician," I said, the words tumbling out in my excitement. "I was able to locate his watch because I'd handled it before. I've worked on it in the past. Its location lit up on the map. If Daniel is still in possession of the coin, and *your* coin is responding to the hoard, and we have a map that shows where that hoard is—"

"We might find him that way."

"Two locations should be revealed," Matt said. "One for the hoard and one for Daniel's coin."

I prayed Daniel had kept the coin with him and the map didn't lead us to his house or the gutter where he'd lost it.

"Put your hand back on the map, Miss Steele," McArdle said quickly. "Let's see if we can replicate the experiment."

"I don't think it has anything to do with me," I said. "There are non timepieces involved. Try it on your own while holding the coin and concentrate very hard."

"Very well." He bowed his head, his palm pinning the map to the door as if trying to push the carriage over. He drew in two steadying breaths and let them out slowly. "The coin is warming again! And look at the map!"

A small pinprick of light pulsed, piercing the surrounding darkness and lighting up that area of the map. It was difficult to see, upside down, with the densely packed streets in that part of London, but I could just make out the street name.

Only it was just one light, not two.

McArdle dropped his coin back in his pocket and the light extinguished, shrouding us once again in near darkness.

Paper scrunched as McArdle took down the map. Then he ran off.

Matt swore and made to go after him.

"Let him go," I said, catching his sleeve. "We have no need of the map now." We watched as the deep shadows on the other side of the street swallowed the figure of McArdle.

"You saw the location?" Matt asked. "I couldn't make it out."

"I did, and I think I know why the map only showed one light."

"Why?" he asked, opening the carriage door.

"Daniel and the hoard are together. Bryce!" With a hand on my hat, I poked my head out the door. "Bucklersbury Street, poste haste."

"Bucklersbury?" Matt said, climbing inside. .

Bryce removed the lamp cover and urged the horses forward.

"It makes sense that both the hoard and Daniel are there," I said as the carriage lurched. "In the case of the hoard, it's there because Bucklersbury happens to have been an important part of Roman Londinium. That's why there are two digs in the street at the moment, one with the mosaic floor where you and Willie were taken, and the other nearby. Whether the hoard is in one of those excavations or elsewhere in the street, I couldn't quite tell from the map."

"But why would Daniel be there? It's too much of a coincidence that someone happened to take him to the same place where the hoard is located."

"Not necessarily. You and Willie were taken to a construction site where building had been halted to conduct an archaeological dig. While the site wasn't in use, it made the perfect place to hide you. No one would stumble upon you and no one could hear your shouts. Whoever took Daniel might have come to the same conclusion and is keeping him at one of the sites."

"Or it may be someone working with Abercrombie, if it was Abercrombie who organized our kidnapping."

"That's certainly a possibility too," I said.

Matt tapped his fingers on the seat beside him and jiggled his knee as if he couldn't stand to sit still. I reached out and touched his knee to stop it moving as opposed to anything more intimate. When I realized how it must seem, I went to withdraw but he laid his hand over mine, trapping it.

"I don't want there to be a connection between Daniel's disappearance and the Watchmakers' Guild," he said gravely. "That links your situation to Daniel's. It's one thing to have them all wary of you, but another entirely to think they would consider...abduction."

Or murder. It was a thought that had crept up on me lately, too; one that I didn't dare dwell on. "Let's not assume anything until we know for certain."

Matt turned away and stared into the inky blackness, his silence creating a void between us. I tried to think of something to say to lighten it, but everything sounded awkward in my head.

It wasn't until he squeezed the bridge of his nose that I realized tiredness might be the cause of his silence. He may have napped while in the cellar, but that had been a few hours ago. He also hadn't used his watch in some time.

He opened his jacket and I thought he'd reach for it, but instead he pulled the revolver from his waistband. "Do you know how to use this?" he asked.

"No!"

"Pull back the hammer, aim through the sight here, and squeeze the trigger. It's loaded with six cartridges."

"Why are you telling me this? I won't be using it."

"Just in case."

"Matt! Nothing will happen to you. Or me. There's no need for a gun at all, surely."

"Just in case," he said again, setting the revolver on my lap.

I picked it up between my thumb and fingertips and set it on the seat beside me.

He rubbed his forehead and bowed his head.

"Are you all right?" I asked.

With a sigh, he removed his gloves and reached into his jacket pocket. "I will be." He pulled out his watch, opened the case, and tipped his head back as the magic washed through him.

***

The boney fingers of the scaffold reached into the black sky above Bucklersbury Street on not one but three construction sites. Bryce pulled up outside the building with the mosaic floor and Matt got out. A figure huddled in a recessed doorway, knees pulled to his chest, bare feet protruding from his trouser legs.

"McArdle was on foot," Matt said, his gaze sweeping the street. "We beat him here."

"Not necessarily," I said. "If he knows the lanes and streets in this part of London, he might already be here. We traveled by the better lit, wider route which is also longer."

"Stay here."

"Why? Only McArdle knows we're here, and he doesn't pose a threat."

"I see threats everywhere. Sometimes there aren't any, and I've over-reacted, but sometimes my caution pays off."

I made a miffed sound in the back of my throat. "You rarely act cautiously, Matt. You're haring off now, aren't you, without a gun and into a dark building?"

"Please, India, just stay here."

He sounded so tired and aggravated that I nodded to ease his mind. "If you're not back in ten minutes, I'm coming in," I told him.

"Fifteen. Bryce, a lamp."

Bryce unhooked one of the carriage lamps and passed it down to Matt.

"If there's any trouble," Matt told him, "drive off as fast as you can."

He crossed the street and disappeared into the building with the mosaic floor. At least this site he knew.

I opened the window and rested my hands on the sill, resisting the urge to check my watch every five seconds. My resolve didn't last long. I couldn't stand it and opened the case. Not even five minutes had passed.

A figure emerged at the end of the street. The vagrant in the recessed doorway lifted his head then returned it to his knees almost immediately, as if it were too heavy to hold up. The figure carried a lantern that swung as he walked, creating an arc of light on the pavement. It wasn't until he passed beneath a streetlight, however, that I saw his face.

McArdle. He must have stopped to fetch a lantern. I wasn't sure whether to alert him to my presence, or Matt's, and was in the process of making up my mind when he slipped behind the scaffold into one of the buildings. It wasn't the same building that Matt had entered.

I waited. The next five minutes dragged, and I considered going inside after Matt anyway. Surely that was long enough for him to search the site.

The horses shifted and the vagrant looked up again as another man approached along the street. This one carried no lantern and I couldn't make out his face.

He paused at the head of the street. What was he waiting for? After a moment he continued and entered the same building site as McArdle. But why? And without a light, too?

Unless he was there for the same reason as us—to find Daniel or the hoard. Could he have overheard us at the guild hall? Someone had certainly been there as McArdle revealed himself, but I'd assumed it to be a passerby who'd walked on. Perhaps he hadn't.

Perhaps he was Daniel's kidnapper and he'd heard everything we said.

I needed to warn Matt. I couldn't just sit here and let him stumble into danger.

I grabbed the gun and my watch from my reticule. I hung the chain around my neck and the case bumped against my breast. "Stay here," I told Bryce. "I won't be long."

"But Miss Steele!" he protested. "You stay. I'll go."

"And leave me with horses I can't control?"

He grumbled something that I couldn't make out. Out of the corner of my eye, I saw Matt emerge from between the scaffold structure. I tried to signal to him, but he didn't see me in the dark, and I didn't want to shout and alert anyone to our presence.

The crack of a gunshot rent the still night air.

My heart leapt into my throat and I stopped dead in my tracks in the middle of the street. Everything else, however, suddenly came to life. The horses reared then bolted, despite Bryce's shouted commands. He managed to hold on to the reins and keep the carriage upright, despite one wheel climbing the gutter. He couldn't stop the horses, however, and the conveyance rumbled out of Bucklersbury, once again plunging the street into near-silence. The vagrant scuttled away, and tiny rat or cat claws scratched the pavement, but otherwise, there were no sounds.

Matt shut off his lamp and slipped away in the dark. He hadn't seen me.

The gun felt heavy in my hand. The watch at my breast warmed then pulsed. Warning me? Urging me on?

All I knew was that Matt had no weapon and had gone to confront a man who did.

I crept up to the building that McArdle and the newcomer had entered. The light was so dim in this part of the street that I had to feel my way past the scaffold by hand. I tripped up the first step. With the gun in my right hand, I was unable to catch myself and landed heavily on my knees. Wincing, I pushed up.

The building's demolition hadn't been completed. The facade was still in place, held up by the scaffold, but the internal walls, floors and ceilings had been removed. A staircase led nowhere and three levels of glassless window frames looked down on my approach like ghostly eyes. Higher still, the open roof revealed the starless London night.

Where were the men? I squinted into the darkness and, at the very rear of the property, saw the glow of a faint light on the floor. I crept closer but was still a considerable distance away when I realized a figure lay flat on the floor near the light.

I didn't dare call Matt's name. It may not even be him.

Hardly breathing, I picked my way across the dirt, careful not to trip over the planks left lying about or stumble into the piles of rubble. I looked around for pits left by archaeological excavations but saw none.

The light brightened as I drew closer, and I realized it came from a cellar below floor level. I was almost within hissing distance of the figure when he swiftly and silently rose into a crouch. I recognized Matt's build, the set of his shoulders. Before I could whisper his name, he placed his palms on the ground then plunged into the cellar.

I hurried to the trapdoor and fell onto my hands and knees. Pain burned my scraped knee. I bit my lip until it subsided and peered through the trapdoor.

Smooth stone steps led down into the cellar. A lamp cast a soft glow over a pit several feet wide and a foot below the cellar floor. An archaeological dig, but not for a mosaic floor. The pit simply contained low, broken walls and little towers of neatly stacked stone, each reaching knee height. Fresh earth filled the far end of the pit and more earth was piled up on the side, ready to be pushed in. It must be the finished excavation Mr. Rosemont from the museum had mentioned.

From my vantage point, I couldn't see Matt or anyone else, but I heard grunting. Someone came into view, bent at the waist and moving slowly backward. He was dragging...a body!

Bile burned my throat. A chill crept up my spine. *Not Matt. Please don't be Matt.*

I searched the room and spotted him in the shadowy corner, crouching behind a wheelbarrow. *Thank God.*

Matt watched the man dragging the body too. The man had shed his jacket and his waistcoat rode up, revealing a gun tucked into the waistband of his trousers. It was impossible to determine the identity of either the victim or his murderer, but one had to be McArdle.

Victim. Murderer.

The words wedged in my brain, their implication so awful, so unfathomable, that I couldn't think past them. All I knew was that Matt was down there in the same room as a man with a gun who'd already used it to kill.

I looked at the revolver in my hand, resting on the ground. I silently repeated Matt's instructions—*pull back the hammer, aim, squeeze the trigger*. It didn't sound too hard.

I clutched it in both hands and pointed it down into the cellar at the man dragging the body. Now what? Alert Matt to my presence? But how without alerting the murderer?

My watch burned fiercely at my chest, the pulsing so strong now that it must be visible. I didn't dare look down and check. At least it remained silent.

The murderer drew closer to the pit and, with an almighty grunt, rolled the body into it near the pile of earth. The body landed face up, wedged between the stacks, legs and arms skewed awkwardly. The murderer straightened and wiped his forehead with the back of his hand. He jumped into the pit and maneuvered the body until it lay flat. The light from the lamp didn't reach to the base of the pit and I still couldn't make out the victim's face.

I watched as the murderer shoveled soil over the body, burying it. Nobody would find it once it was entirely covered and the floor replaced for the new building. The murderer intended for the victim to disappear, for his family to be left in the dark, forever to wonder what happened to him. Who would do such a callous thing?

Matt still didn't reveal himself. He must be waiting for the man to get closer.

Sweat dampened my brow, despite the cool air, but I didn't dare let go of the gun to wipe it away. I didn't dare take my gaze off the scene below me. I waited, like Matt, for the murderer to leave.

He finished burying the body and threw the shovel aside. Breathing heavily, he hauled himself out of the pit and dusted off his hands. He surveyed his work and, with a nod of satisfaction, picked up the lamp that I'd seen McArdle carrying earlier.

He approached the steps and suddenly looked up, directly at me.

Ronald Hogarth!

The apprentice reached for his gun. "Throw your weapon down here," he shouted. "I know you won't use it so don't pretend to get cocky."

I had no time to consider my options. Matt lunged, but Hogarth heard his approach and kicked out at the last moment. The boot hit Matt square in the chest, knocking him back. He coughed and wheezed, trying to catch his breath, but the force had winded him. He pressed a hand to his chest where he'd been struck, and where his watch sat tucked away.

What if it had broken? *Oh God.*

"Don't move." Hogarth aimed his gun at Matt. "Neither of you move or I'll kill him."

CHAPTER 19

My watch pulsed wildly on the outside of my chest, matching my heartbeat on the inside.

"Stand in the pit!" Hogarth ordered Matt. "You," he said to me, "I told you to throw down the weapon or I'll kill your husband."

I didn't correct him. He must still think us to be Mr. and Mrs. Prescott. "No," I said, my voice shaking. Every part of me shook, from the hands that held the gun to my toes. "You think I won't shoot you, but I assure you, I will. If you pull that trigger, I pull mine."

"You'll miss." Hogarth smirked. "You're shaking like a leaf."

"You're a gambling man, are you?"

Hogarth swallowed. His gaze darted between me and Matt, unsure where to look or who to point the gun at. In that moment, he looked so young, so innocent and scared. Yet this man had murdered McArdle, and perhaps Daniel, too.

"You'll either die or go to jail, Mr. Hogarth. It's your choice." I glanced at Matt, hoping to see some advice in his expression. But he still had not caught his breath. He labored for every one, sucking in great gasps that barely made his chest rise.

The watch...it must have broken under the force of the kick. The thing that kept him alive had stopped, and that meant Matt's heart had stopped too. *Please, no.*

"Matt?" My voice squeaked. My hands trembled more. I had to get to him. And do what? "I'm coming down. Don't shoot. Our driver is outside and if we don't return, he'll fetch the police. You can't kill everyone, Mr. Hogarth."

"Stay there, India," Matt rasped. Then he doubled over, hands on his knees.

I stepped through the trapdoor and descended the narrow steps, the gun trained on Hogarth. He swiveled and pointed his weapon at me. Apparently he deemed me the greater threat, with Matt struggling to breathe.

"Don't move, Mrs. Prescott. I will kill you. The world needs to be rid of people like you anyway."

"You mean magicians," I said.

Behind him, Matt continued to wheeze loudly, but he also straightened. His face looked normal. Tired, but not pale. Was he pretending to be winded? He made a circling motion with his hand, a signal to me to keep Hogarth talking, perhaps.

"You overheard our conversation with McArdle," I said. "Is that why you killed him? Because he's a magician?"

"I didn't plan on shooting him. That was an accident. I came in here looking for you and him, but he startled me. The gun went off. Not that it matters. As you say, one less magician." He lifted the gun higher, aiming at my head.

Matt crept forward, his footsteps silent.

"What about Daniel?" I asked, although I already knew the answer.

"Buried in the pit over there, waiting to be sealed up forever beneath the new floor."

Oh no. Poor Daniel. Poor Miss and Mr. Gibbons, and Commissioner Munro. They'd lost something a parent should never have to lose. My heart weighed heavily for them. If we'd found him sooner, could we have saved him?

I had to know. "When did you kill him?"

"The day after he was kidnapped and brought here. I shot him." He made a gun with the fingers of his spare hand and placed it against his temple. "They'll never find him, and good riddance, too."

I frowned. "*You* didn't kidnap him?"

"Duffield did."

My gasp filled the thick silence. "Duffield! Why?"

"Because Daniel was a danger to us. He could ruin every mapmaker in the city. Duffield saw it. He knew what would happen if men like him were allowed to start their own businesses. They'd ruin us, and every last legitimate member of the guild. He couldn't let it happen."

"Duffield ordered you to kill him?"

"No, I did it because Duffield wouldn't. I overheard him planning the abduction with another man."

"Who? Abercrombie?"

"I don't know the man's name. I never saw his face. He urged Duffield to kidnap Daniel, and to try to reason with Daniel and stop him using his magic." He snorted. "You can't reason with an unreasonable braggart. So I followed Duffield here and killed Daniel, since he lacked the spine for it."

I clutched the gun tighter. The youth's cold retelling of the story chilled me further. He had no qualms about killing Daniel, and would have no qualms about killing Matt or me either.

"Daniel deserved it," Hogarth went on.

"Why?" I didn't dare glance at Matt, although I knew he was still too far away from Hogarth to disarm him.

"He was the worst kind of magician. Cocky. Arrogant. He thought he was better than us, but he wasn't. You want to know why?"

"Yes."

"Because he never had to work for his craft. It came easily to him, he was born with it. I, and every other hard-working cartographer, pour time and effort into the maps we create." He shook his head and bared his teeth. "Yet all the accolades, all the money, were showered on him. He hadn't even worked as an apprentice for a month when commissions came to him like kittens led to milk. He didn't have to do anything to earn his reputation."

"He had to create wonderful maps."

"You call those vile things wonderful? They're evil. Magicians are evil, ungodly *freaks*." Spittle flew from his mouth and landed on his lower lip. "You're dangerous people, unpredictable."

"There's no danger from a map magician, Mr. Hogarth. How can a map or globe harm you?"

"I've heard the tales of how maps used to come to life. How rivers flowed off map edges and drowned entire villages. How the tentacles of monsters drawn in the oceans reached out of the paper and pulled real ships under the waves."

"Those are just stories."

"My father told them to me, as his father told him, and his father before that. Not all stories are lost in the mists of time, Mrs. Prescott. What about your magic? What does it do?"

"Does Mr. Duffield know what you did?" I asked, not daring to head down the path he wanted to take. If I riled him, or frightened him, he would want to rid the world of me too. At the moment, he seemed a little reluctant. Because I was a woman? Or was it that I wasn't a cartographer?

"After I told him, yes. He didn't appreciate my efforts to protect him and the guild members." He shrugged, as if that didn't matter.

"Yet he employed you as his new apprentice."

"A happy outcome. I did have to work hard to secure the position, by reminding him that he would be in a great deal of trouble with the police if I spoke to them. He did, after all, kidnap Daniel. Now, any more delaying questions?" His lip lifted in a sneer, baring his teeth.

Matt was so close now I expected him to leap the remaining distance. He continued to breathe heavily, coughing and wheezing so that Hogarth would think him incapacitated.

"Just one more," I said. "Why here?"

"Duffield brought Daniel here upon that other fellow's urging. Apparently he'd heard from some East End roughs that it was a good place to hide people."

"You had nothing to do with Matt's—Mr. Prescott's—kidnapping earlier today?"

"My my, what a busy day you've had. No, that wasn't me."

Another thought occurred to me. "Did you hire a thug to warn me outside church last Sunday?"

"How would I know which church you attend?" No, Mrs. Prescott, that wasn't me either. You do seem to have quite a few enemies."

So it had been Abercrombie too, after we'd confronted him over his knowledge of Daniel's disappearance.

Hogarth glanced toward Matt and, seeing him near, swore and swiveled the gun in his direction. Matt dove low. The gun went off.

My heart stopped.

But Matt was unharmed. He tackled Hogarth just as I was about to squeeze the trigger. I lowered the weapon, afraid I'd hit Matt if I fired. I watched them rolling on the dirt, locked together. Hogarth circled his legs around Matt's waist but Matt caught Hogarth's wrist and forced the gun to point harmlessly away.

I scrambled down the remaining steps to the cellar floor and aimed the gun at Hogarth's head. "Surrender," I ordered. "And I assure you, I'm feeling much more willing to shoot you after your confession. At this distance, I won't miss."

He stopped struggling and released his gun.

"Kick it away, India," Matt said.

I did and stepped back as Matt got to his feet, hauling Hogarth with him. He dragged Hogarth's hands behind his back and marched him up the steps.

I picked up Hogarth's gun and followed them upstairs and outside.

Bryce had returned, thank goodness. He reached into the box under his seat and tossed some rope to Matt, who bound Hogarth's wrists together. Matt bundled the apprentice inside, took one of the guns and trained it on him.

"Vine Street Police Station," he ordered Bryce.

***

We spent too long at the police station. We were interviewed extensively, then had to wait for the detective inspector to send for Commissioner Munro, and for Munro to arrive with the Gibbons family in tow. By then, Mr. Duffield had also been arrested, and a constable returned with confirmation of what we already knew—they'd uncovered Daniel's body in the Bucklersbury Street cellar.

Miss Gibbons's distressed wail followed me out of the building and into our carriage. "Poor woman," I murmured to the inky black sky. "Her only child."

"At least Munro is supportive," Matt said. "More supportive than I expected, to be honest."

"Daniel was his son too. Perhaps he even loved Miss Gibbons, at one point."

"Perhaps he loves her still, but circumstances have precluded him from marrying her. Not every couple can be together, no matter how much they want to wed."

"Being already married is something of an impediment."

He leaned his elbow on the window sill and rubbed his temple. "India…" He sighed heavily.

"I know."

He stopped rubbing and frowned at me. "You do?"

"Of course. This evening's adventure proved to me that you were entirely correct all along. I should have listened to you."

He lowered his hand and half shook his head. "While I like that you've admitted I'm right, I think we're talking at cross purposes. What *am* I right about, by the way?"

"Me keeping my magic a secret. I thought your warnings were simply a matter of you being overly cautious, but after seeing the lengths Duffield and Hogarth went to to protect their business and reputation…I find that I am more inclined to keep my magic to myself, in future."

"I'm glad to hear it. I don't like that you have to stifle this part of yourself, when you've only just discovered it, but it's for the best." He rubbed his forehead where the grooves had deepened in the last hour. "Unfortunately it's too late to keep it a secret from Abercrombie and the other Watchmaker's Guild members. Even more troubling is his apparent link to this sorry saga."

"Hopefully Munro can convince Duffield to reveal who urged him to kidnap Daniel." I shivered at the thought of Abercrombie going to the lengths that Duffield and Hogarth went to. Would he do that to me?

Matt removed his jacket. "You're cold."

I leaned forward and he draped the jacket around my shoulders. It smelled of his scent, a mixture of spices I couldn't name that were uniquely his. He lifted the collar, stroking the underside of my jaw with his gloved thumbs. Then he sat back, all the way on the other side of the cabin.

I drew in a fortifying breath, but my nerves remained frayed. "Cross purposes," I muttered. "What were you talking about?"

He stared down at his hands and stretched his fingers apart. "I was mistaken. I did want to discuss magic with you." He cleared his throat.

"Oh."

He looked up. The shadows smudging his eyes had darkened, the lines radiating from their corners multiplied. It was almost midnight, and he must be exhausted. "McArdle said magic provides what everyone wants most from the object. So gold multiplies, a mapmaker wants to locate something, and a watchmaker wants accuracy in timekeeping. The combining of two types of magic means two things are wanted."

"Giving you back your life for a longer time," I said quietly. "It's not quite what the horology magic is supposed to do."

"Nor does it explain how your watch saved you against the Dark Rider."

The watch still hung around my neck. I removed it and rubbed my thumb over the silver case. It grew warmer. "No, it doesn't."

"It's not just your watch either—the clock in the Jermyn Street gambling den hit Dennison."

I dropped my watch into my reticule and pulled the drawstring tight. "It doesn't make sense."

"It does if your magic is strong, as Mr. Gibbons suggested. Stronger than any other we've encountered so far."

I made a scoffing sound. "How can that be? I didn't know I was a magician until very recently. How could I have passed twenty-seven years unaware of something like that?"

He shrugged. "You've only just begun using it. Perhaps using it makes it grow in strength. The more you practice your magic, the stronger it becomes."

It was an interesting theory, but I didn't think I'd practiced my magic all that much. Certainly no more than Mr. Gibbons or Mr. Onslow, and neither had mentioned being saved by their maps. Their maps only did one thing—reveal locations.

I opened my mouth to tell Matt but shut it again. He'd closed his eyes and leaned his head back. His shoulders had lost some of their tension too, and his body rocked to the motion of the carriage. It was good to see him get some much needed rest.

I closed my eyes, only to open them upon his muttered, "You were remarkable tonight, India."

"Oh. Thank you."

He blinked sleepily back at me. "You're the bravest woman I've ever met."

"Now you're flattering me. *Willie* is a brave woman. She would have held the gun steady, whereas it shook like an autumn leaf in a strong breeze in my hand. I was utterly terrified." I wanted to tell him I was afraid I wouldn't be able to stop Hogarth from shooting him, but decided against it. I already felt raw, exposed, and didn't need to add fuel to the fire burning within me by admitting that.

"And yet you didn't run off. That's what makes you brave." One corner of his mouth lifted and he closed his eyes again. "We make a formidable team."

"Does that mean you'll no longer order me to remain behind when you hare off and endanger your life like you did tonight?"

He grunted. "It means I should stop introducing you as my assistant and start calling you my partner."

"That would be quite a promotion, but no one will believe I'm your equal."

His smile widened, but he kept his eyes shut. "They will once they get to know you."

***

Matt slept late, or so Miss Glass and I thought. Her first batch of callers, Mrs. and Miss Haviland, came and went without seeing him, much to their disappointment. It wasn't until he strolled in at midday sporting a fierce expression tinged with tiredness that I wondered if he really had been asleep the entire time.

"There you are!" his aunt cried. "No leaving the house today. You're all mine." She patted his cheek as she passed him on her way out of the drawing room.

"Why?" he asked darkly.

"You have new visitors this afternoon, Lady Abbington among them."

"With her unwed daughter, I assume. Or is it daughters, plural?" He threw himself into the chair and loosened his tie.

His aunt clicked her tongue. "You look like a vagabond."

"Aunt..." He sighed. "Never mind." He stretched out his legs and crossed them at the ankles.

"Lady Abbington doesn't have any daughters, as it happens, and she's coming alone."

"Then why do you want me to meet her? Am I off the marriage market already? Or are there nieces?"

"Your mocking does you no credit, Matthew."

"You're right. I'm sorry. Tell me about Mrs. Abbington and why you want me here for her visit."

"It's *Lady* Abbington. She's the widow of Lord Abbington—"

"Aha. So she is eligible after all."

Willie, Duke and Cyclops entered. They'd given up on waiting for DuPont to reappear at Worthey's factory. I'd apprised them of the investigation into Daniel's disappearance earlier, but I didn't know where they'd gone after that. They certainly hadn't remained at the house to greet Miss Glass's guests.

"Lady Abbington is twenty-six and widowed almost a year," Miss Glass said, peering down her nose at her nephew. "She's sensible, clever, pretty, and not at all like the other girls I've introduced to you. I suspected she might be more your type since..." She lowered her gaze to the floor. "She seems like the sort of woman who could catch your interest."

He drew in his legs and stood. He clasped her elbows gently. "Aunt Letitia, I know you mean well," he said gently. "But I've already told you I can't wed, and I'll tell each and every woman you bring here the same thing. I am not on the market. I am not eligible. I am not going to marry, no matter how wonderful the lady in question is."

"Not even if you fall in love with one of them?" Her voice changed from dramatic to thin, frail. She blinked up into Matt's face, so far above her own.

"Especially then. You see, Aunt, I've been ill. Nothing for you to worry about, but it means I get tired a lot. I couldn't tie a woman I love to a sick man."

She touched his cheek where the gray pall made the hollows appear starker. Her wistful, sad smile made my heart trip. "When you're cured, then." I suspected she'd already guessed that he wasn't well.

He kissed her forehead. "When I am cured."

She pressed her palms to his chest, as if wanting to be reassured by the steady rhythm of his heart. "Have Bristow send lunch to my rooms. You ought to do the same, Matthew. You look like you need a rest."

He did indeed, but I wouldn't tell him until after he told me where he'd been. I asked him as soon as his aunt left.

He crossed his arms over his chest and stood by the fire, his feet a little apart. The defensive stance piqued my curiosity, and I arched my brows. "We paid Abercrombie a visit," he said.

My mouth fell open. I glanced at the others, but none met my gaze. "You went without with me!"

"You do recall our discussion about not putting you in danger."

"Yes, and I also recall our discussion about you treating me as an equal partner."

"Abercrombie can't be trusted."

"What could he possibly do to me with all of you around?"

Willie marched up to me and poked me in the shoulder. I blinked at her, surprised. "Matt did what he thought was right, so stop arguing with him."

Damn her logic. I pressed my lips together, but it cost me to remain quiet.

"Hush, Willie," Duke snapped. "This ain't nothing to do with you."

"Course it is," Willie snapped back, hands on hips. "He's my cousin."

"I can fight my own battles, thank you, Willie." Matt took her by the elbows and steered her to the sofa. "Now listen." He may have been addressing everyone but he looked directly at me.

I bristled. "I am on tenterhooks since no one has yet told me what you learned from Abercrombie."

"Nothing," he said. "That's the problem. Abercrombie denied having anything to do with Daniel's disappearance, or with our abductions."

"Not even sending Eddie to warn me against investigating? And that other hooded fellow?"

"He claims Eddie talked to you off his own bat, and he knows nothing about the other man. According to him, Duffield and Hogarth acted on their own, too. While I do believe Hogarth killed Daniel without being urged by anyone, I'm certain Abercrombie knew about the abduction, perhaps even orchestrated it. Duffield's not talking."

"But I don't think Abercrombie is a murderer. If he was, he would have tried to get to me before now. That hooded fellow could have knifed me." The thought chilled me.

"Perhaps," he said darkly. "But you must still be careful."

"What about moving Mirth to another facility and spying on him at the bank?" I asked. "Did Abercrombie say why he did that?"

"Apparently the newer facility is better," Matt said. "As to the bank, he claims he simply had his own banking to do, that's why he was there."

"That's ridiculous. He was loitering outside for an age."

"He denied it all," Cyclops said, sitting beside Willie. "He's slippery. We couldn't pin him to anything for certain."

"There was no solid evidence," Matt agreed. "The police won't act without it."

"*We* can act without it," Willie muttered, picking dirt out from under her fingernails. "We know he's an evil snake."

"We won't be acting without evidence either," I told her. "I won't have that on my conscience."

"Your conscience is dull. It needs a little adventure."

"I've endured quite enough adventure, thank you. I'd rather sit here with a good book, right now. If you think that dull, then that says more about you than me."

Willie simply sniffed and wiped her nose with the back of her hand. She tossed a grin my way as she made a point of rubbing the snot on her trouser leg.

I handed her my handkerchief. "You missed some."

She snatched the handkerchief and dabbed at her nose.

"We need to find DuPont." Duke flicked his gaze toward Matt. "Urgently."

"How?" Cyclops asked. "He's disappeared and we know nothing about him or where to find him."

"We know something of his nature," Matt said. "We know what he wants, what he desires above all else. We can use that to find him."

We waited for him to elaborate, but he didn't. He simply changed the subject. "I have a new hobby," he announced. At our bewildered looks, he added, "Archaeology. I'm going to invest in Mr. Young's excavation."

"You want to save the mosaic?" I asked. "How noble."

"Noble?" Willie said with a shake of her head. "You've finally lost your marbles, Matt."

"I have all my marbles and I'm not all that noble," Matt said. "I just want all the damned pits in Bucklersbury Street closed."

I laughed. "I agree completely. The sooner the better."

"What about the hoard?" Cyclops asked. "Are you going to tell Young its buried somewhere near where Daniel's body was found?"

"I think we'll leave it there," Mat said. "Perhaps a future generation of archaeologists will find it."

"That thing has created enough problems as it is," I said. "I agree it should be left buried. Good riddance to it."

Bristow entered. "Luncheon is served in the dining room, sir."

"Thank you, Bristow." Matt held his hand out to me. "Will you walk in with me, equal partner?"

"Only if you promise not to hare off without me again. Not even to see Abercrombie."

"I can't make that promise." He stood there, his hand extended, his smile slipping. "India? Are you mad at me?"

I took his hand. "Matt, you're the most agreeable person I've ever met. Trying to stay mad at you is like trying to make clock hands go backwards."

"Impossible?"

"No, actually it is possible, but it's pointless. Why would anyone want to do such a thing?"

He placed his other hand over mine, sending a thrill whispering across my skin. But he spoiled the tender moment by laughing. "Thank you, India."

I tipped my face so that I could see him better. Our noses almost bumped. His breath warmed my lips. "For what?" I whispered.

"For brightening my moods when they'd otherwise be dark." The shine of humor in the depths of his eyes would imply now was one of those times. "And for not staying mad at me. I wouldn't like it if you did. I wouldn't like it at all."

LOOK OUT FOR

THE APOTHECARY'S POISON

The third GLASS AND STEELE novel.

To be notified when C.J. has a new release, sign up to
her newsletter via her website: www.cjarcher.com

ABOUT THE AUTHOR

Photograph by Melbourne Images

C.J. Archer has loved history and books for as long as she can remember and feels fortunate that she found a way to combine the two. She spent her early childhood in the dramatic beauty of outback Queensland, Australia, but now lives in suburban Melbourne with her husband, two children and a mischievous black & white cat named Coco.

Subscribe to C.J.'s newsletter through her website to be notified when she releases a new book, as well as get access to exclusive content. She loves to hear from readers. You can contact her in one of these ways:
Website: www.cjarcher.com
Email: cjarcher.writes@gmail.com
Facebook: www.facebook.com/CJArcherAuthorPage
Twitter: @cj_archer

87138107R00185

Made in the USA
Lexington, KY
20 April 2018